Dedication

This book is dedicated to 'Dr Leonard Croft', whose magisterial work, *The Master*, inspired portions of it.

—❀—

Acknowledgement

The catalogue entry on p. 88-89 is reproduced with permission from the website of Peter Harrington, 100 Fulham Road, Chelsea (www.peterharrington.co.uk).

—❀—

Foreword

This book is a piece of shameless and unadulterated fiction – but the incident in chapter 1, on which it is based, took place as reported in the press and so is wholly in the public domain. I have altered all names and concealed the location, and I am happy to inform the reader that the seemingly less than competent police exposed in the narrative of this first chapter did not belong to any British or American force.

A Fearful Madness

Julius Falconer

PNEUMA SPRINGS

04819025

First Published in 2013 by:
Pneuma Springs Publishing

A Fearful Madness
Copyright © 2013   Julius Falconer
ISBN13: 9781782282617

Julius Falconer has asserted his right under the Copyright, Designs and Patents Act, 1988, to be identified as Author of this Work

British Library Cataloguing in Publication Data. A catalogue record for this book is available from the British Library.

Book cover image - "Hypnotic tunnel to the light" by "Piku/Piotr Zabicki"

Pneuma Springs Publishing
A Subsidiary of Pneuma Springs Ltd.
7 Groveherst Road, Dartford Kent, DA1 5JD.
E: admin@pneumasprings.co.uk
W: www.pneumasprings.co.uk

1

It has been said, by whom and when I have forgotten, that the four ingredients of a good story are religion, sex, aristocracy and mystery. In line with this recipe, one practised hand penned the following line:

'My God,' said the duchess, 'I'm pregnant. I wonder whodunnit.'

This might qualify as the shortest short story ever told – and I doubt whether it could be expressed in more compressed form even in an inflected language. The following account of the case of a death by curtain-tie will, I hope, provide you with more extended interest on the basis of the same recipe. It begins with sex and religion, and, if the circumstances strike you as sordid, I cannot help it: I recount the facts as I find them, and they are a necessary prelude to what follows. To protect the living, I have altered all the names, and we shall locate the events in an unnamed city. The aristocracy (but alas! not a duchess) and the mystery follow in due course. The events begin with the discovery, the day following his death, of the near-naked body of a seventy-three-year-old retired teacher and part-time cathedral verger, James Thwaites, who had been hit on the head and then strangled with a curtain-tie, which was still round his neck. Four days after the murder, a fellow-parishioner and fellow-cathedral worker, Jonas Chimes, was arrested on suspicion of murder, his motive being resentment at a man who had made unwelcome advances. The parish was shaken to its foundations. The clergy refused to discuss the matter: they commented only that the events besmirched the cathedral's reputation; that the events did not concern the general public or the press; that the matter was not important. The parishioners were more forthcoming. The fact of their verger's homosexuality came as a surprise to most, although one commented that 'they might have guessed, his house was furnished so carefully – often an indication of a man with that sort of problem'. The general feeling, however, was that Jonas Chimes was an unlikely murderer. This was all in the July of that year.

The cathedral gradually regained some of its customary composure – until March of the following year. Chimes' lawyer, Josephine Finch, became concerned that the police had not yet produced a single piece of evidence against her client, although the prisoner's statement was said to have contained a full confession. She demanded to see the video of the interrogation, and on it, although her client was certainly confused and hesitant, he made no such admission. The officer in charge of the case was reprimanded, suspended and finally dismissed from the force.

The investigation, handed to another team, then took three different directions. Traces of semen on the victim's underwear, which had been originally ignored, were found to belong to another parishioner, sixty-two-year-old Matthias Biddulph, who at first denied any relationship with the deceased but eventually confessed to weekly meetings for sexual purposes: every Tuesday, after lunching together at a particular café, they went back to the verger's house to watch pornographic films and provide mutual relief. This was the last straw for the parishioners, who could see no end to the squalid saga. The police had still not identified the finger-prints found on the statuette believed to be the weapon used to hit the deceased. And a neighbour testified to having seen a bearded man outside James Thwaites' house on the evening of the murder.

As for the constabulary high-ups, they were not this time to be hurried into endorsing a hasty conclusion. Mr Biddulph was merely 'a witness'. The investigation was proceeding normally with the routine identification of all Mr Thwaites' partners, including particularly the bearded gentleman. As far as Jonas Chimes, now released from prison, was concerned, he protested that his life was destroyed. 'The cathedral was my life,' he said, 'all the family I had. I can't ever go there again, so many people still believe me guilty.' With his round spectacles and child-like face, it was difficult to believe him capable of a vicious murder. He explained that he had had a painful childhood. Abandoned by his parents and brought up by a woman who beat him and left scars on his face to prove it, he became an introverted and solitary adult whose sole comforts were his work as a bookshop-assistant and the cathedral, where he carried out menial tasks. The week before the murder he had spent on retreat at a remote centre in the Welsh hills, undergoing short fasts, enduring silence and listening to twice-daily talks from the retreat-master. 'This priest,' he said, 'spoke of his happy childhood and the many joys of his family life. I found this very difficult to deal with.' He returned home at the end of his retreat in a state of confusion and physically ill.

He telephoned a doctor, but, when no doctor came, he persuaded a friend to drive him at once to a psychiatric hospital. He was kept in for forty-eight hours – the forty-eight hours immediately following James Thwaites' murder. A deacon attached to the cathedral who visited him in the hospital recorded Jonas Chimes's 'delirious remarks on death' and ramblings about having 'murdered the bishop'. Two days later, three policemen barged into his house, put him against the wall, handcuffed him and threw him into a police van without a word of explanation. Later, one of them claimed that a surveillance camera in the town had caught him entering the dead man's house. (This was proved later to be sheer bluff.) Chimes confessed that, if he had done it, he had no recollection of it. As the accusations continued, he began to believe he might be guilty of the murder. He recounted Thwaites' advances. 'How handsome you look,' the dead man had told him, 'in your white surplice.' He rejected the advances, and Thwaites stopped; but if the police asserted he was guilty of murder, perhaps he was. On paper he was said to have confessed to killing Thwaites 'by accident', but the video contained the record of no such confession. Chimes moved out of the city and was living a withdrawn life - in the hope that the case would be solved and he completely exonerated – when he disappeared.

2

If you know North Yorkshire, you will know also that the county is compact except for the southern projection of the Selby district, which pokes out into what would otherwise be East or West Yorkshire. If you proceed a fraction south of due west from Selby and cross the A1s old and new, you come to a haven of tranquillity bordered by the bird sanctuary at Fairburn Ings on the south and the A63 on the north, by the old Roman road, the modern A656, on the west (beyond which lies west Yorkshire) and by the A1 on the east. These few square miles of near-paradise centre on the villages of Ledsham (pop. 162) and Ledston (pop. 400). The *National Gazeteer of Great Britain and Northern Ireland* of 1868 has this to say of the former:

> The surface is boldly undulating and well wooded. The soil is in general fertile, and in parts luxuriantly rich. The substratum abounds with coal and limestone, which are extensively worked. The village is situated in a vale near the source of a rivulet which flows through it [to join the Aire at Fairburn Ings].

Of Ledston the same source has this comment:

> The surface is varied and the land extremely fertile. Ledstone Hall is situated in the midst of a wooded park enclosed within a stone wall. It was formerly the seat of the Witham family, and afterwards of Thomas Wentworth, Earl of Stafford.

One of the area's glories is the network of well-maintained and well-used footpaths threading through the woods, fields, lanes and equestrian gallops, and the estates of both local mansions, Ledston Hall and Ledston Park (or Lodge). If you do not believe me, you have only to consult the hundreds of geographers online!

In a cul-de-sac known as Park Lane, whence a footpath leads up through woodland and then the parkland of Ledston Lodge towards the A1, there stands a modern cottage which is, at the time of this chronicle, home to a poor family housed there by the local authority, for reasons which would be too much of a diversion to explain here but which involved the enlightened view that a dysfunctional family is better placed in a civilised environment than on a 'sink estate' if the children are to reap the full benefits of twenty-first-century Britain and all it offers by way of culture and lofty standards of living. The family consisted of Dawn and Bert, parents, and Max, Chloe and Leo, children, in that order. The children attended local schools (when they did), Brigshaw High in Max and Chloe's case, Lady Elizabeth Hastings's Primary in Leo's. The family lived in a permanent state of chaos, with multiple social and personal problems which were reflected in the state of the house. They were a local nuisance, but their stay at Ledsham was intended by the authorities to be temporary only.

Max, all fifteen years of him, was always in trouble at school. He was undersized, wiry and bold, given to picking cigarette-stubs off the streets, permanently and irredeemably scruffy (despite school uniform, simple though it was), often involved in fights, the source of headaches among the authorities, resistant to academic learning in all its forms, dishonest, unreliable, impertinent and, as a consequence of these traits, an offensive, boorish, ill-humoured and disagreeable youth. (And who was to blame for that? you ask. I leave you to decide!) His sister Chloe, a little over a year younger, did not trail behind him in the infamy stakes. She was aggressive, surly, dishonest, unreliable and impertinent, given to whims and fancies, more of a dreamer than her brother, but equally disruptive in class and in the social order. If these two creatures sound odious and not the stuff of ingenuity and heroism, know that they were to prove an essential and beneficent ingredient in the life of Mr Alex Carter.

Lorna and Alex Carter had moved into the cottage next door shortly before the Bromleys had been housed in the same Ledsham street by the caring and far-sighted authorities. At first they were something of an enigma to the villagers, preferring, it seemed, to keep themselves to themselves, but gradually information about them leaked out. Mr Carter was, it came to be understood, at the start of his current contract as a carat[1] worker with the prison service, concerned with prisoners who had a 'substance problem'. As part of a team, he visited the sixteen institutions in the North Yorks and Humberside region, identifying problems, counselling and recommending treatment. (His qualifications included a tolerant, unprejudiced and broadminded approach to society's misfits and scoundrels, knowledge of drugs, other illegal substances and HIV, discretion, and an ability to be

---

[1] Counselling, Assessment, Referral, Advice Through Care.

organised and systematic.) His wife, on the other hand, had a more modest job. She worked part-time as a relief receptionist and hospitality assistant at a hotel in Castleford, putting in her twenty-five hours a week without, perhaps, a great depth of enthusiasm but with commitment and efficiency. The couple, in their mid-fifties, were understood to be childless.

In appearance, Mr Carter was taller than average and rather thin, getting short of thatch at the temples and with a fine beak of a nose. (One website makes the following comment on 'Roman nose', addressed to those who sport one:

> 'You hate tepid qualities like measure, temperance, sweetness, slowness and objectivity: either you love something or you hate it. You need to believe in and invest your energy in the things that matter to you.'

Can there be anything in this, do you think? Not *chez* Mr Carter, at any rate, if I am any judge.) His measured voice and calm ways gave every impression of mental and emotional depth and moderation. He was almost always casually, if smartly, dressed. His wife was in some contrast. She was on the short side, and the carping might call her plump, but there was nothing dumpy about her face, which was austere and yet animated, with fine skin, high cheek-bones and blue eyes full of lustre, laughter and life. Neighbours and fellow-villagers were not to know, either that they were not married, despite their rings and affectionate ways, or that their tranquil way of life concealed ulterior purposes.

Alex Carter and his young neighbour Max Bromley struck up a perhaps unlikely friendship. They first met, within hours of the Bromleys' arrival, when young Max, without a by-your-leave, climbed into the Carters' garden to retrieve some object thrown there by his irate and careless father, and Alex, collaring him metaphorically, had words, stern but kind, which were so unlike the treatment usually meted out to him that Max was impressed. From then on, the two would often chat in the street or over the fence, Alex usually taking the lead in inquiring about Max's school-work – where it existed – and his current projects, without cavil or judgement, much less condemnation. If Alex ever gave well-concealed advice or caution, Max did not dismiss it as the interference of an inevitably duplicitous and prejudiced adult. Lorna Carter did not find Max so endearing, but she always treated him with respect. She preferred his sister Chloe, impudent and slovenly as she was. Although not academically, musically or socially gifted, restful on the eye or stimulating in conversation, Chloe had about her a certain spirit which appealed to the older woman as revelatory of considerable potential if properly nurtured. Contrariwise, the Carters realised that they had nothing in common with the Bramleys senior apart from their humanity and did not attempt to fraternise beyond the exiguous limits of bare neighbourliness.

3

A first test of the friendship between Alex and Max came shortly after the latter's arrival at Ledsham. Exploring his new neighbourhood after years on a squalid Leeds estate, Max made it his business to investigate every gateway and opening in the village, running off with obscenities on his lips and at his fingertips when challenged and spreading alarm among the staid inhabitants, who began to consider urgent ways of persuading the authorities to shorten the length of time which they considered appropriate to house the family at Ledsham. In his explorations, Max was frequently accompanied by his sister. There is a direct footpath that leads from Ledsham to Ledston, the first half-mile of it on the road, the rest along a wood and across two fields. Max, on his own on this occasion, decided that it would be fun to open the gate to a field where cows grazed placidly. A bit of judicious shouting and a few pokes with a stick persuaded the heifers that their salvation lay beyond the gate, and the cattle duly ran on to the road, careered into Ledston and did considerable damage to several cars. There could be only one culprit responsible for this piece of high jinks, and a member of the constabulary duly called at Orchard Cottage to interview the young tearaway. It so happened that Alex Carter was in his front garden when PC Rhynd drew up and, suspecting trouble, strolled over to intercept the policeman before he could knock on the door of his neighbours' house.

'Well, now, officer,' he said affably, 'you'll be calling about young Max, I daresay.'

'That's right, sir. Up to his old tricks, I understand. Didn't take him long, did it?'

'What's he done this time, officer?'

'Let cows out of a field, and they wandered into Ledston, where several cars sustained damage. Nasty business.'

'Japes, officer, high spirits. Was he seen?'

'No, not exactly; but everyone knows it was him.'

'I see. What if I had a word with him, and you went quietly on your way?

How would that be?'

'And what'm I going to tell my sergeant?'

'Tell him you met a kindly neighbour who promised to see it won't happen again. No point in making more trouble than we need, is there?'

'Or anything like it.'

Thus soothed, the constable, removing his helmet to scratch his head in time-honoured fashion, returned to his car and went on his way. Alex had severe words with Max, and their friendship was sealed.

4

After their cautious start, the Carters began to make themselves known in the village, through the public house (the Chequers) and the church (All Saints), getting to know the locals and the quiet history of the locality. The history is one of uneventful labour in the fields for the majority and the social round of a wealthy family who chose to build and settle there. The calm waters were disturbed only by the death of a servant-girl at the Hall, one Mary Panel (variously spelt), accused of witchcraft in the late 1590s and apparently hanged and/or burnt in 1603. The superstitious believe she still haunts the hillside where the final indignities were heaped on her. Much, of course, has changed over the centuries. The school no longer functions as a school, nor the almshouses as almshouses. The Hall is no longer home to a wealthy family. The adjacent stable-block no longer witnesses the passage of coaches and carriages. Bodies are no longer carried down the Old Corpse Road from Fairburn for burial at Ledsham, as in times before the former village acquired its own church in 1846. Workers no longer tramp out each morning to the surrounding farmland for a day of manual toil. The roads are metalled for ease of vehicular traffic. The present residents being the affluent retired and commuters to local towns, the villages now give the impression of a comfortable dormitory amidst prosperous and well-mechanised farmland. On the other hand, the centre still floods regularly when rain-water washes down from the surrounding slopes, blocks the route of the Wetherby-Wakefield buses and makes the road impassable for cars and pedestrians alike.

The Carters stopped to chat to others walking through the limestone meadow at the east end of the village. They leaned across gaps between tables at the Chequers to exchange comments with other drinkers. They stayed behind after a church service to gossip with the reverend or the other departing worshippers. Occasionally they rang the changes by popping into the White Horse Inn at Ledston on a Sunday, when the Chequers was closed. They chatted with others standing at the bus-stop. Gradually and discreetly they built up a picture of the community – and, without seeming to, of one family in particular: the Becketts, consisting of Mr and Mrs Roddy Beckett, married daughter Stephanie and married son Philip. Stephanie and her husband Leo lived in Garforth, a few miles to the north-west, Philip and his wife in Pontefract to the south, while the Becketts themselves occupied a house in the main street of Ledsham, stone-built, slated, with mullioned windows and standing back from the Ledston road ('Claypit Lane') behind a sloping front-lawn, clearly the residence of a comfortably well-off, middle-class, unobtrusive couple.

The Carters suspected that, behind the respectable façade, not all was as it should be – legally speaking - in the Beckett household. Stephanie and Leo seemingly made a filial visit every week, as did Mary-Ann and Phil. The two junior families were sometimes there together. There was a frequent passage of boxes, usually of a certain size: larger than shoe-boxes but smaller than tea-crates – the size often known as medium moving boxes (I think). In the course of a casual conversation, a neighbour volunteered the information that they had been given to understand that the boxes contained antiques and that the Becketts senior, who, they understood, had been in the antiques business, were advising and assisting the younger couples, who were in the same line of work. The younger couples had no premises but, it appeared, worked online out of a number of web addresses. It was clear to Alex that the neighbours could not know more than this, because the Becketts' house lay back from the road, screened on all sides by a thick hedge. Once a car went through the gates that led off the road, it would be visible only to someone standing directly outside the premises, on the public road – or to someone standing by chance at the neighbours' upper window. For Alex Carter, the puzzle was why the contents of the boxes were never seen in public: if antiques were the real nature of the business, one would expect to see chairs and tables, bureaux and wardrobes, cupboards and commodes, bookcases, perhaps even statuary – items not easily or cheaply boxed - being wheeled in and out. Furthermore, no items seemed to be stored at the house in Ledsham: a car, not the materials of an antiques business conducted online, sat in the garage. Of course, the Becketts might specialise in smaller items: jewellery, clocks and watches, silver and porcelain, paintings, perhaps, or glassware. There were plenty of specialisms that could keep a family in business without having to cover the whole gamut of what is termed 'antiques'. None the less, it was curious that the usual clutter of an antiques business should be so smoothed over and hidden from the view of all but those immediately concerned.

Alex Carter racked his brains to think of a method of identifying the Beckett family's business, not out of idle curiosity but for a specific purpose. It would be foolish to contemplate illegal means such as breaking and entering. On the other hand, he could not realistically adopt an honest approach either: 'Hello, we're near neighbours of yours. I wonder whether you'd be kind enough to let us know what's in all those boxes you handle. Just curious, you know.' What about calling at the house when one of the children were there and surprising them at it – 'it' being whatever the family were up to? The response to that was that, if there were anything illegal afoot, the Becketts were hardly going to let him in the house to have a look. Carter also thought of training a pair of binoculars on the house to penetrate the interior but, despite a discreet reconnaissance, could not find a suitable vantage point without himself being the object of scrutiny. Could he invite the police to call? But on what pretext? In any case, he preferred to proceed on his own until circumstances should dictate otherwise. It was at this point in his deliberations that he brought young Max and his sister to mind. Here were two youngsters who could perhaps act as spies – or scouts, as he preferred to think of them – without endangering his own reputation. Alex called Max over to him that very day, in the privacy of their back gardens.

'Fancy earning a few quid, Max?' Alex asked the scruffy teenager.

'Mm.'

'This must be deadly secret, mind you.'

'OK.'

'Not even your parents must know.'

'OK, Mr Carter. What about Chloe?'

'She's all right – we might need her help anyway - but she's got to be sworn to secrecy as well.'

'OK. What's it about?'

'Do you know the Becketts, up on Claypit Lane?' Max shook his head. 'Right, let's walk up there now, if you've got nothing else to do, and I'll show you. I'll tell you the rest as we go.'

The two met out at the front and walked purposefully up the road, as if they had some business in the woods towards Ledston. As they passed the Beckett residence, Alex remarked on it but enjoined on Max the need not to turn his head. A quarter of an hour later, they returned home the same way, neither of them calling attention to the fact that they had registered the

Becketts' house as an object of interest. Immediately opposite the house was the cricket club, and Max thought it would be 'a doddle' to keep watch on the house from behind the hedge that bounded the pitch on that side. He would start at once: but what was he looking for? He, and Chloe if he decided she should be recruited, were making a note of the visits of the junior members of the family. They were to register the make and number-plates of their cars and the times and lengths of their visits. Alex wished to build up a clear picture of activities at the house without arousing anyone's suspicions; and he undertook some of the spying himself, from a slightly different vantage-point, where he thought he could conceal himself without being noticed, provided that he exercised the greatest caution.

I shall not weary the reader with an extended account of those weeks of – well, of scouting. Hours were spent recording comings and goings, but no particular pattern emerged. The Becketts conducted an unremarkable quasi-suburban life. Their off-spring called in weekly, at seemingly random times, sometimes (it was surmised) for a meal, on other occasions for shorter meetings. Each time there was an exchange, or a passage, of boxes, but Max would not say that the activity, although unfussy and rapid, was noticeably 'furtive' (when the meaning of the word was explained to him). Perhaps the Becketts relied on the seclusion of their house-frontage and saw no need to take further precautions, such as being active only at night.

That initial reconnaissance being concluded within the limits set by prudence and patience, Alex Carter had to devise some means to see inside the boxes. He dreamed up a series of schemes, each more Bondesque (or perhaps St Trinianesque) than its predecessors: nocturnal burglary, car-jacking, a mock arrest, a road-block, tear-gas … Eventually he thought he could do better than that, even though the results might not be so direct. He reasoned that such activity as he and his team had witnessed must leave some discardable traces behind and that these would find their way in due course into the Becketts' dustbins. Such debris might conceivably give a clue. One night, therefore - the vigil of dust-bin day – at a time when the village was at its darkest and quietest, Alex, Lorna and Max left their respective houses, joined forces and strolled purposefully up the road, covering the two hundred yards in a few moments. There being no resident policeman in the village and, for most of the way, houses on one side of the road only, they did not expect to be seen. When they arrived outside the Becketts' house, they went swiftly into action. Lifting the lid of the wheelie-bin, Alex and Lorna tipped the contents into two black plastic bags held by the willing Max. They then tipped into the now empty bin the harmless and unidentifiable contents of another two bags that they had brought with them, closed the lid again and beat a hasty retreat. They knew that they had made some noise – inevitable when dealing with such recalcitrant material as discarded waste in all its splendid variety – but hoped that the noise could not be heard by soundly sleeping villagers.

Max insisted on assisting them on the following morning in going through the bin-liners' contents. Have you ever sifted through your neighbours' dustbin? Probably not. It is an odious task – even when needs must. The Carters closed the garage doors before spreading their loot out on the garage floor, preferring to run no risk of being seen by neighbours, callers or passers-by. They all wore thin plastic gloves and moved carefully for fear of jagged edges and also for what Aldous Huxley once called 'the busy ferments of putrefaction'. Every item was shaken clear of attached items, carefully inspected and put to one side for later disposal. Max, who compensated for whatever he lacked in conventional learning with shrewdness and who had a full complement of youthful interest in excitement, entered fully into the spirit of the exercise. However, the team were disappointed. Nothing attracted their attention any more than anything else. The contents were what might be expected in any random sample of household waste: wrappers, cartons, tins, kitchen scraps, envelopes, paper, supermarket receipts; not a single sinister or revealing item.

The Carters were disappointed, even discouraged, and it was Max who raised their spirits by suggesting another attempt the following week. (Oh, 'the brisk intemperance of youth' – even in one whose grasp of the decline and fall of the Roman empire was as foreign as chemistrianity.) The following week, therefore, when climatic conditions were even better than on their first escapade, the three miscreants again sallied forth in the wee hours and repeated their act of thievery. (Alex and Lorna argued that there was nothing illegal in emptying your neighbours' dustbin – surely there was not? If such an act had reached the English [and Welsh] statute-book, what was civilisation coming to?) There was one anxious moment when an empty tin of pineapple segments escaped the lip of the bin-liner that Max was holding up and bounced on the pavement, tinkling loudly into the gutter, but there seemed not to be any alarming consequences: the team made it back to their beds without being accosted and challenged. The following morning, they repeated the inspection of their haul, and this time they struck lucky. The Becketts had emptied their vacuum-cleaner and put the dust into one of the bin-liners that later went into the dust-bin. Alex, half-knowing half-guessing what he was looking for, spotted flakes of old paper such as are shed by books of a certain age. These fragments had been hoovered up so as not to leave tell-tale signs in the house – and to keep the house tidy, of course – and they were as gold-dust to the Carters.

'Bingo!' Alex shouted in triumph and enthusiasm. Neither Lorna nor Max immediately cottoned on to the significance of the scraps in the palm of Alex' hands. 'Don't you see?' he went on. 'Antique books! Probably stolen – that's what all the secrecy's about. A black market in stolen rare and ancient books: that's it! Didn't you see the recent case of the Girolamini library in Naples?' No, they did not. 'The curator and one or two of his assistants, including, I may add, a Roman Catholic priest, were systematically creaming off the best of the 150,000-volume collection and flogging them to collectors at vast prices. You've got to know what you're doing, of course, but apparently they had a discreet network set up, with depositories in various places and channels of sale all over the place, hidden from the eyes of the indiscreet. And I may comment that they were aided in their work by slipshod security arrangements and an almost total lack of oversight by anyone in higher authority, but even so, they had quite a sophisticated scheme in operation.'

'And people buy old books?' Max asked incredulously. 'I can't see why people buy new ones, let alone old ones.'

'You'd be surprised,' Alex said. 'Some books go for thousands, tens of thousands, of pounds in auction rooms. Of course, you don't get that much on the black market, where thieves are often happy to get what they can for their haul, but to a thief who has a clear idea of the value of what he's dealing with and has good contacts, it's a lucrative, if risky, business all right.'

'Well,' Lorna asked, 'if this operation at the Girolamini was so sophisticated, as you say, how come they got caught?'

'It's quite a story,' Alex went on. 'The short answer is, carelessness: they got too sure of themselves. One day, a respectable professor of the history of art at the university of Naples called at the library to check a reference. He was known to be punctilious over the use of public money: he'd not long written an article denouncing the Berlusconi government for buying a crucifix attributed to Michelangelo for three million euros without any of the necessary safeguards of authenticity. Anyhow, in he goes, and he's conducted by the conservator, this priest I mentioned, to the Vico room, where the book he wished to consult was apparently housed. As the two men crossed the main hall, a sulphurous blonde in a jogging suit crossed in front of them with her wash-things. The priest asked her how she'd slept and whether the director was up yet. Once arrived in the Vico room, the visitor was astounded to see the disorder: books heaped anywhere, any old how, vying for room with empty Coca-Cola bottles and other rubbish. A dog came in and squatted under a table. There were hold-alls stuffed with ancient books and manuscripts. The visitor, unable to believe his eyes, wasted no time in reporting the matter to the authorities. Investigation showed that surveillance cameras in the reading room had been switched off. Unfortunately for the director, surveillance cameras in the corridors hadn't, and there was enough evidence there to put him and his assistants away for some years: the prosecutor asked for fifteen years for crimes including the misuse of public funds. The sorry thing is that the authorities haven't recovered all the books stolen. They never will, of course, because there was no proper inventory of the library's holdings. So far only 2300 stolen books have been recovered, including some valued at a million euros apiece, and the gang's haul probably runs into many thousands of books. It's a disaster for the Italian patrimony. Who knows what the director and his merry men – and merry women – would have got away with if they'd been more careful?'

'But then the collectors are equally to blame: if there weren't a market out there, there'd be no incentive to pillage.'

'But do collectors know the works they buy are stolen? The Girolamini director took care to remove anything which could betray his books' origins. Even a well-known auction house in London was taken in.'

'So what do we do now?' Lorna asked. 'We've got to go to the police about this, I suppose – our civic duty, and all that.'

'No, I don't think so,' Alex said slowly. 'We haven't any evidence.'

'The police could soon find some – proper evidence, I mean.'

'Look, Mr Carter,' Max piped up. 'What's all this about? We've been watching this family for months, and then, when we find what yer seem to be looking for, yer hold back. I don't geddit.'

'Max, it's probably time Lorna and I took you into our confidence. We may need further help from you, and it's not fair to keep you in the dark. Let's go into the house and sit round with a cup of coffee, and I'll tell you the story.'

20

5

They cleared up all the rubbish, stowing it away in a couple of black plastic bags, and returned to the house. Max plumped for hot chocolate instead of coffee.

'Right, Max,' Alex Carter began when all were seated. 'This is the story. And you're to tell no one, not even yourself: it's a deadly secret.' The boy's eyes widened. 'First of all, Alex Carter isn't my real name, and Lorna and I aren't really married. We're under cover.'

'What, like in the movies?'

'Well, yes, I suppose so, but this is for real. Two years ago, I was wrongly accused of a crime, and my name's never been cleared. I had to leave where I lived because I couldn't bear all the suspicion. Because the real murderer – '

'Murderer?'

'Yes, I was accused of murder. As I say, because the real murderer wasn't found – and still hasn't been - people still suspect me, and I can tell you life was impossible. I lost my friends – the few I had - gave up my job and moved away. It was so bad, I ended up in a psychiatric ward – you know, a mental hospital, loony-bin, whatever you want to call it.'

'What, *you* did?'

'Yes, I did. Well, while there I was seen by a really fantastic psychiatrist who recommended me to consult a woman called Mrs Tukes, who specialised in childhood traumas – you know, people who'd suffered as children and couldn't get their lives on track. This Mrs Tukes was a wizard. She turned me right round, from a shy, awkward bloke with few friends and few interests to the self-confident, dynamic and fully rounded individual you see before you today – ahem. Mrs Tukes encouraged me to talk to her about how I'd suffered as a child and what I felt about things – everything, really. She was really patient, as she must have been bored stiff listening to all my ramblings. I told her the story of the murder as well, and she was very sympathetic. She helped me see that, although the police had apparently given up, there was no need for me to. I had to keep asserting my innocence to myself and defying the world to do its worst.'

'So who are you, Mrs Carter: are you Mrs Tukes?'

'No, Max, my name's Rita, and I'm Alex' cousin. Because I'm widowed, I'm free to join Alex in his hunt for James Thwaites' killer.'

'And what's *your* real name, Mr Carter?'

'You mustn't tell anyone, Max: Jonas; but nobody's to know that.' The boy stared at the two adults, but whether in incomprehension, admiration or sheer wonder was not apparent.

'So why are we watching the Becketts, Mr Carter?' Max asked, gulping down whatever emotion had seized him.

'Well, it's like this. After the murder, I was in some state, I can tell you, largely for other reasons, but the way the police treated me was awful, just awful, and I couldn't get myself together. I spent eight months in custody – you know, in prison – while the police tried to get evidence against me, and if it hadn't been for a clever lawyer, I might still be there. In those eight months, I had plenty of time to think, and one thing I thought about was the murder victim and what I knew of him. Let me describe him to you. Early seventies and looking it. Medium height and build. If you know the word raddled, that'll give you the right idea: run down, seedy – not in his clothes, which were always neat, even smart, but in his face and general appearance. He'd obviously led an unhealthy life, and his vices were showing in the way he looked. A grating voice and a sort of wheedling manner. He'd lean his face right into yours and give you the impression he was treating you as an intimate friend. His breath smelt, as well. I knew him through the church but didn't often speak to him at any length – we just didn't seem to have anything in common; but we didn't live far from each other, and I quite often saw him coming and going from his house. This was even before he retired from teaching. Anyway, you never saw him with a woman, always with men. That's all beside the point, though. He worked part-time in the cathedral, and so did I, and he'd often say, "Must go now – got an appointment, you know. Mustn't keep the people waiting." Made him sound important, I suppose. You can understand him having an appointment every so often – dentist, doctor, hairdresser – yes, quite understandable, but it was always happening, over the years, and I wondered who all these appointments were with. It wasn't any of my business, of course, and I didn't like James Thwaites well enough to bother my head unduly about it. Then we had a bit of a kerfuffle in the cathedral about some books that went missing from the vestry – old Bibles mostly, I think. There was an inquiry – just within the cathedral, you know – and the dean came to the conclusion that someone had gained access to the vestry in daylight hours and had simply walked off with the books. Now I'd seen Thwaites leaving the cathedral once with a parcel under his arm, and I'd idly asked myself what was in it, as he hadn't come in with it.'

'Why didn't yer say anything about it, then, Mr Carter – yer know, when there was an inquiry?'

'I was too shy. I was frightened of him as well, and I guessed that, if I mentioned the matter and it was proved to be perfectly harmless, he'd force me out of the cathedral. I didn't want that. Anyway, anything of value in the vestry was taken out, and the thefts stopped: there wasn't anything left worth stealing. Now in those days I used to work in a bookshop: no, not the owner, not even the manager, just a dog's-body, doing the jobs nobody else wanted to do, and I knew that the collecting bug gets to some people. They want all the works of one author, or they don't buy anything but first editions, or they hunt out rare books – we had a second-hand section upstairs, and I'd see them rooting around the shelves looking for things they thought we hadn't spotted. I idly wondered whether Thwaites was mixed up in something like that, although I never saw him in the shop, but it's not illegal, and I didn't either like or know the man sufficiently to wish to improve my acquaintance.'

'But I don't see how yer got on to the Becketts.'

'Spot of luck, really; and of course we still don't know we're right, so it's a bit of a long shot. The last time I spoke to Thwaites, he propositioned me – look, Max, you're old enough to know all about that, so I won't elaborate. He'd come round to my house to invite me over to his, and I didn't exactly slam the door in his face, but I made it quite clear he wasn't welcome. One day as he left, he dropped a letter he'd been going to post – he had quite a few in his hand - and I noticed the address: Beckett at Ledsham Yorkshire. It wasn't the address that got me thinking, though, it was the words on the back of the envelope: "Sorry: the Ravenna to follow". "Ravenna", I happened to know, was Oscar Wilde's first published work – well, his first work published in book form - and much sought after by collectors: you won't get one for under a thousand quid, and it's only got sixteen pages in it altogether! A first edition, I mean. Well, I didn't think twice about it at the time, as you can imagine. I just posted his letter for him when I next went out, and that was it; but in prison I began to think about it – time on my hands, you see. The police thought I'd committed the murder because I objected to Thwaites' advances, but that didn't make any sense to me. Why should I, or anybody else, commit murder just because an acquaintance had made himself disagreeable? OK, it's a sensitive subject, but murder? No, just not on, except, possibly, in extreme cases, and there you'd be dealing with a psychopath. The police didn't seem able to focus on anything else but the sex side of Thwaites' death – perhaps they were looking for a psychopath with a sexual hang-up and thought I was it. OK, Thwaites was murdered while still in his underwear, but it needn't have been by his partner, need it? Perhaps the sex session was over, and Thwaites was just wandering round in his sitting-room, still in his underwear, when the murderer surprised him. The police found evidence of someone else in the house at around that time, but they didn't hurry to make an arrest, did they? In fact, they didn't arrest anyone at all. If they didn't arrest Thwaites' most recent sexual partner, wouldn't that point to someone else? In my view, the police just gave up at that point. Couldn't be bothered. Not enough evidence. Too much trouble to hunt for some bearded creature who might have been seen in the area – or not, as the case may be. Ruminating on all this, the only thing I could come up with was trafficking in rare books. Perhaps Thwaites had got mixed up in some shady deal and paid the price. It was all I had to go on, you see.'

'So why didn't yer go to the police with this idea, Mr Carter?' Max asked, completely absorbed in the story.

'They might have thought I was just making it up to get myself out of trouble. I had no sympathy with them, none at all. They'd ruined my life, and they could go and stew, as far as I was concerned. They'd simply turn it against me and use it to argue that I had some sort of grudge against Thwaites – which I suppose I had, but not to the point of murdering him or even fabricating accusations against him. They focussed on me, you see, because I'd spent time in a mental hospital and was what they thought an unbalanced individual. I was unmarried, too: didn't that indicate a gay person? It all added up, and they couldn't see beyond the end of their noses; well, the nose of the investigating copper. Can I just tell you why I'm not married, Max? It'll probably sound ridiculous, but I don't want you harbouring doubts about me. I was in love once – desperately, head over heels in love. Still am. We got engaged. Life was rosy. Then she was killed in a car accident. It nearly destroyed me; but I came round and vowed never to marry, because I'd be true to her. So you see, young Max, Thwaites had picked on the wrong person, only I was too feeble to tell him never to darken my doors or speak to me again. Well, I went over all this with Mrs Tukes, and she set me on my feet again, but I knew I could never really rest until I'd cleared my name in the estimation of the great British public. I was discussing this one day with Rita here – well, Lorna – when she came up with the idea of doing a bit of snooping ourselves. She had the money to buy this little house, and we moved in with the hope of discovering something worthwhile.'

'And have yer?'

'Have we what?'

'Discovered something worthwhile.'

'Well, what do you think? We've discovered that the Becketts are dealing in rare or old books – at least, in my opinion we have – and that's a good start, isn't it? It certainly ties in with my suspicions about the late and little lamented James Thwaites. And we know that Thwaites corresponded at least once with the Becketts.'

6

Meanwhile, Mrs Quentin Bursnell, née Serenity Thwaites, was operating to an agenda of her own. Serenity (which is how she would wish to be known to the reader) was a spry sixty-five and claimed to feel years younger than her age. Since her widowhood, she had lived on her own, quietly pursuing her work as an independent re-upholsterer. When her husband was alive, she rented a shop in Ripon's Kirkgate, welcoming the well-to-do burghers of the city with their settees and stools, voltaires and love-seats, savonarolas, fauteuils and bergères, of which the woodwork was sound but the fabric worn, torn, stained, faded, out of fashion or simply no longer the right colour or pattern for the room. Since her husband's death, she had her garage adapted to act as premises instead. This was perfectly feasible, because her house, in Mallorie Court, was no great distance from the city centre and perfectly accessible to clients. There was room for her store of fabrics, braids, webbings, springs, tacks and the other paraphernalia of her trade, as well as an area which served as her work-shop, as she teased old chairs down to the bone and re-built them in the style selected by her clients. Of course, she was expensive – she knew that – but then expertise commands a high price. You could let anyone loose on a chair, and that didn't matter provided you weren't fussy about the finished product, but to anyone with taste and discernment, the professional had the absolute edge over the amateur, knowing, as she did, when to tuck, when to pinch, when to twist, to smooth, to ruffle, to overlap, what size large-headed nails would look best and how to compress the springs so that they gave years of life without compromising the seating experience.

Her objective in moving out of rented premises just off the Market Square was not to save money, although of course savings were always welcome, but simply to be more compact in her business. She did not really need public frontage: it was not as if some stray shopper, intrigued by her window display, were suddenly going to pop in to order the re-upholstery of six dining-room chairs. No, householders planned these things in advance, and selected advertising outlets were all she needed; and heaven knows, they were expensive enough.

Her brother's murder had shocked her. She knew that he was not an entirely admirable character. She remembered his youthful escapades, which had gone down in family lore as pardonable and expected indiscretions. He had done well at school, failing only in French and excelling in science, but even then his predatory instincts were apparent. Expulsion was not an option for such trivial lapses in decency and taste as he perpetrated, but the headmaster viewed with repugnance each new manifestation of an undisciplined and unsocial libido. From school, James had proceeded seamlessly to university, where he had graduated in chemistry with a view to entering the teaching profession. One or two homosexual encounters, of his engineering, had not endeared him to the majority of his fellows, but he cared not two hoots for others' opinions, secure in the knowledge that he was being true to himself. Although the schools in which he had then taught were aware of – or had guessed - his proclivities, his brilliance as a teacher, once proved, was the passport to several august educational establishments, where his rapport with pupils male and female was justly and highly valued. Like many homosexuals, James had never settled for long with one partner but roved around, eying up the market and helping himself where he could.

It was not a distinguished way of life, and Serenity contemplated it with aversion - as, indeed, had her husband. She could not account for it in the context of her parents' upbringing of their children. James, the first-born, had been followed by Zachary, Rebecca and herself, and the family had been both cohesive and animated. (Zachary had died in an accident in early adolescence, and Rebecca had had nothing to do with her remaining brother for years.) They played games together, holidayed together, were interested in each other's activities and friends, shared common jokes, juvenile vocabulary and tastes in food and were, to all appearances, a loving and religious family. Money had never been exactly plentiful, but the children had not gone short on the things that mattered, and Serenity was unsure why James had turned out so ambiguous a character: a gifted teacher but a poor advertisement for human fullness and balance. She sighed. There was nothing she could have done. James was her senior by eight years, beyond any control or influence she might have tried to exert, and in any case a stronger personality than she was, so that, even if they had been of a similar age, she could not envisage her having been able to exercise any sort of restraint on his wayward personality. She had been fond of him – of course: he was her brother; but she was not surprised that someone had seen fit to murder him, and, in a sense, she was not sorry to see his passing, as he exercised, she thought, a deleterious influence on those who came within his reach. She also remembered the wisdom of *The Anatomy of Melancholy*:

> There is no content in this life, but all is vanity and vexation of spirit; lame and imperfect. Hadst thou Samson's hair, Milo's strength, Scanderbeg's arms, Solomon's wisdom, Absalom's beauty, Croesus his wealth, *Pasetis obolum*, Caesar's valour, Alexander's spirit, Tully's or Demosthenes' eloquence, Gyges' ring, Perseus' Pegasus and Gorgon's head, Nestor's years to come, all this would not make thee absolute; give thee content and true happiness in this life.

James lacked the one thing that would have made his life a success (in her opinion): a loved and loving wife. It had never happened, of course: never even come close to happening, and she regretted it.

Now she was faced with what to do in the light of his violent death. Doing nothing was an option. The affair had been put in the hands of the proper authorities, right from the beginning. There did seem to be room for doubt about the professionalism and effectiveness of the subsequent inquiry, but then she was not in possession of all the facts; but how could she hope to discover, much less compensate for, any shortcomings in the police investigation? The police had not made an arrest; but then no arrest was better than a false one. She had no experience in such matters. She could number on the fingers of one hand the number of detective novels she had read – and how close were they to realistic detective procedure? They were designed for entertainment – escapism – like all novels. Of course, many of them, she supposed, shed light on the vagaries of human behaviour, the labyrinths of motive, the complexities of relationships. Perhaps they drew on all sorts of outside interests: bell-ringing, it might be (she recalled *The Nine Tailors*), or mediaeval philosophy (*The Name of the Rose*), or the Syriac language (*Tempt Not The Stars*). They exploited, she had no doubt, all sorts of reactions in the reader, from horror and dread to surprise and admiration. They were gory, gentlemanly, literary, hard-boiled, fast-moving, intriguing and so on, depending on the writer's taste. Some, no doubt, reflected accurately and in detail modern police procedure. Their main motive, however, was to *entertain*, and she could not see that any amount of reading Ngaio Marsh, Ruth Rendell or Ian Rankin could inspire her with ideas in the case of her brother's murder. She expressed these thoughts one day to her eldest-born, Reuben.

'Mother,' he said, 'don't be such a wimp! If you think justice hasn't been done – and clearly it hasn't – it's your duty to do something about it. There's a murderer out there wandering round unpunished – after nearly two years!'

'But,' she offered tentatively, 'what if your uncle James deserved to be murdered? I mean,' she added hastily as she saw the look on her son's face, 'he wasn't really a very nice person, was he? I can say that, as his sister. He had many qualities, and his professional life was extremely successful, but how do we know how many people he'd upset – or worse? His wasn't an engaging life-style, and we all have to die some time.'

'Mother,' Reuben answered impatiently, 'you take such a short-sighted view of things. Human justice is fragile and to be treasured in consequence. You can't just let murderers get away with their crime, as that jeopardises the whole justice system, and, as I say, that's shaky enough to start with.'

'We could leave it to God.'

'We could, but we're not going to.'

'"We": does that mean you're taking part as well?'

'Well, I'll do what I can, as his nephew, but I've got work and a family to consider.'

'And what about my work? Isn't that important?'

'It is, of course,' he said soothingly, 'but you work for yourself, and you can take on as little or as much as you like. It won't hurt you to take a bit of time off, or to reduce your load so that you've time for other things.'

'But I don't know where to begin,' she complained. 'I'm a complete novice. That's what I've been trying to tell you.'

'We don't need a lot of expertise,' he explained. 'Look where that got the police: precisely nowhere. OK, they made an arrest, but they had to release him for lack of evidence. They swanned around interviewing uncle's possible partners; they had DNA samples, they had all the scene-of-crime data, but none of that got 'em anywhere, did it? What we need is common sense, that's all.'

'Common sense? How's that going to help?'

'OK, let's think about it a bit. Uncle James was found in his underwear with another man's semen on it. That pointed to murder by a sexual partner. But did it? Wouldn't uncle James have rather been naked in that case? The game was presumably over. I'm not speculating on what it was – too gruesome for words – but it seems to me that the murder could've been completely unconnected. Whoever was in the house or whoever had dropped in to commit murder needn't have had anything to do with the sexual goings-on, need he? So what else was uncle James up to? Didn't the police interview you at the time?'

'Of course they did, but it was only to discover the names of partners if they could. I wasn't asked about anything else.'

'Well, I'll ask you now: what else was going on in uncle James' life that could have a bearing on his murder? What was he up to, apart from seducing people as perverted as himself?'

'Reuben, don't talk like that about your uncle!'

'OK, OK, only joking. So what about the bloke who was arrested and then released: could he have done it? What was his name again?'

'Jonas Chimes. An inadequate individual, as far as I could gauge. I never met him, and James never mentioned him, that I remember, but, from what the papers reported, he seems to have had a history of mental illness, to be shy and awkward, a solitary creature haunting the precincts of the cathedral, skulking around keeping himself to himself – an unlikely murderer, I always thought. Wouldn't have had it in him.'

'No, but he had motive and opportunity, didn't he?'

'Maybe, but then so presumably did others.'

'Didn't you find anything in uncle's papers? What happened to them, by the way?'

'They're all here, in the garage. Quite forgot about them after all this time. The thing is, Reuben, the police had access to all this stuff. They must have gone through all his things – address book, correspondence, papers and so on – and they found nothing, so why should I?'

'The police were fixated on the sex, because they were convinced that explained the murder, but what I've been trying to argue is that there could be something else entirely they never thought of or never bothered with. I suggest you have a look. Can't do any harm, can it?'

'Oh, but there's masses of stuff! I sold all his furniture and books, but the contents of his desk I simply shoved into a suitcase and, well, it's been in the garage ever since. I couldn't see the whole of James' life simply disappear in the flames, and I suppose I intended one day to go through it all and salvage what I could. There must be something there that will recall the happy days we spent together. I don't know, photos or letters or something.'

'Look, mum, one suitcase of papers isn't "masses of stuff", is it? Shall I get it?'

'Oh, all right. But we'd be wasting our time.'

Reuben disappeared and was not long absent. He returned with a standard leather suitcase, wheels at one end and retractable handle at the other. He placed it in the middle of the floor, on its base, and opened the lid. Just papers, seemingly, an untidy heap, some in bundles, others loose, the detritus of a life lived on the edge of respectability with no inkling, presumably, of its sudden ending. He began to empty it.

'So what are we looking for?' she asked.

'I don't know, do I?' said Reuben. 'Anything unusual, I suppose. We'll just have to go through it all and hope something strikes us. Here, mum, you start with this wodge,' he invited her, handing her a packet of papers loosely tied with a piece of kitchen string. The two worked on, getting quite absorbed in even innocent papers, raking over the embers of James Thwaites' worldly existence before the glow faded for ever. It was surprising what their owner had thought fit to hoard: academic certificates, ragged book-markers, old exam papers, odd utility bills, some class-notes dated thirty years back, newspaper cuttings, miscellaneous correspondence, dog-eared photographs of unidentified persons, a couple of old school magazines.

'What about this?' Reuben asked suddenly, holding up two printed sheets.

'What is it?'

'A couple of letters.'

'Well, go on: who from?'

'That's just it: I'm not sure. There's no signature, just an initial, P, but it's headed "The Anti-Church of Jesus Christ".' When he stopped, Serenity prompted him.

'So what does it say?'

'Here, read it for yourself.' He passed a sheet of paper over.

> Dear James [she read] Good of you to reply so rapidly. We're gathering strength, and your support has been invaluable. My particular thanks for your contribution these last few months: I promise you full public acknowledgement when the time comes – which we hope is not far away. The purpose of this brief note is to tell you that our next meeting is at No. 18, as usual, on the 7th, and we hope you can make it.

'Is that it?' she asked, turning it over – but the other side was blank. 'What's it all that about, then?'

'Search me,' he replied. 'Here, here's the second one.' She reached out for a similar sheet again headed "The Anti-Church of Jesus Christ".

> Dear James [it read] Things are going according to plan. We've got the required 250 signatures, the dean's with us, it's all set – only the date to be fixed. Will be in touch. Don't let us down. Yours P

'Well,' Serenity asked her offspring, 'what's it all about, then?'

'Search me,' Reuben replied with a shake of his head. 'All very mysterious, if you ask me. What on earth had uncle James got himself into? One thing's obvious to me: we're talking cathedral here, aren't we?'

'Not necessarily,' his mother said. 'You get deans in all sorts of establishments: well, universities, colleges and parishes anyhow. Could be anyone anywhere. Almost.'

'No, it couldn't, mother. Uncle James was tied up with the cathedral, and that's what all this is about.'

'So what now?'

'Well, I suggest we finish going through these papers, and, if this is all we find, we can consider our next move.' They made their way through the remaining contents of the suitcase, but neither of the searchers stumbled on anything remotely sinister or mysterious.

'Right, high time for a cup of tea,' Serenity announced. 'Shall I make it or will you?'

'Let's consider things,' Reuben began. 'Uncle James was murdered. The police are convinced it was sexual, but so far, after two years of inquiry, they haven't come up with anything concrete: just the figure of a bearded man outside his house, whom they haven't traced. We've uncovered fragments of a correspondence which has all the makings of a mystery: no dates, no venues, no names, under the menacing heading "The Anti-Church of Jesus Christ". We've got to investigate: it's the only lead we've got.'

'OK, I suppose you want me to go and see James' old cathedral dean – presuming that's the one meant?'

'Wouldn't be a bad start, would it?'

'What if I get murdered?'

'Mother!'

'Right, I'll go, but what I'm to say to him I've no idea.'

'Rely on the inspiration of the Spirit. You know the text: "The Holy Spirit will teach you at that time what you should say."'

'Yes, but rather a different context, wouldn't you think?'

'Oh, I don't know. But seriously, you can't really imagine you'll come to any harm. Just see what he says. He may have heard of this Anti-Church business. Well, he obviously has, if he's agreed with it, and he may be able to shed some light on what these letters are about. Take them along with you, just in case.'

7

Two days later, Serenity made an appointment to see the Rev. Harrison Booth at his place of work. When asked what her business concerned, she confessed unashamedly that it concerned the death of her late brother, James Thwaites. Mr Booth was a stocky creature, seemingly without a neck, with short-cropped, grizzled hair on a completely round skull and two small eyes peering out from a florid and fleshy face. His complexion struck her as unhealthy, and she concluded almost at once that she found the Rev. Booth unappealing. However, she persevered in her request. The two were seated in the dean's office, somewhere in the heart of the buildings that surrounded the cathedral. His attitude was brisk but not hostile.

'What can I do for you, Mrs Bursnell?'

'Did you know my brother, Mr Booth?'

'No. By name only. I haven't been dean here for two years yet, so I never had the pleasure.'

'I see. Then I'm probably talking to the wrong person.'

'Try me anyway.'

'Well,' Serenity ventured after a pause, 'I've been going through his papers, and I found these two letters. Can you help explain them to me?' The dean took the letters, read them through with every appearance of keen attention and ended by uttering the single syllable, 'Ah!'.

'So they mean something to you?'

'Yes, they do, but I'm not sure you want to bother your head with it.'

'Shall I be the judge of that, dean? Somebody murdered my brother, and I should like to find out who and why. The cathedral, as you may know, was very much a part of his life, and he seems to have got mixed up in this Anti-Church business which also involved your predecessor, if I've read matters rightly. I need to know more. At the moment I just don't know what's what.'

'OK, Mrs Bursnell - '

'Do call me Serenity: everyone does.'

'Very well – happy to do so. Well, then, Serenity, let me tell you what I know about this business. The Anti-Church of Jesus Christ is a movement founded by a man called Len Croft, who's lecturer in theology at Nottingham. He's written two books: *Taking Miss Fanshawe Seriously* – little more than a pamphlet, really. The reference is to a novel by Benson, where one of the characters – the Elizabeth Fanshawe in question - says something like, "It's only by dreaming that you can get close to the world and hope to get at its meaning" – so in the pamphlet Croft dreams away; and a weightier thing called *The Master – Prolegomena to a Deconstructionist Christian Spirituality*. I know about these things because my predecessor left copies behind in the, er, vestry of all places.[2]

'What Croft does is reduce Christianity to its barest bones – to start again from scratch, if you like, on the grounds that most of it is time-bound, irrelevant, obstructive, alien or simply unnecessary. Two things, you see, went wrong from the very beginning – according to Croft. Firstly, men got hold of Christianity and made it their own, excluding women from all the structures. The result was a macho, aggressive, intellectual and systematic perversion of Jesus' original message. Secondly, the men – frightened to entrust anything so precious as Jesus' heritage to unlettered peasants – my eye! - excluded all democratic involvement. The result was a two-tier church, consisting of clergy on the one hand, who were everything, and the laity on the other, who were nothing. This, according to Croft, was quite foreign to Jesus' thinking. To crown it all, Croft argues that Jesus didn't even intend to found a church, so that Christianity is actually a mistake of monstrous proportions: a man-made structure that puts itself in place of the Master, claims to control all access to the Master and sets out to explain the Master's teaching to the world with exclusive authority. Croft simply sweeps the church aside.'

'So what's he put in its place?' Serenity interrupted.

'Nothing. There's no church, no clergy, no buildings, no creeds, no liturgy – nothing but what the author calls "an eschatological persuasion".'

'What on earth does that mean?'

'It means that you put your trust in a God who's going to bring an end to injustice, poverty and misery. What you have to do is to prepare yourself for the ensuing cataclysm, which'll be like nothing the world's ever known before. Actually, I'm not really being fair to Croft. He proposes a loose association of small groups of Christians who meet weekly to discuss Jesus'

---

[2]*Taking Miss Fanshawe Seriously* was subsequently withdrawn by the author on the grounds that it was superseded by *The Master*. The latter is available, Dr Croft tells me, at www.lulu.com.

teaching and its application to our times, but it's not a church – just an idea, a way of living which puts the fight against injustice at the forefront of people's minds.'

'OK, dean, go on. None of this explains what's in the letters.'

'Well, it does and it doesn't. The letters are nothing to do with Croft; well, not really: they concern a local disciple of his, if I may so phrase it – a man carried away by Croft's ideas, whose name I still don't know. He's the "P" of the letters. His idea was to stage a massive Anti-Church protest here in the cathedral. Hundreds of people would turn up for a service. They would move all the chairs round to form a circle – no leader, you see, all equal – promise to withhold all contributions until certain changes were introduced – such as democratic structures - and generally use the cathedral to launch a programme of deconstruction and renovation. I'd have been surprised if P could have rustled up so many demonstrators, even summoning them from the four corners of the country, but I hand it to him for chutzpah!'

'So what happened?'

'P had got so far as to persuade the dean – my predecessor – to go along with this. The dean was near retiring, and I suppose thought he hadn't much to lose. Talk about a fifth-columnist! Anyway, also on the dean's side was your brother – and I suppose others, although I've no idea who.'

'But the letters hint at the need for extreme secrecy. From what you're saying, all this was out in the open.'

'Then I've given you the wrong impression, Serenity. P was determined to stage a thunderous coup: not some minor demonstration that would irritate a few people and fade away like a damp firework. I think it was more than a demonstration he wanted: nothing less than the complete capitulation of the cathedral to Croft's views, which P had made his own. The bishop would be unseated, because his seat – his *cathedra* – and all who sailed in her would have succumbed to the Anti-Church. In the end, it was proposed, I believe, to flog the cathedral for cash and distribute the proceeds to specific charities. Complete pie in the sky, of course, as it would have been illegal, apart from being totally unrealistic.'

'But then perhaps P would've argued that Jesus was unrealistic.'

'Maybe so, but the fact remains that P's scheme failed. Well, you probably know it did, otherwise you'd have heard about it. The thing was, P knew that if his little scheme leaked out, the authorities would simply have shut the building, or put a police guard on it, or prevented the disturbance in some other way. Sacking the dean would've been a good start. Oops, sorry! Shouldn't be saying these things. So P was determined to keep things under wraps until it was too late for the cathedral authorities to prevent the demo. Hence the secrecy embedded in these letters.'

'So what happened?'

'Your brother got cold feet, that's the long and the short of it, and betrayed the movement. Apparently he went to the bishop and disclosed the plot. The bishop acted swiftly and organised a fake meeting of ecclesiastical high-ups which gave him an excuse to close the cathedral for the day on the grounds that it would be required for the august assembly. All baloney, of course, but the press never got hold of it, and it all passed without remark. When the demonstrators assembled in dribs and drabs and found the cathedral closed, they simply dispersed, believing that the demo had been called off.'

'But how do you know it was my brother who tipped the authorities off?'

'I don't know for certain, but it was some remark the dean made which led me to that belief. You see, the bishop couldn't tolerate him in place one day longer, after all this business, and sacked him, but to maintain appearances, it was given out that he was taking early retirement on the grounds of ill-health. The bishop asked me to negotiate the hand-over so that no suspicions were aroused that not all was as it should be. I hurried over to see the dean and discussed the situation with him. He was in a way repentant. He agreed with Croft but had begun to see that what P planned wasn't the way to go about getting things changed, and he moved out without fuss. He made some silly comment like: He supposed Thwaites would now be promoted from verger to dean, and it dawned on me only later that this was perhaps a shaft aimed in anger but based on some knowledge hidden from me. So there you have it.'

'Didn't you go to the police with all this?'

'I did mention it when I was first interviewed, but, with the bishop so anxious to hush things up, I made it plain to DI Whatever-His-Name-Was that I didn't think there was much in it. And I still don't. Serenity, let me be quite frank with you. Your search for your brother's murderer – a completely laudable undertaking, don't get me wrong – is doomed to failure if you think you can find clues here. We're a house of God, not a cauldron of intrigue and murder. Whatever P's errors, I can't think that a man so dedicated to the heritage of Jesus Christ, however deluded his understanding, would consider murder an appropriate weapon. What's the matter with the police's theory that your brother was murdered by a partner who turned on him – sexual frustration, rage, jealousy, I don't know, there are plenty of motives to choose from.'

Although Serenity was no nearer liking this bullish man in front of her, she had to admit that, as far as she could judge, he had been perfectly fair with her.

He seemed to have concealed nothing, not to have made excuses, not to have fobbed her off with lies or half-truths. On the other hand, his opinion that James' death had nothing to do with the cathedral was a little ingenuous. The failure of a plot seemingly conceived on no small scale could well have prompted murder, on the part of P himself or of a lieutenant. Religious fanaticism takes on all shapes and sizes, and James' martyrdom in the cause of religion would not by any means be the first. So she reasoned as she caught her bus back to Ripon.

Reuben telephoned her that evening.

'Well, mum, how d'you get on?'

'OK, I think. As you can hear, I wasn't murdered, and in fact the present dean is quite affable. He seemed perfectly honest, and he was certainly helpful, telling me what he knew about the Anti-Church of Jesus Christ and what he knew about your uncle James' part in it.' She proceeded to outline her conversation with Dean Harrison Booth.

'So are we any further forward, do you think?' Reuben asked. 'How do you feel about things?'

'Well, I'm now convinced that the riddle to the mystery of James' death lies there, and I'm determined to do what the police should've done in the first place.'

'But you're no nearer knowing who P is. So where d'you start?'

'I thought of starting with the other members of the cathedral staff, but I don't think that's a good idea if the bishop and present dean are so keen to let the matter rest, as they obviously are. Don't want to stir up a hornets' nest, do we? Another possibility is the religious bookshop which has been selling Croft's book. P presumably bought his copy there, if he's a native of the city, and they may know who he is. After that there's always Croft himself, tucked away in his Nottingham eerie: he started all this, and he can jolly well help unravel where it's gone wrong.'

'The trouble is, mum, the Anti-Church itself may be all above board and quite beyond suspicion, but the plotting of a demo at the cathedral – that's the thing, isn't it? There was secrecy surrounding that from the start, and nobody's going to speak openly about it to some random dame swanning in from Ripon demanding answers to impertinent questions.'

'You're right, of course. I shall obviously need to put you on a retainer as guru-cum-chaperone-cum-body-guard.' She smiled, and, although he could not see it, he sensed it.

'Now, mum, don't do anything foolish. This may be dangerous, we don't know. Keep me informed, and we'll see it through together.'

8

Meanwhile, sixty-four-year-old Matthias Biddulph was turning over in his mind the disastrous sequence of events which had led him to abandon his house in the city of his birth and move to the city of York, principally to avoid his detractors. The police had interviewed him time and again, trying to break down his resistance to an admission of guilt in the death of James Thwaites; they had forced him to admit a relationship with the deceased of a kind which struck the cathedral authorities, the parishioners and his neighbours as wretched, grubby and proximate to bringing the parish and neighbourhood into disrepute; and they had abandoned the enterprise only because they had found not a shred of proof with which to belabour him. Here in York he achieved something approaching anonymity. Nobody bothered very much with this council employee whose official title was 'assistant parks and cemeteries manager', who minded his own business when he was allowed to and whose life was in ruins. All but arrested on a murder charge? pointed at in the streets? paraded in the local press with details of his private life? Intolerable. Not that he was beyond murder. He had enough insight into the human condition to realise that, while many, perhaps even most, would not and could not commit murder in cold blood, unless they had allowed themselves to be led into situations where the normal standards of decency, pity and right-doing were abandoned in an orgy of violence, many would be capable of murder in moments of personal stress: anger, intoxication, fear, extreme provocation, defence of loved ones and so forth. He knew, however, that nothing in Thwaites' life would goad him to such extremes. He knew the man intimately, was, he supposed, his friend, but there had not really been a meeting of minds. Thwaites was a learned man, member of a disciplined profession with responsibility for young lives and bearer of the traditions and good repute of the institutions in which he had worked. He himself worked only with flowers and plants, which had no intelligent life or, philosophically speaking, a mind of their own, were powerless in his hands and did not provide anything that could pass as conversation. He had no habit of abstract thought, speculation, analysis – just not trained that way. He regretted it, of course, since he felt that his life would be richer for a bit of philosophy, at however humdrum a level, but he knew that, as things stood, he could never really be James Thwaites' *friend*, except at a prosaic and, for Thwaites, an unsatisfactory level. On the other hand, he would, he supposed, have been prepared to die for his friend, but he did not think that was the situation when he was being pilloried and hounded on suspicion of his friend's murder. He was dying inwardly, yes, but not out of friendship for Thwaites – merely out of police incompetence and the pressure of circumstances.

Matthias Biddulph had been born in Truro, almost within sight of the cathedral, the runt of a family of three boys. His father worked as a radiographer at the hospital (which was at that time in the city), while his mother, when she returned to work after rearing her family sufficiently, managed a dry cleaner's in the city centre. Of the three boys, only Matthias attended Truro School, the fee-paying establishment on the hill overlooking the upper reaches of the creek on which the city is built. Those who have not lived in Cornwall cannot appreciate the peculiar atmosphere that pervades the county ('duchy') south of the Tamar and particularly south of the Fal – an atmosphere compounded of an unhurried life-style, hostility to the English ('emmets'), pride in the coast-line and countryside and regret for the loss of tin-mining and fishing. There is also a pseudo-mystique whipped up by certain members of the tourist trade, anxious to cash in on king Arthur, *Jamaica Inn*, Poldark, Rosamund Pilcher and so forth. The expansion of the school matched the expansion of the city in the 1980s, which Matthias considered a degeneration, because it brought the city into line with other cities up country.

After school, Matthias made his way to Askham Bryan agricultural college, which is how he came to be acquainted with the Vale of York. There followed a series of horticultural jobs, some in his native county, others up country, until he settled in the city which was to prove his undoing.

Mulling over his present plight, he decided to consult an oracle, in this case an old school-teacher of his, now in his late eighties, whom he had always regarded as a fount of wisdom. Hadrian Wallace, retired teacher of English, lived quietly with his wife of nearly sixty years in a bungalow on an estate in Pontefract, in the so-called New Town. He was a man of diminutive proportions but formidable intellect. Matthias Biddulph was one of the few ex-pupils with whom he was still in touch, having maintained a sporadic correspondence over the intervening forty-five years. The elderly couple received him warmly and, after an initial cup of tea together, Mrs Wallace discreetly withdrew to attend to some matters of her own.

'Now, young man,' Mr Wallace said, 'what's all this about? Not a social visit, I take it.'

'The fact is, Mr Wallace - well, you see, I'm not really myself – can't seem to get my life on track – well, it's a bit difficult to explain.'

'Why not just give me the facts from the beginning, and we can take it from there? That'd seem to be the best thing.'

'You'll think me such a fool.'

'My dear boy, do you think I haven't done things I now regret? Nobody's immune from regret – or embarrassment. So just get on with it.' Biddulph swallowed and paused before speaking.

'I don't know whether you heard of the so-called Thwaites Sex Murder two years ago – doesn't matter if you haven't. James Thwaites, a cathedral verger, was found dead at home, in just his underpants. The main suspect - after the police had fumbled around fruitlessly for a day or two – was a fellow-cathedral worker called Jonas Chimes, a rather ineffectual creature who mooched about on his own and did odd jobs round the cathedral. History of mental illness, and all that. Anyhow, the police couldn't find any proof that he was gay or get him to admit to any involvement in Thwaites' death, so they had to let him go. They then cottoned on to a bearded man reportedly seen in the area at the time, but that slender thread came to nothing as well: how do you trace a bearded man lurking about the place without any further description? The next victim the police latched on to was – me! They had finally got round to analysing traces of semen found on Thwaites' underpants, and, amongst all the men they got a DNA sample from, I was the only one that matched.'

'So you had been there?'

'Yes, I couldn't deny it – and I didn't – but the police couldn't produce a shred of evidence that I'd murdered the man. You see, before being strangled with a curtain cord, Thwaites was hit over the head with a statuette found in his house, and the police still hadn't identified the finger-prints found on it, so they couldn't really charge me with anything, could they, knowing that someone else had been in the house as well?'

'So what's your story?'

'Look, Mr Wallace, it may sound stupid to you, and I suppose most people would find it distasteful as well, but Thwaites and I met once a week

41

for a friendly session – a café meal, bit of a film, bit of, well, you know – and that day had been no exception. I left his house at, what, three o'clock, I suppose. There was nothing unusual, it was the same every week. And that's it. I saw nobody else, James didn't tell me about other visitors he was expecting, so I'm as much in the dark as anybody else.'

'Was James in the habit of having more than one partner to his bow at a time, if I may so phrase it?'

'Yes – a bit of a randy devil, if the truth be told, and his appetite didn't seem to dwindle with age.'

'Why, how long had you known him?'

'Oh, it's not that, it's just things he'd say which led me to believe he was a much-practised man and had no intention of slowing up.'

'If the police preferred no charges, what's your problem?'

'I've become a pariah. The cathedral authorities and usual parishioners knew nothing about Thwaites' activities – a complete shock to them to find out – and they couldn't come to terms with it. As for the rest of the city, well, it was all over the local press, wasn't it, and so was my name. Most people are pretty tolerant of gays these days, but two old gents fumbling about after a porn film every week – well, they couldn't take it. Just disgusting. Old folks should know better. The fact that it was two consenting adults minding their own business in the total privacy of their own homes seems to have escaped their attention. There are no doubt mysterious psychological reasons behind the phenomenon. Anyway, Mr Wallace, life just became intolerable. I felt so uncomfortable, I gave up my flat and moved to York. No one knows me there, and my name means nothing to people. I was lucky enough to get a job straight away with the council, and now I'm trying to pick up the threads of my life again.'

'What family have you left, Matt?'

'Two brothers, both married, and a couple of cousins. Parents and all aunts and uncles long since gone.'

'And how have they reacted?'

'I think they were a bit shocked by it all, but none of them has disowned me, if that's what you mean.'

'So: you've got a job, a new flat, your family's standing by you: what's the problem?'

'The problem is, Mr Wallace, my name's not been cleared. I feel – oh, I don't know – sullied, somehow - sordid. People think I'm capable of murder, a man of violence, and I'm not. I can't settle. I can't just ignore it all – the innuendos, the snide comments I had to put up with before I left. And of course I can't go back.'

'So who do you think murdered your, er, friend, Thwaites?'

'I'm no wiser than anybody else, but I had my suspicions that James wasn't above a spot of blackmail. Perhaps one of his victims turned against him.'

'Go on. What gave you cause for – "suspicion"?'

'I'm not sure. Chance remarks. I'll be perfectly honest with you, Mr Wallace, although you'll regard me as even more of a fool than you do already, but I don't think James was actually a very nice man. Oh, he was good at his job, from what I could tell, no trouble there, but there was a selfish and ruthless streak in him. He told me once, "Don't ever cross me, Matt, or I'll see that your activities are all over the papers" – something like that, and that led me to believe that he could prove a pretty nasty acquaintance if you got the wrong side of him. I was stupid, I know that. I kept in with him because it was easier than trying to find another partner. And now I'm reaping the fruits.'

'Is this bearded man relevant, in your opinion?'

'How do I know? I suppose he could be – if he exists.'

'So why don't you chase him up?'

'How, if the police couldn't manage it?'

'No, but had you thought of hiring a private investigator? If there was blackmail going on, there must be some traces of it somewhere. It probably needs only a bit more persistence than the police showed – or had time to show, to be fair to them.'

'A private investigator? How do you get one of those? And don't they cost the earth?'

'To answer your last question first, Matt, how much is your peace of mind worth to you? Have you got any savings?'

'Well, yes.'

'There you are, then. Approach a firm of private detectives, one which offers a first consultation without obligation, and see what they say. You can't lose, can you?'

'No, but - '

'Give it a go, then.'

'How?'

'Go online. You'd know more about that than I would, as I've never really understood computers. Or try the library. Yellow pages: do investigation firms advertise in yellow pages? Anyway, I'm sure there are plenty of firms – and individuals – out there, anxious to get hold of your custom.'

'Your idea, I suppose, is that doing something will relieve the tensions in my twisted psyche.'

'Look, Matt, you know full well I can't tell you what to do – I can't "advise" you, in the usual meaning of that term. I can only make a few suggestions and see what you think. You quite rightly say that the police have done what they can, but I'm simply saying that there's obviously – since they haven't come up with anything - scope for somebody else to have a go. Not you: like me, you probably wouldn't know where to start; but a private firm of investigators might be just the trick. You'll have to decide how much it's worth to you, particularly in the light of the realisation that they mightn't come up with anything either. I really don't know what else to suggest.'

9

Matthias Biddulph left the house in a state of great perplexity. He saw the force of Mr Wallace's contention, but he shrank within himself at the thought of exposing his anxieties to a complete stranger and spending his savings on a possibly doomed enterprise. The move was beyond him, psychologically. On the other hand, could he come up with an alternative? No, he could not, was the short answer. He decided to pop into St Giles' Church in the Market Square to see whether the Almighty might take the opportunity to address him with a few pertinent words (either 'Yes' or 'No' he thought would be a good start). He crossed the elegant space of the Market Square and entered the church. He walked slowly up the main aisle, paved in herring-bone wood, admiring the Tudor ceiling and the simple but pleasing architecture around him and sank on his knees on the steps of the main altar. Nothing happened. He murmured an inchoate prayer for guidance before rising and wandering at random round the church. His eye was caught by a piece of stained glass high up on a window depicting a multicoloured angel – purple, white and golden robe, red, green and white wings, golden hair, blue and silver halo. It was difficult to see clearly from his position on the ground: the angel was probably at prayer, but to Matthias Biddulph the celestial figure seemed to have raised his hand in blessing. That was it; that was the sign he hoped for. He was not entirely sure that he believed in angels, but this one was so real his doubts fell away like autumn leaves on the breeze.

He hurried home to go online before his courage failed him. Seated at his laptop, he googled 'private investigator' and came up with a plethora of firms, all claiming to be the leading agents in the business with an unbroken record of success. Metaphorically sticking a pin into his monitor, he chose a big firm with a wide range of services wherein, he thought, his privacy and insignificance would not be compromised. He rang, received an immediate answer and was promised, by a smooth-voiced receptionist no doubt used to dealing with the distraught, the puzzled, the hesitant and the malicious, a visit within twenty-four hours. Mr Biddulph waited impatiently and uncertainly. The operative who called the following morning turned out to be a young woman in her twenties, blonde, tall and brisk. He offered her coffee, but she declined. Her efforts to elicit from him the precise nature of his problem met with embarrassed stammers and a total lack of substance. He just could not bring himself to describe his problem to this modern, sparky young woman whose experience may well not have stretched to murder in a cathedral precinct and doubtful goings-on after doubtful films. Red-faced and squirming, he apologised for troubling her and showed her the door – to her astonishment. (To her credit, she took her expulsion in good part, thereby demonstrating that she might have been a very suitable operative for Mr Biddulph's circumstances. Too late, regrettably.)

For some days he proceeded no further. He was flustered and mortified. He wavered between a downright refusal to countenance hire of a private detective one minute longer and a desire to follow Mr Wallace's suggestion to its conclusion, for his peace of mind. Finally he returned to his laptop to google 'private investigator' once again. He hesitated. He prevaricated. He dithered. Finally he took the plunge and fixed on a(n apparently) one-man firm in York called The Jorvik Probe, with an office on King's Staith. He decided to call in person, the better to vet the firm's public face. Feeling insecure and rather wretched, he mounted the steps and knocked on a black door on which a notice in gothic script told him to Please Knock and Enter. He was faced with an older woman sitting at a large desk in a room that was uncluttered, even austere, yet there was a sense of warmth and efficiency that he appreciated. The receptionist looked up immediately and greeted him in a straight-forward, business-like and cordial way.

'Good morning, sir,' she said, peering over her horn-rimmed spectacles. Her dark hair was gathered at the nape and pinned into an assortment of coils and twists. She wore a waterfall-front blouse in cobalt and looked (he thought in his confusion) a million dollars. 'What can we do for you?' For a moment he said nothing.

'I want a consultation with the investigator, please,' he managed to stammer. 'Just an initial consultation, you understand.'

'Quite so, sir, perfectly in order. He'll be delighted to meet you, I'm sure. Now's he out of the office at the moment, but he'll be back directly. Will you wait, or would you prefer to call back later?'

'I'll call back later. This afternoon?' He made an appointment and went his way, some of his misgivings soothed by the stylish receptionist and her courteous friendliness.

When he returned that afternoon, the receptionist was again all smiles.

'Mr Ravensdale will receive you immediately, sir. This way, please.' She rose, moved to the door behind her, knocked and opened without waiting for a reply. 'Mr Biddulph for you, Mr Ravensdale,' she announced. Mr Ravensdale was far from the Philip Marlowe stereotype and impressed the still hesitant Biddulph with his aura of competence and quiet discretion. His suit was sober and unthreatening. His open face was that of a middle-aged man familiar with the ways of the world but not cynical: a broad forehead, a broad smile and lively eyes. He rose, moved round the desk, shook Matthias Biddulph warmly by the hand, then gestured him into a chair.

'Mr Biddulph, what can I do for you? I'm here to help.' Having got thus far, Matthias found a resurgence of confidence and told Ravensdale his story without flinching and without gloss. It was a relief, and he felt at once that he had made a wise choice in climbing the steps up to Jorvik Probe. Mr Ravensdale said nothing for a time.

'It's a slender thread, isn't it: a bearded man seen in the vicinity at the time, and we're going back two years. I'll tell you what I can do for you – like a no win, no fee arrangement. I'd like to take your case on, but you'll realise that we haven't much to start with. So I propose to charge you our full fees - £25 per hour – only if I'm successful. If I'm not successful, I'll charge you less than half that.'

'But it all sounds rather open-ended, Mr Ravensdale: you could spin it out into weeks and months, and I'd find myself unable to pay your bill.'

'My dear Mr Biddulph, I pride myself on running a business for the good of the clients: we're here to help; but I see your point entirely. What if I put a cap on it of £500, and then we can review the situation?'

'Very well. I've no choice, really. When can you start?'

'As soon as possible – before the trail gets even colder than it is!' He smiled wanly, but his manner oozed confidence. 'You may rely entirely on us, Mr Biddulph. May I ask what happens if we trace this bearded man? What can you do about it?'

'I don't know. I may go the police if they haven't given up all interest in the case. Otherwise I shall just have to see. I'll cross that bridge when I come to it.'

'And do we know the name of the witness who claims to have seen the bearded man?'

'No, but I daresay the police do, and of course the press must have some idea.'

'Quite so. We shall take it from there, then. Leave it with us, and I'll get back to you just as soon as I possibly can.'

'And I can rely entirely on your discretion?'

'My dear sir,' Ravensdale said, spreading his hands out, 'Discretion is my middle name.'

10

Back in Ledsham, Lorna and Alex Carter were discussing how best to exploit their discoveries. The theory, which had yet to attract any sort of confirmation, was that Thwaites had become involved in an illegal traffic in old and rare books, had fallen foul of his masters or of his fellow-traffickers and had met an unhappy end as a reward for his infidelities. The only lead Lorna and Alex had on this business was the Becketts at Ledsham.

'We've got to infiltrate their organisation, Lorna,' Alex said at length. 'It's the only way. They're never going to talk to us, let alone take us into their confidence, unless they see us as one of them; but how do we do that?'

'"Infiltrate their organisation"? That's rather grand, isn't it? Get an insight into their seedy little operation, more like. Let's look at the options.' She counted the options off on one hand, using the index finger of the other, and spoke deliberately. 'One is that you pretend to be a friend of Thwaites keen to carry on his work.' Pause. 'Another is that you approach the Becketts as a would-be operator offering your services and hope to lead them round to Thwaites eventually.' A further short pause. 'A third, I suppose,' she concluded, 'is that you are looking to start some organisation of your own and thought the Becketts would be willing partners.'

'I see drawbacks to all of those little schemes.'

'OK, let's go through them. The first one is that you claim friendship with Thwaites - I mean, he's not around to refute you, is he? - and you're keen to take his part in the operation.'

'Right, how do I know he was part of an illegal trade, and how do I know he was in contact with the Becketts?'

'You need some story, obviously. For the first part, you could say you surprised Thwaites with some stolen books – the ones taken from the cathedral vestry will do – challenged him and threatened to go to the police, only he won you over and offered you a sweetener to keep your mouth shut. Or he was going to set up in business and offered you a partnership.'

'So why didn't I take it?'

'He died before that could come about.'

'Hm – doubtful.'

'For the second part,' Lorna pursued, '– how you got on to the Becketts – that's a trickier one. Any ideas?'

'What if Thwaites told me that, if I wanted to get involved, I should approach them?'

'The trouble is that that presumes the Becketts are the leading lights in the racket, and we've just no idea. If they're minor cogs, Thwaites would hardly recommend them as your first port of call. And if Thwaites threatened to betray them, they're probably not going to take very kindly to his nominee, are they?'

'That's a risk we might have to take. What's next?'

'You keep Thwaites out of it and go to the Becketts offering your services.'

'How do I know the Becketts are involved in an illegal trade?'

'Intuition?'

'Come off it, Alex – you might as well say "ESP".'

'OK, ESP.'

'That's hardly going to convince them, is it? Be sensible. They're running huge risks daily, because they could go to prison for years: they're hardly going to embrace the first geezer who comes along laying claim to inside information through some psychic medium.'

'One of the parcels meant for them was delivered here by mistake, and we opened it inadvertently.'

'But their parcels don't seem to be delivered by post: they're all picked up by hand. In any case, it's difficult to see how the postman could make such a stupid error – we're not even in the same street.'

'No, you're right. I know, what about my old bookshop: couldn't I have picked up some whisper there about the Becketts' illegal activities?'

'How?'

'I overheard Thwaites being indiscreet.'

'Hm, that might work, but it would have to be a pretty good story. I mean, Thwaites is hardly likely to come out with a name and an address in a public place, is he?'

'He wrote it down, and I happened to see it round the corner.'

'Furthermore, if the Becketts did have anything to do with Thwaites' death, they're going to be doubly alert if anyone mentions his name. Well, we can come back to that. In third place, you're looking to start an illegal operation of your own and wondered whether the Becketts would come in on it. But why the Becketts?'

'Because they're a dodgy couple who stand out like sore thumbs in the village.'

'Alex! This is serious.'

'Sorry. Well, why not the same reason as above: I was thinking of involving Thwaites but he was murdered? I'd approached him, and he'd suggested the Becketts.'

'Yes, that might work.'

'But one thing worrying me about all this is, Aren't we running a heck of a risk of falling foul of the police ourselves? Shouldn't we tell them first what we're planning?'

'Yeah, and they're going to stand by while you do their work for them. Hardly. The minute you spill the beans about the Becketts' operation, they're going to wade in – they'd have to – and there'd be no chance for you then to work things round to Thwaites.'

'Well, we go to the police with our suspicions, Thwaites and all, and let them take it from there.'

'Are they going to take you seriously? They'd cotton on to the Becketts' racket, but why should they bother to go to the trouble of tying them in with Thwaites' death, now two years old and in any case in another police authority? But they might, of course.'

'Then I write a letter and lodge it with a lawyer, and he can produce it in case of trouble.'

'Ye-e-s. We'll think about that. He might not take kindly to being party to an illegal activity.'

'Then don't tell him what's in the letter.'

'I can't see him taking custody of a letter without knowing what's in it.'

'No, maybe not. So which of our three options are we going for?'

'Well, there's a fourth option if none of those appeals to us, but it's probably just as risky.'

'And that is?'

'Thwaites confided in you that he had doubts about the Becketts' expertise. He roped you in because of your knowledge of the book-trade and asked you to sound them out or find out more about them or make their acquaintance and put them to the test. It sounds the sort of devious thing Thwaites might get up to. Instead of doing that, however, you decided to go over to their side.'

'So why have I waited two years before doing anything about it?'

'Because you've been ill and didn't know Thwaites was dead. You just wished to warn them that they couldn't trust him any longer.'

'But that's open to the same objection as two of the options above: as soon as I mention the name Thwaites, they're going to clam up.'

'Maybe not, if you tell them you didn't know he was dead. All that side of it is a closed book to you – so to speak.' After much further discussion, Lorna and Alex thought they had enough material, when polished up, to form the basis of a little plot.

11

A few days later, consequently, Jonas Chimes, in the person of Alex Carter, felt confident enough to present himself at the Becketts'. It was a quiet evening, with brisk white clouds scudding across a sky of brilliant blue as the sun began to set behind the Roman ridge that mercifully shrouded Ledsham from the blot that was Kippax (to those in the know, pronounced Kippx or Kippu^{u}x) further to the west. In line with Mrs Tukes' recommendations of months before, he had abandoned his round spectacles in favour of something rather heavier and more imposing, and his upper lip sported a large moustache in the style sometimes known as a chevron. With his curly black hair, it might look to the hostile that he was trying to out-Burt Reynolds Burt Reynolds in one of his particularly macho roles. Inside, however, he was nervous, knowing how much depended on this first interview. The door was opened by Mr Beckett.

'Good evening, Mr Beckett,' Alex said with as much confidence as he could muster, 'I wonder whether I might have a private word.'

'What's it about, may I ask? You're not selling anything, are you?'

'No, nothing like that. I'm hoping you'll find what I've got to say to your advantage.'

'Well, come in then – but not for long, mind, as we're due to go out shortly.' Beckett led the way into the lounge, sat his caller down and invited him to begin without more ado.

'Mr Beckettt, my name's Carter, Alex Carter, and you may know, since we live only a few hundred yards from each other, that I work for the prison service. However, I used to work in the book-trade until there was, well, shall we say a little unpleasantness, and I felt it advisable to seek employment elsewhere.' He felt rather than saw that Beckett's interest quickened. 'However, my job doesn't pay all that well, and Lorna – that's my wife – and I feel we need a bit extra to prepare the way for our retirement. We wondered about a part-time return to the book-trade – even though times are hard for publishers.' He allowed a thin laugh to escape.

'I hope this story is going somewhere useful, Mr, er, Carter.'

'Oh, yes, but of course you must tell me at once if I've got the wrong end of the stick. Anyway, as I was saying, Lorna and I are contemplating a return to the book-trade, but not with the old firm - not advisable, we feel – and only part-time, to, er, allay any suspicions.'

'Suspicions?'

'Yes, well, you know, people will talk, and in the light of my previous, er, troubles I prefer to be regarded as a devoted servant of our criminal friends behind bars.'

'Mr Carter, I hope you'll get to the point quickly, I'm still not sure what all this is about.'

'Mr Beckett, may I ask whether you've ever read Ruiz Zafón's *The Shadow of the Wind*? No? I can strongly recommend it: a really fascinating tale of post-civil war Spain. Now one of the characters in it, Fermin, who's an ex-prisoner, begins to work in the book-shop of the hero's father. Part of his job is to hunt out old and unusual books for the shop's clients, and he is an expert, not precisely because of a great store of knowledge but through determination and savvy. The book appeals to me particularly because I fulfilled a role very similar to Fermin's. Haunting the novel is a stranger with a badly burnt face who has set himself the task of destroying all remaining copies of the works of a long-dead writer called Julián Carax. There's also a tragic love-story at the heart of it, involving Carax and a girl who dies at nineteen years old. However, I digress. To cut a long story short, Mr Beckett, I was talking recently about this book to a prisoner - one of my clients - patients, if you prefer - and because he knew I lived not far from Leeds asked whether I'd ever come across you.'

'Me?'

'Well, you know what prisoners are - too much time on their hands, given to speculation and romancing, dreaming their life away.'

'Who is this man?'

'I'm not allowed to tell you, I'm afraid - professional confidentiality. You see, I try to help people with certain kinds of problems, almost like a specialist doctor, and it would be more than my job's worth to breach the confidentiality of any consultation I have. But our conversation about the Ruiz Zafón was marginal and casual. He just told me that if I really wanted to make a spot of money in a trade I knew something about, I should contact the Becketts of Ledsham. That's really all he'd tell me. "Give the Becketts a call," he said, "you never know, they may just have some advice for you." So I've just called round to ask whether you know of any openings.'

'I see. I understand from that that you don't trust me very far.'

'Not at all, Mr Beckett. You probably don't know the prison fraternity as well as I do, but I can assure you that betrayal of a source is not to be undertaken lightly. It's not that I don't trust you, but until we get a little better acquainted with each other, well, it's probably not in your interest or in mine to have too much information. I hope you understand that.'

'Very well. For the moment we'll leave it there. So, you're looking for openings in the, er, book-trade. It's a tricky business, ours; full of pitfalls; a minefield for the unwary; easy to get one's fingers burnt. Ever heard of Olaus Magnus' *Historia de gentibus septentrionalibus*?'

'Oh, yes: Dutch guy, somewhere round 1562, that work?'

'And what about Blandin's *Traité d'anatomie topographique*? Mean anything to you?'

'The Atlas or the full two volumes? Well, either way, quite a collectors' item: Brussels, some time in the 1820s, if memory serves.'

'I see you're quite well informed, Mr Carter. Yes, quite well informed. Now I wonder. Did your criminal friend mention that our work, like yours, is highly confidential?'

'Yes, he did, and of course that appeals to me, as I'm not anxious to draw attention to myself, and the fewer people who know of my involvement the better.'

'Well, you call providentially, Mr Carter, as Ava and I have been discussing taking someone else on board, but you can imagine how difficult it is to find someone with the requisite degree of, er, discretion – and, of course, background. You say your wife knows why you've called on us today?'

'Oh, yes. Couldn't do without her support.'

'As I said earlier, we haven't time to talk at any greater length at the moment, as we're going out shortly, but we've had an interesting conversation, haven't we, and I should like to continue it at greater leisure. What do you say to joining us for supper in a couple of days, the two of you, and we can chat some more?'

'Well, that's very kind of you. I'm sure Lorna will be delighted to accept.'

'Good, good. Shall we say Thursday? half-six for seven?'

Alex was under no illusions: the first encounter had proceeded according to plan – in fact, probably better than he had dared hope – but a single slip could jeopardise his entire enterprise. He returned home encouraged but determined to polish his performance even further. He and Lorna went over their joint story again and again, creating fictional biographies for themselves, fictional incidents and fictional relatives. They had to agree on everything, it had all to sound plausible and, above all, it had to have no reference to Thwaites and the sordid business of two years before, except obliquely. They were treading on egg-shells, but now that they had – to mix our metaphors – burnt their boats, they were committed to seeing their inquiry through until, if possible, Alex's name was freed of all taint. It would be very unfortunate if the story they told could be challenged on any point by their hosts.

12

The dinner party scheduled for the Thursday proceeded without a hitch in an atmosphere of increasing – if on one side faked - mutual regard. Ava Beckett turned out to be an attentive and efficient hostess. Their dining-room was comfortable even if not, perhaps, the most spacious one imaginable. Ava produced mint and aubergine bruschetta for starters (a bit too crunchy for Lorna's taste, but then that is the nature of the beast), cider pork with spring vegetables, a cheese-board (not an exciting one, but adequate, with the emphasis not on good old English cheeses but on some French varieties) and a choice of desserts: chocolate ginger tarts and plum clafoutis. Roddy served a Pinot Noir burgundy to complement the main course and the cheese.

Conversation began by being exploratory, round people's backgrounds and relationships and interests: the reader will readily imagine the tentative nature of a first encounter on which so much hinged. The Becketts were busily assessing their guests as prospective partners in an illegal but lucrative trade, while the Carters were anxious to ingratiate themselves with their hosts in order to be taken on as partners in an enterprise which was to lead to the unmasking of a killer. The Carters' pretence over some months at Ledsham before making contact with the Becketts proved its worth, as it had given them the chance to work themselves into their unaccustomed roles. Eventually the conversation reached the crucial point of more detailed negotiation. Roddy Beckett grasped the nettle.

'Well, now,' he dropped into a pregnant pause over the coffee, 'Alex tells me you two are interested in joining a little money-making venture Ava and I are involved in.'

'We are, but only if we think it suits us and you think we'd make suitable collaborators.'

'Yes, of course. Let me ask you first of all whether you've ever been in this line before.' Lorna thought it safer to let Alex do the talking. He was in any case the moving spirit behind their relationship and enterprise.

'Not to say exactly in that line of business, no,' Alex answered carefully. 'Perhaps I could just give you a brief sketch of my experience in the field and also an idea of what I'm looking for.' He had rehearsed these fictional details endlessly with Lorna, balancing grand outlines with more detailed comments interspersed, to give them the requisite patina of conviction. 'I did a BSc in Information Management and Computing at Loughborough – thoroughly enjoyed it, I must say, although I was no great genius and had to work hard to satisfy my tutors that I was up to it. It was there I first came up against pilfering from libraries, but of course it was largely volumes students needed there and then, not recondite tomes to be sold on the, er, black market. There probably weren't many such recondite tomes at Loughborough anyway,' he added as a little joke. 'The course whetted my appetite for older libraries rather than, say, modern public lending libraries, and I was lucky enough to land a first job at the St Bride Library in Fleet Street, London. Do you know it? Fifty thousand books – which is where I worked – not to mention trade journals, artefacts and so on, all on the history and techniques of printing - calligraphy, illustration, music and all that as well. I wasn't particularly interested in printing as a specific subject, but librarianship's librarianship, isn't it? From there, after gaining my initial experience, I moved on to the Old Library at Trinity in Cambridge, and that was much more exciting – for me, I mean. It was very satisfactory work, and I'm sorry it had to come to an end, although I knew I ran that risk. You see, I took a particular liking to several old books which were never consulted by a member of the public in my time there, and I began to wonder whether they wouldn't be of more interest at home with me than mouldering away in an ancient library.'

'I see,' Beckett intervened. 'Can you remember what they were – just out of curiosity?'

'I can, Roddy, as it happens. One was a first edition of Rousseau's *Du contrat social*, in the original Amsterdam edition, calf binding, very good condition – worth about £8000 at a guess – and the other was a first edition of Stephen Crane's *George's Mother*, worth a fraction of that, of course, but even so ... I didn't like to start by being too ambitious, so I decided to see what I could do with the Crane. Unfortunately I was lowering the book out of the loo window on a piece of string, with a view to retrieving it later, when it caught the gardener's eye, and that was that. I hadn't done my surveillance carefully enough, had I? The authorities were generous in a way, in that they didn't take the matter any further, providing that I left immediately and forwent my final month's salary, but it was the end of my career as a librarian. So I went into the book-trade as a seller – well, assistant seller, in a large emporium with a second-hand section as well as new stock. It was then I witnessed another kind of pilferer – the thief who poses as a genuine shopper and skulks round the shelves waiting for an opportunity to slip a likely acquisition into his inside pocket when the staff aren't watching. I tell you, we got 'em all there. You could generally spot them at fifty paces: sleazy geezers with soiled raincoats, or student-types with flapping overcoats, or little old ladies with capacious handbags. I was eventually put in charge of the antique section, with responsibility for buying and selling, and if one or two volumes went surreptitiously missing, no one but myself was any the wiser. Not much really good stuff came our way, but occasionally you'd get some old chap come in with a couple of volumes from his grandfather's attic and sell them to us for what he could get, and you found you had a bargain on your hands because the old codger hadn't done his homework first. A very nice copy of Samuel Fisher's *Testimony of Truth* came my way like that, and I still treasure a half-calf edition of John Webster's *Elements of Mechanical and Chemical Philosophy* – simply gorgeous woodcuts – always an attractive feature of a book for me. Of course, the receipts and invoices needed a bit of juggling, but I didn't find that too difficult. That's about it, really.'

'Why did you give the job up, Alex?' Ava inquired.

'I was in danger of overreaching myself. You see, I'm not really a collector. I mean, I like old books and treasure the ones I've got, but I'm more interested in old books as a source of income. I just wasn't making enough money there, and there's no point in risking exposure for a few decent volumes every so often. So I decided to get out before I'd gone too far for too little and give my energies another outlet altogether. I'm now looking for something, well, not to put too fine a point on it, something more lucrative in line with my old, shall we say interests and skills.' He paused. No comments were made, but he judged that his discourse had been favourably received. 'Now,' he projected into the silence, 'do you think we can do business?'

'How do you know our, um, business methods will suit you, Alex?' Roddy asked.

'I don't, of course, I'm guessing, but I hope you'll enlighten us.' Beckett made no answer for a while, and the only sound in the room was the gentle noise of a quartz clock.

'OK,' he said eventually, 'let me tell you a little about how we operate. Forgive me if I tell you what you already know. The key to success in any operation such as ours is to know how to put those who acquire books in touch with those who collect them. We act as middlemen, but we need a constant supply of acquisitions on the one hand and a network of outlets on the other. Because none of it's legal, we can't advertise, so most of our business is done by word of mouth – and I needn't tell you how difficult discretion and secrecy are to maintain in those conditions. There are a few websites, including our own, which function on the basis of a code, but we have to be even more careful there. Over the years, we've established lists of trustworthy suppliers and of eager collectors, and our job is to satisfy the former, so that their good work continues, and to provide the latter with what they require to complement their collections. The whole thing is in permanent flux. On the one hand, suppliers depend on the circumstances of the moment - what's available at any given time – while collectors begin their collections, turn up their toes or simply shift the focus of their interests.'

'Do you see any limit to the capacity of your business?' Lorna put in.

'Yes – our ability to do the job without compromising safety through haste or inattention. That's where any, um, partner would come in.'

'And do you see any threat from the recession?'

'No: wealthy collectors are mostly beyond the reach of financial fluctuations. If you can spend 1m€ annually just on the upkeep of your yacht, you're not going to worry about a temporary rise in the price of bread! Talking about yachts, did you know there are 8000 yachts worldwide over 24 metres long? As a matter of slight interest, half of those call in or moor at the south of France every year: Monaco, Antibes, Cannes, Saint-Tropez, La Ciotat. A new yacht can set you back 100m€ or more. And when an owner can no longer afford one, someone else comes along who'll buy it off him: otherwise he'd be waiting up to ten years for a new one to be available. So, no, we don't see our business constituency declining appreciably. On the other hand, most of our customers aren't the mega-rich, in so far as we can judge, but simply wealthy people with an interest in a particular author or printing-house or subject and enough money to satisfy their curiosity, and we think there will always be enough of those to keep us afloat.'

'It looks as if you're the right people to come to, then,' Alex said.

'Well, before we go any further' - Roddy sounded cautious – 'perhaps we should just sound a word of warning. You'll appreciate that there's a lot at stake: our liberty, for one thing, but also our life-style – we've got one of the yachts I mentioned earlier, moored at that expensive little place, Le Ciotat. So – let's be quite blunt – we have to be able to protect ourselves against those who, um, abuse our trust. I know, it's not a pleasant subject, so, if we understand each other, let's say no more about it.' Lorna and Alex nodded their understanding and agreement. Roddy became brisk again.

'Good, good, but we also need to check security at your house. Our idea would be that we called round at your place periodically to deliver and collect, but could your neighbours see us?'

'No. Even in the daytime, once a car's come into our drive, that's it: complete privacy.'

The conversation continued as the couples discussed details of their collaboration: finance, logistics, codes, methods of communication, division of labour. The evening came to an end eventually with a toast to the couples' cooperation, drunk out of glasses that contained grapefruit juice, grand marnier, rosewater and champagne in the appropriate proportions: a 'moonwalk'!

13

Mrs Quentin Bursnell, née Serenity Thwaites, widow, re-upholsterer of Ripon, North Yorkshire, and mother of Reuben, Abigail and Jocelyn, sat in her living-room the evening after her eldest had goaded her into taking action in the matter of her brother's murder. The clues she held were minimal: two hand-written letters from 'P'; the name of a shadowy organisation; and the name of a university lecturer. The venue of meetings of the Anti-Church, given as 'No. 18', not seeming very helpful as a lead, Serenity decided that Len Croft was her best bet. Accordingly she went online to consult the staff-list at the University of Nottingham, contacted the object of her search and made an appointment to visit him at his house in Hucknall. The latter turned out to be a comfortable detached house in Bolingey Way, looking out over the fields that border the M1, troubled only by a little suburban traffic and the distant hum of the motorway. Mrs Croft welcomed her husband's guest warmly, sat them both down with a pot of tea but then excused herself on the grounds of jobs to be done.

Dr Croft turned out to be younger than she had, for some reason, imagined: a paunchy man in his late thirties, with a straggly beard and untidy hair, ruddy cheeks and spectacles perched on his squat nose. He might have stepped out of the pages of some Dickens novel, where his role would have been a pawnbroker or, if that sounds in the context too disreputable, an apothecary or perhaps, age apart, proprietor of an old curiosity shop. He was warm in his welcome. Serenity surveyed the well-proportioned sitting-room, furnished in modern style: on the minimalist side, a little chilly, aesthetically speaking, presumably to match the proprietor's trimmed-down theology (if her understanding was correct). She cast an appraising eye over the upholstery, where she detected a woman's eye for colour and pattern.

'Well, Mrs Bursnell,' he said, 'what can I do for you?'

'It's Serenity, Dr Croft.'

'In that case, I'm Len.'

'I'm interested in the Anti-Church of Jesus Christ, and I believe you can help me.'

'Only obliquely, I'm afraid.'

'Well, you founded it!'

'Oh, no, who on earth told you that?' The trouble was, Serenity had not rehearsed her approach to Dr Croft. She had no idea what she wanted to say, what she needed to say or how to react to any information imparted. Taking a rapid decision, she decided to trust her host with her story. She saw no alternative – apart from stumbling through an ill-conceived web of distortion and deceit, of which she did not consider herself capable. She ran the risk, she knew, of exposing herself to a master-criminal already up to his elbows in the blood of his opponents, but Croft did not really look the criminal type – if that made sense (and she knew it did not). She outlined the murder briefly, stated her relationship to the murdered man, explained her intention to find his killer if possible, gave an account of the reasoning which led her to connect the murder with the Anti-Church of Jesus Christ and which had decided her on her present mission. Croft listened to her narrative without interrupting her and then expressed his regret at her brother's death. Yes, he knew something of this through his clerical acquaintances, but her account had given the matter a human dimension. He promised to help if he could.

'I'm going to tell you two things,' he promised. 'The one's a bit of a hobby-horse of mine, and don't mind me if I seem to be wandering off at a tangent. You may have heard of Dr Augustus Jessopp, schoolmaster and Norfolk country parson, who died in 1914 in his early nineties. In his sixties he wrote a short series of historical essays which were all published in the periodical called *The Nineteenth Century*, now defunct. Can I ask you to read a bit of one of his essays? I hope it won't bore you.' He reached up to a periodical on his shelves, selected the appropriate page, handed it over to her and settled himself back into his seat. 'It's the passage I've marked in pencil.' This is what she read:

> Rome has never been afraid of fanaticism. She has always known how to utilise her enthusiasts fired by a new idea. The Church of England has never known how to deal with a man of genius. From Wicklif to Frederick Robertson, from Bishop Peacock to Dr. Rowland Williams, the clergyman who has been in danger of impressing his personality upon Anglicanism, where he has not been the object of relentless persecution, has at least been regarded with timid suspicion, has been shunned by the prudent men of low degree, and by those of high degree has been—forgotten. In the Church of England there has never

been a time when the enthusiast has not been treated as a very *unsafe* man. Rome has found a place for the dreamiest mystic or the noisiest ranter — found a place and found a sphere of useful labour. We, with our insular prejudices, have been sticklers for the narrowest uniformity, and yet we have accepted, as a useful addition to the Creed of Christendom, one article which we have not formulated only because, perhaps, it came to us from a Roman Bishop, the great sage Talleyrand — *Surtout pas trop de zèle!*

She looked up from the paper, clearly not seeing the passage's relevance.

'Let me explain, Serenity, if you'll allow me,' he said, divining her unformulated question. 'I'm what some people here – at the university, I mean – regard as a fanatic. My Anglican colleagues turn from me in distaste, theologically speaking, as a radical – an extremist, if you please. I think they acknowledge my competence in the field – otherwise I shouldn't still be teaching here – but they can't accept my disallowance of all that makes Anglicanism a unique part of the Christian communion and of so much of the tradition of conventional Christianity. They complain that I've taken one strand of the New Testament and blown it up out of all proportion. Needless to say, I don't see it like that at all: I've removed some of the extraneous matter to focus on the essence, that's all. (Well, when I say, "That's all," it's actually a major step, when all's said and done.) I'm viewed askance as a dangerous man, and I ask you, Serenity, does that match the figure you see before you now? Of course it doesn't!' Anxious to stem the flow of self-justification, although gratified to be confirmed in her opinion, Serenity chipped in.

'What's all this got to do with Dr Jessopp, Len?' she inquired mildly.

'Rome is so sure of itself that it can allow fanatics free rein. It knows that they'll rattle around for a time and then get forgotten or merge with the background. At least, that's Jessopp's theory, although I'm not sure it's borne out in practice. However, I wanted to bring to your attention his comments on Anglicanism – which is, after all, what you're researching. Anglicanism regards the fanatic as essentially unsafe, a danger, because he's taking things too far or too seriously. Moderation in all things! Aristotle said it, the Buddha said it, and it has been repeated endlessly since. Now all I've done is publish a book. It carries the snappy title *The Master*, but the subtitle – *Prolegomena to a Deconstructionist Christian Spirituality* – is designed to give potential readers an insight into what it's about – and also, I suppose, to impugn those who might be tempted to dismiss it as light-weight. It's seen by my peers – those who've taken the trouble to read it, of course, or even to dip into it - as taking the gospel too seriously, and I'm dismissed as a crank. However, the ideas I put forward are now in the public arena, and the author of an idea loses control of his brainchild. The idea is picked up by others and transmogrified in the light of their own existing conceptions. It draws in other ideas, like a theological Higgs boson, changes its shape, feeds into other systems – and all without the begetter's knowledge or consent, much less governance. So what I'm telling you is that I disavow all responsibility for the so-called Anti-Church of Jesus Christ. I know nothing about it – well, very little about it. I'm told it owes its existence to ideas promoted by my book. That may be so. As I say, however, I cannot be held responsible for what others choose to make of ideas put forward in all seriousness on the basis of a detailed, punctilious and professional view of the Christian tradition. I've done my part, and if the result speaks to others, all the better, and if somebody chooses to make it the basis of his or her own system, well, I can't stop them, can I?'

'I think I follow that, Len, although I'm no great brain, heaven knows. So what's the other thing you're going to tell me?'

'I'm going to tell you who P is, so that you can get in touch with her if you wish.'

'Her?'

'Yes, why not? Had you been imagining all along that it was a man? Sorry, I'm being mischievous! P is an amiable, perhaps slightly eccentric person called Pyrena Hembry.'

'You know her, obviously. A student of yours?'

'No, not at all – except, I suppose, indirectly. I've met her just the once.'

'Let me guess: she read your book, was bowled over by it and came for the author's signature!'

'Almost: she made the pilgrimage to my door, to consult the oracle.' He smiled broadly. 'She'd read my book and decided to pay me a visit. That's all there was to it.'

'But you know of her in connection with the Anti-Church?' Serenity insisted.

'Yes. I told her I didn't approve, but she wouldn't listen. You see, her idea was to set up a non-church in opposition to the Anglican communion – hence her chosen title – and challenge Anglicanism on its home turf. My view was – and is - that "church" gives quite the wrong impression today of what Jesus was about, and I studiously avoid giving any impression that I propose, or wish to see established, or am in any way in favour of, or would endorse even under the threat of instant annihilation, the idea of a church, either separate from or in opposition to the established Christian churches: non-church, anti-church, it's all equal misleading. We don't need churches, which are creators and purveyors of cumbersome bureaucracy, with all that bureaucracy implies: authority and subservience, red tape, laws and people to administer them, spokespeople, official statements, buildings, conventions and hide-bound traditions – the list is endless. The worst thing of all is the bovine, mechanical, deadening mentality bureaucracy inevitably breeds, quite foreign to what I believe, on the basis of a detailed examination of the gospel evidence, Jesus the Master, the eschatological prophet, was about. In the lapidary words of Camilleri: "Down with officialdom!"' Here he smiled broadly again, but his words carried both weight and conviction.

'Can you tell me anything else about Pyrena?'

'No, not much. She lives on her own, I gathered, with a maid and a ferocious dog in a rambling great house that's as eccentric as herself. I don't know what she does for a living: maybe nothing. Maybe she inherited family money. She's quite intense and certainly determined. Incidentally, she told me the dog's called Savonarola – that's how it came up in conversation.'

'Age?'

'Not sure: forties? early fifties?'

'Clued up?'

'She is now, having read *The Master*! Sorry, only joking. Yes, she seemed pretty familiar with standard theology. Perhaps she has a degree in theology, I wouldn't know.'

'So she came to you just to make your acquaintance?'

'Well, no, as I said, she came to consult me. She really wanted me to expand on the two chapters in the book where I talk about the idea of Christian community: she thought the fourteen or fifteen pages I'd devoted to the subject insufficient; but really I had nothing else to tell her. All my thinking is there in the book. Anyway, we chatted for a long time, and I got the impression not just that she was enthused but that she was going to take the matter further. I expressed my strongest misgivings about trying to set up any sort of organisation and told her quite peremptorily that I would not allow my name to be associated with any such endeavour. In fact, I think she was a little taken aback by the vehemence of my feelings!'

'So where do I find this Pyrena?'

'Look, here's the address. You can say you got it from me, she won't mind that. Go easy: if you're right about your brother's involvement, you may be playing with fire. I don't see Pyrena having any role in that, but one never knows, I suppose.'

14

Serenity was aware that she should not blunder into a situation which, if she was right, had proved her brother's undoing, but what choice had she but to make contact with this Hembry woman? Having left Dr Croft, she sought refuge in the first small café on the way to see Pyrena Hembry, beguiled by its name, Aesop's Tables. Over a hot chocolate and a bun, she turned Croft's words over in her mind. She realised that, although he had obviously tried to keep things simple for her, the matter was over her head. She just had not the training or the turn of mind which would enable her to come to grips with theological matters at this theoretical level. In that sense, her visit had been a waste of time, as she could not cope with the ideas. On the other hand, she felt she had achieved a rudimentary grasp of what this Hembry woman was about. She sounded rather headstrong: an organising type; 'intense and determined', Croft had called her. So be it. She, Serenity, could be equally determined. On the other hand, a woman who took her theology seriously enough to consult the author of a radical book on deconstructionist Christianity (whatever that was) and propose the setting-up of an organisation in opposition to the Church of England – well, surely she was above criminal behaviour? She wouldn't stoop to murder, would she? On the other hand again, Serenity knew, merely from reading the press, that murder and assassination were daily weapons in the lives of some so-called religious people. Was not pope John Paul I himself an assassin's victim in 1978, if the media were to be believed, for announcing his intention to institute an investigation into the Vatican bank? All Serenity could do in the circumstances was to be circumspect and to keep Reuben informed of where she was going and what she was doing.

Having somewhat assuaged any anxieties Croft might have raised by putting her in touch so swiftly and easily with the Anti-Church of Jesus Christ, Serenity continued her journey and drew up eventually outside The Old Priory, her destination, situated in a hamlet of several dozen houses snoozing gently in the countryside in the warmth of a summer's day. The gates were closed and padlocked, and a vicious-looking animal, about the size of a small horse, growled and snarled at her as it leapt up and down in response to her push of the bell: a great beast in the tradition of the Baskerville hound (but without, as far as she could tell in the sunlight, the phosphorescence). A human head appeared at an upper window and inquired after the visitor's business. When Serenity told the head that she would welcome a few words with Miss Hembry, it withdrew wordlessly. Shortly afterwards, a door in the side of the building opened, and a hand beckoned her inside. All very mysterious. She was ushered along a corridor, round several corners and through a hallway into a small room that might be called a cosy or perhaps a boudoir: two or three arm-chairs, some books scattered about, a pot of cut flowers, an elegant round table, a small window looking out over an orchard; peaceful. A large grey cat eyed her suspiciously from its perch on a fat cushion in the window embrasure. Miss Hembry appeared in a few minutes: an angular woman, clearly bra-less, dressed in an artist's smock, her hair disordered, small splodges of paint on her face.

'To what do I owe the pleasure?' Miss Hembry said without betraying any pleasure in her voice.

'Um, well,' Serenity managed to utter, 'I've not long come from seeing Dr Len Croft in Nottingham.'

'Oh, him, pusillanimous little toad.'

'I beg your pardon?'

'Pusillanimous little toad: all mouth and no trousers. Spouts off about this, that and t'other but hasn't the guts or the gumption to see it through.'

'I see.'

'Do you, though? You look to me to be in the same mould: limp-wristed, namby-pamby. Who was it that called Christianity the refuge of the weak and sickly? Not far out, it seems to me. The trouble is that the image projected has all too often been of Jesus meek and mild, Jesus gentle of heart, Jesus whose yoke is light, and so on, and it just gets my goat. What about the Jesus who chased the traders from the temple, who publicly derided the leaders of his own people, who faced down the Roman governor? *That's* the man I believe in, not some soppy prophet drooling over little babies and counselling pacifism. Fight the bastards all the way, that's what I say.' She glared defiantly at Serenity, who was baffled by this reception, as well she might. 'So what was it Croft had to say?' Mrs Hembry went on. 'No doubt something about eschatological values, apocalyptic visions, Septuagintal readings and other such tomfoolery, and no doubt also something derogatory about me. Words, words, words – no action. What this world needs is ACTION' (spoken in capital letters), 'not more theology in the same mould as the theology peddled over the centuries by all those dreary little men in their cloisters, with their bottled-up fantasies and gloomy misogynistic war-mongering.' Having got all this off her (unsupported) chest, Mrs Hembry unbent so far as to ask Serenity again the purpose of her call. Serenity swallowed the retorts that struggled inside her for expression.

'Miss Hembry,' she said simply, 'I wanted to ask you about the failed attack of the Anti-Church on the cathedral two years ago.'

'Huh, that! We owed that fiasco to the snake in the grass known to all and sundry as Mr James Call-Me-Nancy Thwaites. Turncoat!' she spat out venomously.

'Could you tell me a little more about it?' Serenity put in quietly, although inside she was boiling.

'Look, I don't know who you are, but there's no reason I shouldn't tell you. You're not a reporter, are you?' she added inconsequentially. Serenity thought that the woman was a nightmare: 'I don't know who you are' – no, you don't, because you haven't bothered to ask me. Well, I'll tell you anyhow: I'm the one that's going to see you put away for years and years for my brother's murder, that's who.

'No, Miss Hembry, I'm not a reporter.'

'Good. What a stupid - and dangerous – brood of vipers they are. I've no time for them, poking their noses in, intent on superficial titillating gossip instead of the things that matter. Croft had the ideas, I'll give him that. He reduced Christianity to a handful of beliefs that nobody in their right minds would quarrel with – but he wouldn't take it any further. He flung out all the excessive baggage that had accumulated over the centuries, most of it really obnoxious and much of it mystifyingly irrelevant, and exposed the core of Christianity as something really worth believing in: a man, a prophet, on a mission to save the world from the final cataclysm brought about by human – mainly male - iniquity. "My ideas will find their way into general circulation," he simpered. Stupid man! Ideas become influential by being wielded, not by sitting around between the covers of some dusty book nobody's going to read. Do you know, Newman's quoted as saying once that it's difficult to wind an Englishman up to a dogmatic level. That's Croft; he writes a book and then sits back, for heaven's sake. If it's difficult, sitting around on your backside isn't going to do the trick, is it? Where was I? Oh, yes, the fiasco of our assault on the cathedral. You asked me about that, didn't you? Let me tell you what happened. Look, sit down, Mrs, er, Mrs - Sorry, what did you say your name was?

'Bursnell, but everyone calls me - '

'Sit down, Mrs Bundle. Have a G & T - I always do at this time of day.' Without waiting for an answer, she disappeared, to return a few minutes later with two glasses on a small silver salver. She poked the tray in Serenity's general direction, took the remaining glass herself, put the salver on a vacant chair and sat down.

'Yes, the assault on the cathedral, as you call it,' she resumed. 'After my consultation with the egregious Croft, I decided that action was what was needed. Ideas are good enough in their way, but they need to be put into practice. Action; that's what gives us women the edge. Don't you think so, Mrs, er, Mrs Birtnel – I think you said your name was Birtnel, didn't you? A gesture would do, then people would get the idea. I thought round the problem and eventually picked on the cathedral because, well, because it's a symbol of all that's worst in Christianity, and, if I could make a mark there, that would be a victory indeed. Quite a few people I knew were influenced by Croft's book, partly because I was putting it in their way, and it was decided to stage a sort of demo - a protest against the excesses and absurdities of the Christian establishment in this country. We aimed to occupy the cathedral, issue a manifesto and invite the general public to support us. We circulated leaflets requesting people to get in touch if they felt any antagonism towards the established church for its obscurantism, misogyny, irrationality, authoritarianism and sheer tedium or had any views about reforming Anglicanism, including its demolition. I thought that victory would lie in the publicity. All right, we announced that we were going to occupy the cathedral, refuse to make any further contributions to its upkeep, flog it for the good of mankind, all that sort of stuff. Completely unrealistic, of course, but the aim was the publicity, don't you see? Anyway, after the leaflet, support grew largely by word of mouth, until we thought we could count on 250 people to turn out on the day. We had a plan: date and time, printed manifesto - of sorts - a couple of star speakers - no, not Croft, whose weasely, nimminy-pimminy simperings wouldn't have had any effect at all - suitable music and so on. All lined up. Then that quisling Thwaites dished us. Ran to the bishop or whoever and spilled the beans. The authorities closed the cathedral - pulled the plug, you might say - and that was that.'

'Any idea why Thwaites betrayed you?'

'Gutless. Lily-livered. Hadn't got the courage of his convictions, that's why. He fancied himself as someone, when he was in fact no one: a jumped-up teacher of I don't know what, prancing around all day in front of a crowd of spotty teenagers. Any fool can do that. But put him in the real world - the world of ecclesiastical politics, the world of proper theology, where thinkers and doers battle it out for humankind's soul – and he crumbled. No spine, you see. Look at history: have doers or thinkers contributed more to its advancement, would you say? Some people like Aristotle and Kant sit in a chair all day and spin gossamer dreams. Others pick up on their ideas and do something about them. Look at Zenobia and Joan of Arc: women of vision and energy! Which kind have moved history on, would you say? I'll tell you: the doers, of course. Thwaites was able to pick up the ideas, but then he was stuck. Simply didn't know what to do with them.'

'You're not quite answering my question, Miss Hembry,' Serenity dared to put in. 'Mr Thwaites believed strongly enough to join your campaign, but then something turned him against it. What?'

'Ambition.'

'Ambition?'

'Yes, fancied himself as a leader - a spokesman for the Anti-Church. Wanted to muscle in on the leadership.'

'But I thought Croft denied the value of leadership.'

'You've misunderstood, my dear. Croft, the chicken-hearted, craven Dr Croft, author of books with fancy titles, wants leaders all right: all movements need beacons, pioneers, people of vision, insight and courage. What he doesn't want is officials, people in authority. Jesus said, "Don't call anyone 'master'." So when Thwaites offered himself as official spokesman – "I've got the public speaking manner," he told me – I had to turn him down. Simple as that. I told him that the moving spirit was me, and there just wasn't room for anyone else. He wouldn't accept a subordinate position, so went off in a huff and, as I discovered later, made straight for the bishop's office – or somebody's office.'

'So he scuppered your plans.'

'Yes, he did, as you phrase it, scupper our plans.'

'And somebody killed him for it.'

'What? What are you talking about? He was killed, my dear Mrs, er, Mrs – sorry, what did you say your name was?'

'Smith.'

'Thwaites was killed, my dear Mrs Smith, by a homosexual lover who turned on him. It was in all the papers. There was no mystery about it, and it certainly had nothing to do with us.'

'But the police didn't make an arrest, did they? Still haven't done, two years down the line.'

'Then you'd better ask the police about that, hadn't you? I can assure you, we had nothing to do with it.'

'May I ask where the Anti-Church is at the moment? Is it growing? is it dead?' This question seemed to cause Miss Hembry a little embarrassment.

'We're – we're marking time. Gathering our strength. Looking forward to recruiting new members.'

'So the failed assault on the cathedral was actually a major set-back.' Mrs Hembry looked uncomfortable.

'You could say that,' she admitted. 'But, you see, recruitment is out of our hands: it must be God's work. That's the key: trust in divine Providence.' Pyrenia Hembry made to rise from her chair.

'Could I just come back to Mr Thwaites?' Serenity put in hurriedly.

'If you must,' was the sour retort as Mrs Hembry subsided back into her chair.

'You can't be absolutely sure no one attached to the Anti-Church was responsible for his death.'

'I can't be, no, I'm just telling you what all the papers said. May I ask why you're so interested in Thwaites? – an almost completely repellent person, as far as I can see; a disgrace to his profession – and to the church.'

'No reason. It's just that I shouldn't wish the Anti-Church to get into bad odour with the public if one of its members were proved to be responsible for his death.'

'Well, we were well rid of him, that's for sure, so whoever it was did us a service; but I really can't help you further on that.' She paused. 'I suppose some Anti-Churchers thought he was an encumbrance and better out of things. He besmirched our name, you know.'

'But not many people knew he was gay, did they? Mr Thwaites was known as a respectable retired teacher, a pillar of the cathedral, a man in good standing with his community. So there would have been no scandal in his membership of the Anti-Church.'

'Maybe not,' Miss Hembry conceded.

'In any case,' Serenity ploughed on, 'homosexuality in itself is not against either what the church or what the Anti-Church stands for – is it?' She was guessing that Miss Hembry was herself homosexual.

'Er, no, I suppose not – but it wouldn't do to advertise it, would it? No, not at all. We're respectable people.' Except that Jesus wasn't, Serenity thought. All she spoke out loud, however, was thanks for Miss Hembry' time and hospitality.

15

Mark Ravensdale, in his eyrie on the King's Staith, York, scratched his head. Like many private investigators, he had risen (or descended, depending on your point of view) from the ranks of the official police-force, irked by the need constantly to follow regulations, work to shifts, obey a superior who might or, more likely, might not be to one's liking, wear a uniform and in general follow the rules and conventions of an organisation which, while admirable in itself and essential to society's well-being, was not suited to his particular requirements for job satisfaction. Since leaving the police-force, he had experienced first hand the uncertainty of life on the seedy fringes of twenty-first-century Britain, where, as for a sheep-farmer – he plucked the example out of the ether – one could not guarantee a steady income or indeed any income at all. There were premises to hire and maintain, staff to employ, advertising to pay for, bills of one kind and another, notably the telephone, to settle, and he was sometimes in the position that his out-goings exceeded his income: a parlous condition for an intelligent, educated and well-bred man of his stamp. On the other hand, he worked his own hours, was beholden to no one, exercised his initiative and ingenuity at will and seemed on the whole to make a decent enough living. The inland revenue were a constant source of irritation which forced him to account for his time and expenditure. Although he recognised that taxes were essential to the country's smooth management, he objected to the often petty and seemingly irrational ways in which they were raised and the wasteful ways in which they were all too often spent. Taking the rough with the smooth, however, in a properly philosophical (to use the word loosely) spirit, he felt that his life in a city such as York was OK.

The reader may have divined from a previous scene in this narrative that Mr Ravensdale's office was not at this moment overflowing with commissions: otherwise he would not have considered lowering his standard fee for the likes of Mathias Biddulph, a scrubby, dilapidated little man if ever he had clapped eyes on one; metaphysically scrubby, that is. However, needs must, and he now sat contemplating the case which had so unexpectedly opened up before him. If he succeeded in tracing a bearded man last seen – fleetingly - two years ago near the centre of a British cathedral town, he was, or might be, £500 better off, which, for say a week's work, was inadequate remuneration but better than a smack in the eye with a wet gudgeon. He determined to begin by visiting the scene of the sighting, dressed down for the occasion so as not to antagonise the locals by seeming too posh or too official. Mr Ravensdale therefore donned a pair of baggy trousers and an innocent jacket, gathered a few night things into a bag in case of an emergency stay-over and set off for his destination with a mixture of determination to win some emolument, come what may, and a sense of the hopelessness of the task in front of him.

His first port of call was the local newspaper offices. Sensing, from the customer's request, some fresh angle on an old story, the offices were happy to cooperate in locating their accounts of the Thwaites Sex Murder: lurid, sensational and far from uplifting. Ravensdale's client had given him an accurate version of the events, in the sense only that the newspaper reports agreed with him, and he was so far encouraged. He next inquired whether anybody on the premises remembered the case well enough to help him with further details, in particular the name of the witness who claimed to have seen the bearded man. Although several such were volunteered, only one was needed, and a Mr Oldchurch was invited into the office to talk with the customer.

'We were never told the witness's identity,' this employee explained. He was an older man, probably on the verge of retirement, with a skewed nose and half an ear missing, but Ravensdale did not consider that these defects warranted wholesale dismissal of his evidence. 'The police were reluctant to disclose it,' Oldchurch went on, 'in case the bearded man returned to batter the informant. That was the story, anyway. I reckon they were covering up for their failure to find him – or even to bother to look for him, if you ask me. What a shambles, eh? Emil and his little gang would've done better than that. But it's all water under the bridge now, isn't it – unless, of course, you think you can do better?' He eyed Ravensdale quizzically but without malice. 'What's decided you to ferret round, then? Private eye, are you?' There were no flies on this old journalist.

'Well, yes, I can admit that,' Ravensdale saw no reason not to, 'but equally I can't tell you – yet – why I'm raking over the embers.'

'You'll give us first refusal of any new development, will you? Otherwise my memory might play me false.' He winked knowingly.

'Yes, yes, of course. Happy to oblige.'

'Well, then, I told you the police refused to disclose the witness's name; but I happen to know it.' The reader will imagine a pregnant pause.

'Yes?'

'It was a woman, minding her own business, but happening to be sitting in her window watching the world go by. She wasn't twitching curtains, or anything like that, just quietly sitting, looking out. She saw this man, who to her looked suspicious – but perhaps I look suspicious to you, governor: who's to say what "suspicious" means, eh? – and thought it her duty, as a citizen and as a moral centre with responsibility to her fellows in an ungrateful and uncertain world, to go to the police.'

'Yes, I see: a noble action. So who is she?'

'Ah, well, there you have me, governor.'

'But you told me you knew her.'

'I do – in a manner of speaking. I know her by sight, and I know where she lives, but she's got some foreign name I've never got my head round, so I've given up trying to remember it.'

'Ah, I see,' Ravensdale said, finding the old gentleman rather wearing, when all he wanted was a quick piece of information. 'So how might I get hold of her?'

'I'll tell you: all part of the service. You won't be able to say that *The Courrier* let you down, will you? Not that I think you would, but we want full acknowledgement, you know. Oh, yes: credit where credit's due! So here's what you do. Hold on a sec, just find a piece of paper.' He scrabbled round for a suitable sheet of paper, spent a minute sketching in a small map, and thrust it across the counter to his customer. 'Look,' he explained, 'there's the High Street, this one leads off it at a bit of an angle. You follow that one down to the bottom, then turn right – into Jove Street. Walk along a little until you come to a pub called the Black Swan. Opposite the pub is a dead-end called – huh, I've forgotten its name – something like Duke Mews, or do I mean Melton Gardens? – anyway, you can't miss it: a little alley-way, really, that's all it amounts to, almost directly opposite the pub. Half-way up on the left is a little cottage called, let me think – no, the name's gone. Anyway, all you've got to do is to ask for some woman with a foreign name, and there you are.'

'Hold on a minute,' Ravensdale said, 'how could she be watching the world go by from the front window of a cottage in a back alley-way?'

75

'You asked me where you could find her now, not where you could've found her two years ago, didn't you? I may not look much to you, governor, but I'm all there, really.' He gave a friendly and self-deprecating smile.

'Sorry,' Ravensdale acknowledged. 'Look, thanks so much for your help. Buy yourself a pint,' he added, pushing a coin across the counter.

'Much obliged, mister. And don't forget: we want the story first.'

'If there is one: yes, I promise, in so far as I have any control of it. Thanks again. 'Bye.' At this rate, his job was not going to be over in a day.

He decided to have a coffee before embarking on his trip to Duke Mews or Melton Gardens, whichever it might turn out to be. He bought a newspaper, dropped into a café and refreshed his inner person to wash away the well-meaning but garrulous newspaper-man. He then made his way to Jove Street, finding nothing to reproach Mr Oldchurch's plan with in the way of accuracy, saw the Black Swan on his right and the lane on his left, boldly labelled Wellington Park. Half-way up was indeed a crooked little cottage which, if Mr Oldchurch's plan was as accurate here as elsewhere, must be the one in question. He knocked, and the door was instantly opened by a crone with a screwed-up face and sharp features who demanded to know his business. Her small eyes, set in a sea of wrinkles, challenged him to spin a tale if he dared.

'What do you want, mister, disturbing honest folk at this hour of day?' He glanced at his watch: half-past two in the afternoon, which he did not consider untoward.

'I wondered,' he told her diffidently, 'whether we might have a quick word.' He brought a fiver out of his pocket and rustled it with unmistakeable intention.

'Come in,' she said, 'yer look all right, you do. Can't trust folk these days. Knock on the door pretending to be the gas-man or some bloke to fix yer windows, and the next thing yer know is yer trussed up like a turkey and the 'ouse done over. Doesn't take long to go through somebody's 'ouse, yer know, just pinching what yer can put in yer pocket: cash, watches and the like. And I'll tell what's caused it: all them politishuns. Wouldn't trust one of 'em to crack an egg properly. Lor', what a shower!' She carried on mumbling as she led Mr Ravensdale into a tiny kitchen at the back of the house. ''Ere, sit yerself down and rest yer weary legs. That's what my old mum used to say, whether yer legs was weary or not. 'Ers always was, yer see, that's why she said it, thinking that everyone was the same as 'er. We're all different though, aren't we? What a stupid world it'd be if we was all the same! Now if yer wouldn't mind getting to the point … I'm busy, I am. Leastways, that's to say I missed the last episode of the *Billy-boys* – fell asleep in me chair, of all the daft things – and want to catch up this arter. Right, young feller, what can I do for yer?'

'Well, I hope I've got the right house,' Ravensdale said apologetically, trying not to sound too posh. 'Would it be rude of me to ask whether you have a surname English people find difficult to pronounce?'

'What: Göröncsér? Me ole man was 'Ungarian, see. Daft bugger got drunk and fell into a ditch. Left me on me own, as yer can see, with 'ardly a farthing to me name. Still, 'slife, innit? If I'd married a dook, I'd be living it up in some palace, I daresay. But I didn't. Nothing like that came me way. What was it yer said yer wanted?'

'Two years ago you told the police you'd seen a bearded man near where James Thwaites lived – you remember, the cathedral verger who was found dead in his flat.'

'Oh, I did, so, but they wasn't interested. Not enough detail, they said, like looking for a needle in a 'aystack. "We can't go searching every 'ighway and bye-way looking for a bearded man, now, can we, madam, must be thousands of 'em out there, and where'd we begin?" "That's your business,' I told 'em, "I'm just telling yer what I saw. Can't do more than that, can I?"'

'So what *did* you see, Mrs, er – '

'Call me Janey. I can see ye'r all right, you are. Yes, everyone calls me Janey. Surname a bit of a mouthful, yer know. Me ole man was 'Ungarian. Not that 'e could speak any o' the lingo. Never been there, 'e told me. Couldn't learn the language if 'e tried. Any'ow, where was I? Yes, what I seen. I'll tell yer what I seen. It came back to me arterwards, only it was too late then, the police wasn't interested any longer.'

Mrs Göröncsér went on to relate her experience to Mark Ravensdale in no small detail. At the time of the murder, which she remembered well, she lived in a flat opposite Thwaites's. It had a little balcony, where she used to sit of an afternoon catching the sun and reading, or knitting, or looking through catalogues or listening to the wireless – all according. She would look up occasionally, just to keep her eye on what was happening in the street, in case she saw something more interesting than her immediate occupation. On the afternoon in question, her attention was caught by a tall man – well-dressed, he was, upright, a gentleman obviously. She did not take particular notice at first, because he was just passing by, but when he passed by several times, sauntering like, she looked more closely. She noticed that he frequently glanced up at Thwaites' window, or one near it, and then consulted his wrist-watch – except that it was not a wrist-watch but a pocket-watch, another mark of a toff, she told herself. She told the police all this, but apparently the information was insufficient for them. So what was it that she had remembered later, when police interest had faded? It was this: the man had a club foot. Well, this was her interpretation. What she meant was that one shoe seemed to be built up and that the man walked with a limp, and she had always thought of that as a club foot. Perhaps she was quite wrong, but her visitor would make his own diagnosis, she dared say. She would estimate the man's age as mid-forties. She had no reason to think that the facial hair was false, although, of course, in this day and age when so much emphasis was put on fashion and appearance and people tried to disguise whatever feature it was that they disapproved of, he could have put on a wig and beard just to disguise himself, if only for the afternoon, couldn't he? It was a full beard, neatly trimmed, the same colour as his hair: black, and it gave him a sort of Russian appearance, although she could not explain why. The man was, as she had already told Ravensdale, tall, and slim with it. He did not seem troubled or agitated, just impatient. When she next looked up from her book or her knitting or whatever it was she was doing, he had gone. She could not see him in the street, but then there was really no reason why he should linger over his departure just to give her the chance to bid him farewell, was there?

16

Ravensdale extracted himself from Widow Göröncsér as soon as he decently could, numbed in his spirits by the barrage of words that had assaulted him in the previous hour. He wondered whether he was further forward and thought that on balance he had made progress. The beard might be false, but the bearing and the pocket-watch were unlikely to be. Furthermore, none was the hall-mark of the typical working-class, or even middle-class, man. The built-up shoe could not be disguised – or a disguise. However, he reasoned, the beard was unlikely to be false. It would be unusual for a man to don a false beard except in circumstances where he was intent on a crime. If he intended to kill Thwaites and was waiting for a visitor to emerge so that he could make his own entry, he would not walk up and down in the street outside Thwaites' flat first, drawing attention to himself. In his experience, the prospect of committing a crime played havoc with one's usual sense of blending into the background, and Mrs Hungarian Widow had specifically told him that the man did not appear on edge or paranoid, merely impatient. None the less, even though the man might not be intent on a crime, he was a possible candidate for Thwaites' murderer, and Ravensdale would do his best to track him down. What happened then, Ravensdale was not quite sure: perhaps his commission could be considered to be at an end.

He thought he could usefully make one or two inquiries to narrow his search. With this in mind, he went down to the main library in the city to locate likely residences of titled people in the area. The bearded man need not be local, of course, but Ravensdale's inquiries had to begin somewhere. The library assistant confessed that the library held no list of the titled living in the area: why should it? She explained that there are approximately 25 dukes, 35 marquesses, 180 earls, 120 viscounts, 400 barons – not to mention all the life peers – and no less than 4000 baronets and knights in the land, and no one that she knew kept an account of where they all lived. Some titles were associated with country seats – the castles, palaces and mansions of the great – but the rest, well, what would you? The assistant suggested that he might try online, using one of the many machines in the reading-room available for public use, and he followed her suggestion. However, whatever information he requested from the screen, he did not succeed in coming up with anything remotely like what he wanted to know: plenty of material on the history of titles, but nothing on the geography of titled persons. He resigned himself to failure at the little screen.

He then thought of that great British institution, the public house, where the great and good, the insignificant and the not so good gathered to sip beer in an atmosphere of civilised equality. It was a long shot, but he had no choice: so little to go on. He asked the librarian for a map of the area, which he studied carefully. He divided the villages surrounding the city into five zones, one for each of the next five days, drawing up a rough itinerary for each day. His plan was to frequent the pubs in each zone, limiting himself to non-alcoholic drinks where possible, until he chanced on some local who could help him with his inquiry. As he contemplated the imminent disappearance of his fee in accommodation in the city, food, pub drinks, bribes and bus-fares, he was minded to abandon the chase, but his investigatory spirit urged him on: he would not abandon his quest so soon. Accordingly, he fixed up accommodation for the night, found the bus-station and was shortly at a village called Thornley seven miles from the city. On his way, he concocted a plausible story which would not arouse suspicion that he was a private eye hunting a potential blackmail victim. He would stand at the bar of the village tavern, or at the bar of one of the village taverns if the village boasted more than one, order a drink and, if the landlord were busy, identify a likely regular who would not be averse to helping him. He would then tell this toper – or the barman or the landlord - that he was the casting-director of a small film company, anxious to trace a man who he knew would be ideal for a part in a forthcoming documentary. The man was tall and thin, a gentleman, bearded and had a club-foot, and Ravensdale's impression was that he lived in the vicinity of the village. He had met him once but lost his details. Could his interlocutor help?

Over the next few days, Ravensdale visited village after village, moving on foot or using local buses, occasionally getting a lift. The names passed in a miasma of improbability: Crofton Parva, Duntisbourne Abbots, East Kyloe, Grundisborough-the-Water, Breasclete, Nether Albrighton and so forth. Nothing. Until he got to Wigborough Green. There he met success. More success than he had been hoping for. The pub stood on the green, proclaiming itself the Cock and Bottle in a florid board swinging squeakily from the façade. The unpretentious exterior did not promise much, but the interior was all a pub should be: cosy, cheerful, intimate, welcoming, and Ravensdale experienced immediately a presentiment of victory after days of foot-slogging weariness. He approached the bar as usual, ordered a half of cider and looked around for a likely contact. He spied a farmer-type sitting on his own in the window. There being no table completely free, Ravensdale felt justified in inviting himself to join the solitary farmer at his drinking, and, the farmer not demurring, he settled down companionably.

'Cheers,' he offered, and the farmer reciprocated amicably.

Do you know Francis Brett Young's 1937 volume *Portrait of a Village*, with its engaging, indeed entrancing, woodcuts by the great Joan Hassall, limned to represent days in which thatch was plentiful and tarmacadam unknown? The book deals with an imaginary village ('Monk's Norton' in Worcestershire) peopled by typical country-dwellers, and the farmer therein described would fit Ravensdale's companion of that evening:

> Mr. Collins is never – or never appears to be – in a hurry. He is a big, lumbering man, with a humorous mouth, shrewd, twinkling eyes, and enormous blunt-fingered hands. For a man of his weight and figure he is surprisingly active, and, apart from an occasional twinge of lumbago, does not know what it is to be sick.

Ravensdale never found out whether his fellow-drinker was called Collins, but he told himself that he might have been. (The pub, however, was definitely not The Sheldon Arms.) After a while, when the two chatted of this and that, Ravensdale broached his favourite topic.

'I'm looking for a gent who I think lives hereabouts: tall and thin, bearded, club foot. Looks like a toff, with a pocket-watch on a chain. Want to offer him a part in a film, and I've lost his details.'

'Ah, you mean old - what's his name? - hold on, it'll come to me - yes, got it: Drechsler. Leastways, I think that's it. Count, I think he is, or some such foreign title. Lives out Sale way: big house set back from the road, called - let me see - some posh name - now what is it? - yes, St Catherine's Court. He's your man for sure. Doesn't mix very much with the likes of me; keeps himself to himself, but then each to his own, I say. I wouldn't want his smooth acres. Give me farm land any day, great clods of black earth, butterflies on the verges, gates twisting off their hinges - proper farm-land, none of your manicured lawns and neat-trimmed hedges for me.' He chatted on about farming and the changes he had witnessed in his life-time, about deceased farmers he had known and their wives and children, reminiscing about his own childhood on his father's farm, oblivious that his drinking-partner was lost in speculation and no longer listening. Eventually Ravensdale slipped his informant a fiver, so great was his jubilation, and took his leave. First thing in the morning he would make his way to St Catherine's Court to see for himself.

17

In the early morning light, the house was captivating. Huge wrought-iron gates set between pillars in a shoulder-height stone wall were closed, but the visitor, peering through the ribs, gazed down a tree-lined drive, several hundred yards long, to an Elizabethan house standing proudly at the end of the vista. Painted a fresh white, wooden gates half-way down the drive marked off the area of park-land where horses might graze freely. The massive lime-trees partly obscured the mansion, but that added to the latter's charm. Ravensdale, having dismissed his taxi and waited for the habitual silence to return, paused a moment to admire the view, pushed open the pass-gate and made his way down the drive, drinking in the bird-song which alone broke the silence of the morning countryside. Although he was anxious to beard the count in his den, he strolled down the drive at a slow pace, prolonging the enjoyment of the moment. He might be forcibly ejected by hired lackeys at any minute; he might be chased by ferocious dogs out of the demesne; he would probably never have another chance to walk down this drive in the morning light; so he would make the most of it.

In response to his knock, the door was opened by a uniformed valet. He had rehearsed this moment but was still unsure how to begin. Should he ask for Mr Drechsler? the count? Count Drechsler? your master? In the end he opted for the first term.

'Who shall I say wants him, sir?' At least the flunkey did not send him round to the back door or pitch him down the steps.

'My name's Ravensdale, Mark Ravensdale.'

'You have no appointment, I believe, sir?'

'No. I was in the area and thought I'd call in. I'm an old school-friend of his.'

'Very well, sir. Please follow me.' The servant led him to a parlour across the main hall, invited him to make himself comfortable and closed the door behind him. Some minutes passed, which Ravensdale spent leafing through a coffee-table book on long-case clocks, before the owner of the house appeared, complete with beard, pocket-watch, aristocratic bearing and limp. Ravensdale put him in his late forties or early fifties.

'I'm afraid I don't recognise you,' Drechsler said. 'Thomas told me you were an old school-friend – or should I say that you claimed to be an old school-friend?'

'Mr Drechsler, I must apologise for giving you the wrong impression: we've never met before that I know of, but I felt it was very important to get in touch with you.'

'I'm sorry I must terminate this interview. Thomas!' he shouted through the door he had not closed behind him as he turned to leave his visitor.

'No, wait,' Ravensdale said hurriedly. 'It's about the murder of James Thwaites.' Drechsler turned back, a look of alarm appearing momentarily on his features before he recaptured his poise.

'Is it? Is it, now? Well, I can give you a few moments of my time.' Thomas had reappeared in answer to his employer's summons. Instead, however, of ordering him to pitch his visitor down the steps – or, less improbably, to show him the door - he said, 'Bring coffee for two to the drawing-room, please, Thomas. Or would you prefer tea?' he asked as he faced his visitor.

'No, coffee's fine, thank you.' Drechsler, now a model of courtesy, waved Ravensdale back into the hall and then preceded him into an elegant and comfortable room that commanded a view of a sumptuous rose-garden.

'Please take a seat, Mr, er, Ravensdale, was it?'

'Thank you.' He looked round him. The room was straight out of a manual on 1930s furnishing styles; it could have been the set for *Dear Octopus*. A fireplace in one of the short sides of the rectangle was flanked by doors. At right angles to the fireplace, two four-seater sofas faced each other across a heavy coffee-table, on which stood some glossy books and a large bowl of cut flowers. On the walls were hung large paintings in flamboyant frames, while the carpet, of a busy floral pattern, stretched from wall to wall. There were other tables, an assortment of table-lamps, a few arm chairs and a grand piano. It was, in short, the sanctuary of a wealthy man.

'Shall we just wait a minute until our refreshment arrives? In the meantime, perhaps you would be kind enough to tell me whether Ravensdale is your real name.'

'It is: Mark Ravensdale – Mark after my father, whom I never knew.'

'I'm sorry.'

'May I in my turn ask whether you have a title, and if so, how I should address you?'

'Ah, well, I don't know how familiar you are with European titles, Mr Ravensdale, but the matter is absurdly complex. To be brief, I am the last of the House of Jülich-Cleves-Berg, and my title, if I cared to use it, would be Wilhelm VII duke of Jülich and count of Berg and Ravensberg; but all that is just so much trumpery, and I don't care for it. I use my mother's maiden name and prefer to be addressed as plain Mister.'

'But you have an ancestral seat?'

'Yes, Burg Nideggen, which is actually in Germany, although we're a Luxembourgeois family. The family haven't lived in the castle for years; it's mostly a ruin anyway.' There was a discreet knock on the door, and Thomas entered with a tray of coffee things, which he proceeded to place on the table within comfortable reach of the host. When he had withdrawn, Drechsler resumed.

'Now, Mr Ravensdale, perhaps you'd be good enough to tell me what all this is about.' Subterfuge becomes second nature to a private investigator, whose safety and effectiveness may depend on secrecy, discretion and artifice, but on this occasion, perhaps lulled into a less suspicious state of mind by the affluence he saw about him, Ravensdale decided that a full confession would best suit his purpose.

'You will know, Mr Drechsler, that a bearded man was seen in the vicinity of Thwaites' flat round about the time of the murder and that the police were keen to trace him as a material witness – or even, I might add, as a suspect.' He paused, and when Drechsler volunteered no comment, he went on. 'I believe I am talking to this man now.'

'What is it you want with me?'

'Look, I'm not making accusations; that's not my job. I'm merely anxious to get at the truth. I'm a private investigator, Mr Drechsler, and I've been hired by another suspect who's anxious to clear his name.'

'Ah, you mean Jonas Chimes, poor chap. You mean he didn't do it after all?'

'No, not Mr Chimes: Mr Matt Biddulph.'

'Ah, yes. I followed the newspaper accounts closely, as you can imagine, and can understand what he must be going through – if he's not guilty, of course.'

'I believe he's not guilty. So I've come to you to see whether you can shed any light on the problem.' Drechsler said nothing for a while. Then he began.

'This is a rather delicate matter, Mr Ravensdale, and, if I tell you what I know, since I too have an interest in getting at the truth, I rely on your honour and complete discretion. I sense that you are a gentleman and not some grubby little snooper out for a scoop. So: I got to know Thwaites when I was at school and he taught me chemistry. We got on well. I did A-level and then went on to university. Thwaites and I kept in touch – nothing unusual in that – and a couple of times we even met in town for a coffee when I was home. James – we were on Christian name terms by then - tried his homoerotic rubbish on me, but I wasn't having any of it. Despite that, we were friends, I think I must admit, at least in a desultory sort of way. He had charm, a good sense of humour, he was lively and sociable – the sorts of things that made him easy to get on with. Anyway, while in my first year at uni, I committed an indiscretion – a stupid act – and he got to know of it. How, I'm not quite sure – perhaps through another student. The next thing I know is that he's badgering me for a "loan", with a veiled threat if I didn't accommodate him. I should've told him straight away to go to blazes, but I was feeling very vulnerable. The girl's family wanted revenge and threatened to go to the police, but of course they didn't want publicity any more than I did, so nothing came of that. I didn't want a stupid scandal hanging over my head before I'd even got out of my teens, so I went along with Thwaites' demands. That was the end of our friendship, of course. At first, his demands were modest. He realised, I suppose, that there was a price above which I should refuse him, but he became over the years a little more exigent and insistent. Anyway, two years ago, I fell in love with a young widow, and we determined to marry. This was an added reason why I was anxious to conceal my university escapade, although I realise now that it would have been far better to come clean at the beginning. When our engagement was announced in the papers, Thwaites came up with a figure double his usual, and I saw red. This time, he *could* go to blazes.'

'So you went along and hit him over the head with a bust of, say, Robert Boyle and then strangled him with a curtain-tie.' Ravensdale smiled, despite himself.

'No, neither of those things, although I was probably capable of them.' Drechsler smiled in his turn. 'I decided to see him – I was in town anyway – and tell him he could do his worst: I no longer cared who knew about an imprudence committed thirty years ago. OK, the girl died, but that wasn't entirely my fault, and no one was going to take much notice these days. As I arrived at the entrance to his block of flats, a bloke in front of me rang his door-bell on the street, spoke into the microphone and, when the door clicked open, went in. I hung about outside for a time and then, when this other bloke didn't reappear, went away. I thought a letter, or even a telephone-call, would do the job just as well. When I read the news of his murder, I lay low, fearing that the police wouldn't believe my story and would fit me up for the crime: "aristocratic count charged with sex murder" – you can just see it, can't you?'

'Yes, yes, I can,' Ravensdale murmured thoughtfully. 'So you think the man you saw at the flats was the murderer?'

'What else am I to think? Look, Mr Ravensdale, I'm as keen as you are to clear this matter up. If you've tracked me down, so, I suppose, could the police, if they're still interested, and I don't want to be mixed up in a murder any more than the next person. So what if we come to an agreement? I'll finance any further investigations you need to make, and in return you'll keep me out of it - altogether, I mean?'

18

The first consignment of books for Lorna and Alex Carter was delivered to their door a few days after their dinner-party with the Becketts. The delivery was made by an unmarked white van at a time of day agreed between them by coded text-messages. The Carters' task was to draw up a list of the books with a photograph of each one and full details of author, publisher, place of publication, condition and other relevant information. They were given this guide:

Author: **SMITH, Adam.**

Title: **An Inquiry into the Nature and Causes of the Wealth of Nations. In Two Volumes.**

Publisher: for W. Strahan; and T. Cadell, 1776

First edition of 'the first and greatest classic of modern economic thought' (PMM)[3]. In his Wealth of Nations, Smith 'begins with the thought that labour is the source from which a nation derives what is necessary to it. The improvement of the division of labour is the measure of productivity and in it lies the human propensity to barter and exchange ... The Wealth of Nations ends with a history of economic development, a definitive onslaught on the mercantile system, and some prophetic speculations on the limits of economic control' (PMM). 'The Wealth of Nations had no rival in scope or depth when published and is still one of the few works in its field to have achieved classic status, meaning simply that it has sustained yet survived repeated reading, critical and adulatory, long after the circumstances which prompted it have become the object of historical enquiry' (ODNB)[4]. Provenance: James Arundell was one of the trustees of Lady Huntingdon's college at Cheshunt, Hertfordshire, a dissenting academy founded at Trevecca, Wales, relocated in 1792 to Cheshunt and in 1906 to Cambridge.

---

[3] The Carters were responsible for obtaining their own copy of *Printing and the Mind of Man* - readily and cheaply available.

[4] The Becketts had to take out their own subscription to the online version of the *Oxford Dictionary of National Biography*.

2 volumes, quarto (288 × 223 mm). Contemporary half binding of marbled boards rebacked and recornered to style with diced russia, smooth spines attractively gilt in compartments, plain green endpapers, sprinkled edges. Half-title only in vol. II, as called for. Bookplates of the Cheshunt College Library, with inscription presenting the book to the college by James Arundell, 1824, on verso of front free endpapers. Title pages with neat red inkstamps of Cheshunt College. Very occasional spotting to some gatherings as usual, a very good copy, in an attractively restored contemporary binding.

In other words, their entries in the Beckett catalogue were to be as professional as those of a reputable bookseller. Under the heading 'Provenance', the Carters were warned to be particularly careful and if necessary to omit it altogether. It was also made clear that the present consignment of books was a dry run, in that the Becketts would be doing their own audit and making suggestions or corrections in the light of what they found in the Carters' efforts. The question of price was a delicate one. The Carters were told that, at first, the Becketts would be pricing all the books, which they did with an eye on the legitimate market. Factors included a book's age, condition, provenance and rarity, but also what the Becketts had paid for it. The big imponderable was what the collector was willing to pay in his or her turn. It was common sense that the Becketts' catalogue must include a guide to the price demanded, but there was also a need for flexibility. A secondary sheet therefore listed the books with a reserve price below which the Becketts would only rarely go – to satisfy a known and frequent customer on that one occasion, for example – as well as the price that was desirable. In the case of the example given above, a price around the £95,000 mark would be required.

The Carters set to work with a will. The expert assessment was, naturally, the work of Alex, while Lorna was responsible for producing the catalogue of the thirty books in this initial consignment. They knew that, to convince the Becketts and allay any suspicions they might have, their work had to be not just accurate but meticulous in its presentation. At one point, Alex exclaimed,

'That's odd!' He held in his hand a leather-bound copy of Macchiavelli's *The Prince*. 'Look,' he told Lorna across the table, 'the frontispiece proclaims it to be a first edition, 1640, but there's something funny going on. The binding's not a contemporary one. See, the thongs and cords are recessed, which wasn't a technique available that early in the seventeenth century. Then if you look closely at the frontispiece, you see it's been tampered with. The date's in a slightly different font and looks to me like a falsification.'

'Does this affect the book's value?'

'Certainly it does. A first edition like this might sell for, I don't know, £30,000 - £25,000 anyway - whereas a second edition wouldn't really be worth much at all – a few hundred quid possibly. I wonder … '

'What are you wondering?' Lorna asked when Alex paused.

'This isn't a test by the Becketts, is it?'

'Could be. You could hardly blame them, though: they've got to get it right, haven't they?'

'Yes, I suppose so.' They continued to work. A quarter of an hour later, Alex gave another exclamation.

'They've done it again! Look, here's a pamphlet pretending to be an offprint of Mary Church Terrell's article, 'Society among the Colored People of Washington', from *The Voice of the Negro* of 1906.' He pushed it over to Lorna. She handled it carefully, turned it over, opened it.

'What's wrong with it?'

'The paper's been deliberately aged – a tea-bag, I should think,' he added, recovering it and sniffing. 'This would deceive only someone in a hurry, not a real collector. What I think's happened is that someone's produced a copy on a computer and then aged the paper artificially to give it a more authentic look. Amateur, really, but I suppose the Becketts are keen to see that we exceed amateur level. It's their right, I suppose, but I do feel, well, somewhat shabbily treated.'

'For heaven's sake, Alex, what does it matter to us? We're not in this business for real. As long as we find out what really happened to Thwaites.'

19

The two worked on, checked their catalogue of the consignment and wrapped all the books up again. The mysterious van called to take the books away and left another parcel, and the Carters emailed their catalogue of the first consignment to the Becketts. The Carters had no idea how they were going to proceed beyond the present state of affairs to something more to their purpose, but the for the moment they were content to establish themselves in the Becketts' eyes as *bona fide* partners. Their next move was decided for them sooner than they hoped. Some months went by in the fashion just described – including the odd dud - when they received a (coded) text from the Becketts: 'Must consult urgently. Please call round.' The Carters wondered whether they had made an enormous error in the cataloguing, whether there was a serious hitch in the operation or even whether their little game had been rumbled – although they did not quite understand how that could happen, except possibly inadvertently through little Max. They decided to obey the summons promptly, partly to satisfy themselves as soon as possible that their situation was not threatened. Accordingly, as the clock in their hall struck eleven, they sauntered out and up the road, as if on a casual visit for a morning coffee. Ava greeted them at the door and invited them in. There was no sign of Roddy. Ava Beckett was an attractive woman, in her mid-forties, who held herself well and made the most of a wide smile that showed perfect teeth. She had high cheek-bones, big eyes and a narrow jaw – the recipe, I understand, for engaging the attention of the male of the species. The only blemish was an unsightly scar under her right eye, visible despite artful make-up.

When they were seated comfortably in the sitting-room round the coffee-pot, Ava told them her news: Roddy had been admitted to hospital after a car accident. His injuries were not life-threatening, but he was likely to be out of circulation for some months, and a lot of Ava's time would be taken up with visiting and nursing him, as well as doing the garden on her own. Ava and Roddy agreed that the Carters would be invited to fill the gap, if they felt able. They would effectively be shouldering the business for a while, which would, of course, mean more work and more responsibility. How did Lorna and Alex feel about it? Lorna remained silent while Alex, the moving spirit in their partnership, replied cautiously that they would like to have more information on what might be involved before committing themselves.

'Fair enough,' Ava said. 'This is how we operate – although you probably realise all this already. We have a number of what you might call accommodation addresses, where the delivery of parcels would not be noticed: a newsagent here, a bookshop there, up and down the country. We have a list of procurers – we tend to call them "sellers" - who "acquire" the books and send them to the accommodation address we dictate. We also have a list of buyers, which includes their specific requirements but to whom we also send out our full catalogue, just in case something else catches their eye. The sellers are never put directly in touch with the collectors: everything comes through us – it has to, to protect our business. A seller acquires a book. He or she contacts us, and we indicate where it should be sent, with the exterior of the parcel marked with a specific logo. In due course the co-worker in his news agency or bookshop or wherever, who has received the book, makes up a parcel of all the books he's received over the previous days or weeks, all of them still in the original, unopened packaging, and the parcel is collected by an unmarked white van – as you know. We receive these parcels and identify the contents. We then contact a collector if there's anything there he or she might be keen to get hold of, but in any case all books are entered fully into our catalogue, which we send out every six weeks by email. The collector, let's say, likes what he reads, puts in his order, and payment follows into one of several bank-accounts we run in various banks under various names. We then send the book, either by white van or by recorded delivery or by ordinary post, according to the buyer's wishes: it depends on their circumstances, I suppose. We then settle with the seller, often in cash through our co-workers. OK, there are risks, but nothing's foolproof. We reckon we've worked out a system which is as risk-free as we can make it.'

'Can I ask a couple of questions?' Alex put in.

'Of course.'

'The first is this. How do the people who acquire the books – the "sellers" – know you're in business? I mean, it's not the sort of trade you can openly advertise.'

'No, you're right: it's mainly through the criminal fraternity – the prison population and the like. "Look, mate, you find yourself with a valuable old book: go to the Becketts at Ledsham, they'll see you right" – that sort of thing.'

'Yes, I see. As a carat worker, I might have guessed that: that's exactly how *we* found *you*! Why don't you get the sellers to draw up their own account of the books they've, er, acquired and email it to you for your catalogue: wouldn't that save a bit of to'ing and fro'ing in white vans?'

'It might, but we couldn't trust them, you know. We need to know the feel of a book. We need to check for fakes – as you've found out for yourselves,' she added with a smile. 'In any case, we've much more of an insight into the market than an individual seller will ever have, and we can't put a price on a book until we can guarantee the accuracy of the catalogue entry in all its details for ourselves.'

'Yes, yes,' said Alex, 'that certainly makes sense. Your system seems to rely a lot on good will. For example, why should the sellers trust you to give them a fair price? How do they know you're not ripping them off?'

'Good question! The answer, I suppose, is that the whole business depends on good will. We could betray the sellers to the police, particularly in the case of thefts which hit the headlines; the sellers could betray us. What the latter realise is that they're going to get less for their acquisitions than if they bought them through a legitimate bookseller. They're limited by the few, er, shall we say dealers like ourselves who'll take their acquisitions for cash, no questions asked. They're not really in a position to play one dealer off against another since, ultimately, the whole business depends on the market, and that's limited to the people out there with the money and the collector's wish to, well, to collect – to accumulate the works of an author, or the editions of a publisher, or books on a particular subject. Of course, if the seller doesn't trust us, or thinks we're, as you term it, "ripping him off", there's nothing to stop him going elsewhere, but then he'll have closed a ready outlet for himself. No, all in all, I suppose it's a game in which we're all hemmed in by fear of exposure by the police or the tax-man – or both.'

'Finally, and this is probably a silly question, why don't collectors go through legitimate booksellers and avoid any risk? Why should they deal on the black market?'

'Oh, some do. Many do, I've no doubt, but there's a simple answer to your question, Alex. Many works never come on the open market, because of rarity, or because they're part of some public or private collection not available for sale or because their provenance is doubtful and legitimate dealers won't handle them for fear of falling foul of the law; but more than that, we offer books for sale at below market price. This has to be the case, because if we don't undercut the legitimate booksellers, collectors wouldn't come to us. Even wealthy collectors want to feel they're getting something on the cheap. That's not to say, to repeat myself, they won't also add to their collections through auction-houses and the like. Now, any more questions, either of you, and any more tea?'

After a refill of tea-cups and another raid on the plate of jammy dodgers, Ava asked them whether she had alleviated their hesitations. Were they now prepared to take on the bulk of the business for the next few months? Alex realised that to combine that with his day-job would be a heavy burden, but Lorna encouraged him to give it a go.

'You see,' Ava then commented, 'we can't simply suspend or even soft-pedal the business for the months that Roddy might need to recuperate: our clients would go elsewhere, and that would be a pity after all the hard work we've put in. It would also mean financial difficulties. So we should very grateful if you'd agree.' Alex and Lorna agreed.

'Good, excellent!' Ava exclaimed. 'Now what we're going to ask you to do is to install a safe, either in a wall or in the floor. It won't be very expensive, but it may take a day or two to set up. Then I'll give you the list of sellers, the list of collectors, the list of safe-houses, as you might call them, with the various logos we use. The van-drivers' details will also be included, for when you need to contact them. All these have to be kept locked up at all times, except when directly in use, and even then the greatest caution will have to be exercised. You've seen our catalogues, and you're to do the next one, and the one after that if necessary, on exactly the same pattern, so that our clients don't suspect any changes at the top. Business as usual, that's our motto while Roddy's indisposed. Now, any more questions?'

'Just one, Ava,' Alex said. 'What if we suspect some hanky-panky? Someone trying to pull a fast one. A seller not being straight with us, for example.'

'My, you are on the ball, Alex. You're a find, you are, that's for sure. I think the best thing to do is to come back to me. We do occasionally have trouble in that direction, and we have to deal with it on an *ad hoc* basis. They're not the sorts of decisions you should have to be bothered with.' The conference ended with the greatest satisfaction on both sides, and Lorna and Alex left the Becketts' to discuss this recent development.

20

When Lorna and Alex, careful not to manifest any jubilation in the street, calmly returned home, they could hardly contain their joy. Here at last was what promised to be a breakthrough. The list of sellers was bound to include the name of James Thwaites, with the words 'murdered' or 'disposed of for jiggery-pokery' or 'silenced for good and all' scribbled beside his name. That would be all they needed to go to the police with their evidence. It was clear to them that Thwaites had been stealing books, not necessarily very often, and had threatened to expose the Becketts if they did not give him the right price. Perhaps he was short of money and had acquired a particularly juicy specimen. The Becketts did not concur with his assessment, he turned nasty, and wham! bam! that was the end of James Thwaites, unfortunately weeded out, it so happened, in the middle of or at the end of some obscure sex game. In accordance with the Becketts' instructions, the Carters set about installing a safe. They went into Leeds, arranged for the delivery of flowers to Roddy Beckett with wishes for a speedy convalescence and then embarked on the serious business of the afternoon. They spent some time selecting a model from the range offered by a supplier of security devices and engaged the shop to fit it at their earliest convenience. On consultation of his books, the shop-assistant informed them that the safe could be delivered and fitted in two days' time, if that timetable was acceptable. The safe was the size of a breeze-block, and the fitter had done his job in an hour or so. The Carters tidied up round the gap, leaving the safe-door snugly showing, and then covered the site over with the large landscape that had hung there before (a print of a Thomas Cole 'Romantic Landscape' from 1826, if you have an interest in these things). Having installed their safe, they invited Ava round to inspect it, and, concealed in her handbag, were the lists they required to continue the Becketts' business. Ava approved of their precautions, was impressed by their enthusiasm and business-sense and went away confident that the enterprise was in good hands.

The door had not closed behind Ava Beckett before the Carters had swung the safe open, found the list of 'sellers' and consulted it. Yes, there it was: James Thwaites, with contact details. However, the only word next to his name was, disappointingly, 'deceased': no help at all. Since they already knew that Thwaites had had dealings with the Becketts, they were no further forward; not one whit.

'Hold on a minute,' Alex told Lorna. 'These lists are fine for running the business from day to day, but there aren't any accounts. What I mean is, the Becketts must keep a record of how much they pay the seller, how much the collector pays, and how much profit accrues to the Becketts on each transaction. They have considerable outgoings as well: the accommodation addresses, the vans and their drivers, postage and packaging – where's all that stuff? They must keep records, surely?'

'They don't trust us with them.'

'Perhaps they don't think them necessary. Perhaps that side of the business takes care of itself. But that's exactly where their dealings with Thwaites are going to be down on paper – well, more likely in some computer file guarded by a password. Damn. Damn and blast. How are we going to crack this one?'

'Max?' Lorna suggested.

'Max? How do you mean?'

'Have a word with him. See what he knows about cracking computer passwords.'

'This is nonsense, Lorna. How's he to get into the house, for a start?'

'Look, we invite Ava round here for a meal. Roddy's safely out of the way for some time to come, surrounded by lovely nurses and his mind on other things. While Ava's here, Max whips in and consults the files. Easy.'

'It's not easy, Lorna, and you know it. For a start, it's illegal, and you'd be getting Max into trouble.'

'If he's caught.'

'Yes, of course, if he's caught. Then how does a sixteen-year-old find the right file?'

'Look, Alex, you're making difficulties. You underestimate the ability of today's kids to manoeuvre their way through complex IT tasks. Let's ask him: it can't do any harm, can it?'

'No-o-o,' Alex said slowly. 'No, I suppose not; but I tell you, we're playing with fire.'

Although Roddy Beckett would be indisposed for some time, according to the information received from Ava, there was no guarantee, given the pressure on hospital accommodation, that he would not be sent home early. Lorna and Alex therefore needed to move fairly swiftly. A conference with Max was convened for that evening, when the three met accidentally on purpose in the churchyard, where a couple of handy benches between the buttresses guaranteed privacy and a good vantage-point. Not surprisingly, Max looked his usual scruffy self, and a less likely candidate for subtle affairs of computer innards could hardly be imagined. The Carters were again mistaken. Max was scandalized that they had so little faith in him.

'Crack a password? Easy!' he told them. 'All yer need is Ophcrack, and away yer go. You load the programme on to a CD or memory-stick – I've already got it on one – download it into the laptop yer trying to get into, and that's it. The programme does all the work for yer. Spells out the password. Then all yer have to do is shut down and re-boot as if it were yer own computer.'

'And where did you get Ophcrack from, may I ask?'

'The net: yer can download it for free.'

'Blooming heck,' was Alex's only comment.

'Look, Mr Carter, what's all this about?' Max asked. 'If yer want a little job doing, I'm yer man.'

'Max,' Lorna said kindly, 'we're not asking you to do anything against the law. Well, not really. We just want your ideas. You remember that house you kept a watch on? - '

'- The Becketts'?'

'Sh, not so loud! Yes, the Becketts'. We want files from their computer, and we don't know how to do it. Can you think of a way?'

'Are yer goin' to pay me if I come up with an idea? And what if I offer to do the job meself?'

'Of course we'll pay you. What'd be your fee for the job?' Alex could not help smiling. Max was certainly a character.

'Well, let me think a bit. I really want "God of War Ascension Part II", but it's out of my range at the moment. How about that?'

'How much is it?'

'Nineteen quid, give or take a few p. Shall we say twenty quid?' Lorna and Alex roared with laughter. The youth's grubby little face lit up with a smile as he joined in, even though he was unsure what the joke was.

There was further discussion concerning the date of the dastardly deed and the likely nature of the files to be accessed and downloaded. Lorna and Alex were content, had to be content, to leave much to Max's initiative, once they had explained to them what they thought they were looking for. When they got home, Alex again raised his misgivings about using Max for an illegal act. What if he were caught? What if their own role should be discovered, as, in the case of Max's arrest, it was sure to be? Their project would come to a definitive, disastrous and ignominious end. Was it fair on Max? Was the risk worth taking? Watching a house and noting the comings and goings was morally acceptable; infiltrating an organization was possibly ethical; but entering and accessing a protected laptop was not. On the other hand, the Carters had already compromised themselves by drawing up details of stolen books. The couple discussed the subject until they were tired of it, but the conclusion was that they would go ahead, as their aim - to unmask a killer with evidence that would be accepted in a court of law - was just, wholesome and laudatory. In one of his poetic *Epistles* (I, 2, 40f), Horace pens the memorable phrase:

Dimidium facti, qui coepit, habet; sapere aude, incipe.

Beginning is half the battle. Dare to taste [or perhaps 'to be wise']: begin!

Lorna and Alex decided to take his advice. (But what of that other apophthegm of Horace's, *Satires* I, 2, line 134: *Deprendi miserum est* [It is wretched to be caught out]?!)

21

A few days later, Ava was pleased to accept Lorna and Alex's invitation to a quiet supper. Lorna had decided on a simple meal, out of respect for Roddy's injuries, which seemed to exclude a lavish meal full of jollity and cheer. The time of the appointment was seven for half-past, but the Carters reckoned that Ava would not be punctual. Max was instructed to watch for Mrs Beckett's arrival at the Carters' and to give her a good quarter of an hour to settle in before leaving his house to execute his mission. Lorna, Ava and Alex enjoyed several glasses of sherry in the sitting-room before moving into the kitchen-diner where they were to eat.

'Oops,' exclaimed Ava, 'I've forgotten my mobile. You don't mind, do you? What if the hospital or Roddy need to get in touch with me? They haven't got this number. I'll just slip home: won't be a few minutes. So sorry.'

'No need,' Alex intervened swiftly. 'Look, I'll phone the hospital now and tell them where you are. I'll ask them to pass the message on to Roddy. Silly for you to walk home again and back, particularly as I think I can hear the rain starting.'

The meal had not concluded when Ava said she did not feel too well and would like to return home. She apologised for breaking up the party. Lorna offered her a bed upstairs if she wished to lie down for a bit, but Ava was adamant. She'd get home, if they didn't mind. It was all this worry over Roddy, she supposed. She hadn't been sleeping well, and she felt run down. All she needed was a few quiet days. Alex insisted on seeing her back, and soon the two of them were setting out in the rain. Alex tried to walk deliberately slowly, but his companion, who, clearly anxious to get back under her own roof, was having none of it, stepped out smartly – as smartly, that is, as her indisposition would allow. They reached the Becketts' house without mishap, and Alex was relieved to see that no lights showed except in the hall, through the window above the door, and Ava herself probably left that on. He hesitated: what if Max were still inside? How could he prevent a confrontation with Ava? He could not risk rousing her suspicions by going inside with her; would that in any case help? He saw her enter the house.

'That's funny,' he heard her say.

'What is?'

'Look, the computer's still on. I'm absolutely certain I turned it off.'

'Couldn't have done, Ava,' Alex said, leaning into the hall through the open doorway. 'I'm always doing that, thinking I've turned it off – or on – and haven't. I shouldn't worry about it. Good night, and sleep tight.' He waited while she closed the door behind her and then held his breath for the first sign of an encounter between the householder and a sleazy urchin on her premises. Nothing transpired. He saw the upstairs light go on, he heard the toilet flush, and then silence. He sighed deeply, relief flooding through his mind. On the other hand, perhaps Max hadn't found anything, or had not been able to break the password. Since it was too late to engineer a meeting with Max that night, he would have to be patient until the morrow; but he was sorely exercised.

The following morning, when the Carters met Max by prearrangement on Mary Panel Hill, Alex could hardly contain himself.

'Come on, Max, how did you get on? Give!'

'Hold on, Mr Carter,' Max expostulated. 'Let me get me breath!' Alex was so impatient he waited only seconds before asking Max how he had got into the house.

'Loo window at the back.'

'You mean, you broke it?'

'Nah, didn't have to. It's got a dodgy catch.'

'You sound as if you knew that.'

'O' course! I've cased a lot of 'ouses in the village for when I need money in a 'urry – if I ever did, I mean; so I knew I'd 'ave no trouble gettin' in.' Alex was flabbergasted.

'Our house as well, I daresay?'

'Yip. Couldn't leave you out, could I, Mr Carter?' He winked.

'Right, so, how did you get on?'

'Piece o' cake. It took my little programme about ten seconds to give me the password – after I'd booted up, and that took some time: blimey, their machine's slow – but then I couldn't find the files you wanted. Mrs What's-It's system is all over the place. Took me ages to discover that "excursions" meant what they pay out to the sellers and "incursions" what the collectors pay *them*. Don't use them words meself, see, Mr Carter.'

'But you found the files eventually? Come on, don't be so long-winded, Max!'

'You asked me 'ow I got on, an' I'm tellin' yer. Well, the files are naturally dated, an' I didn't know 'ow far back you wanted me to go: no point in downloading a 'ole lot o' useless stuff, was there? Then I accidentally deleted 'em all - '

'What: on their machine?'

'Nah, on me memory-stick – so I 'ad to start again. Anyways, I got 'em, an' 'ere they are.' He produced a silver plastic memory-stick from his pocket and handed it over with a broad smile. "Ave I earnt me twenty quid, guv'nor?'

'Of course you have, Max. Let's just hope you've got the right files.' Max's face dropped.

'Yer don't trust me, do yer, Mr Carter? You probably think I can't read an' write.'

'Max,' Lorna reassured him, 'don't be silly. Alex is on edge because this means so much to him. Take no notice. Here, here's twenty-five pounds for you, with our sincere thanks.' She handed the notes over.

'Gee, thanks, Mrs C. Let's 'ope me mum an' dad don't ask where I got it. Better not let 'em find out.'

'You know you left the laptop on? Nearly gave the game away.'

'I know. I 'eard voices outside the front-door and scarpered quick. Just 'ad time to pull the flash drive out and 'ead for the downstairs loo. I was still wrigglin' out the winder when I 'eard 'er come in.'

'Well, you've done great work, Max,' Alex told him, 'and we're proud of you – aren't we, Lorna?'

'We are. We'll get along home now, to have a look at this stuff. See you around, Max!' They walked home fast, trying not to look as if they were in a hurry.

Alex fed the flash drive into the side of his laptop and impatiently scanned the titles of the files on it. As Max had told them, there were "excursions" and "incursions", all dated, but not in order. Whether that was owing to Max or to the Becketts they neither knew nor cared. When Alex thought he had digested the list sufficiently to understand it, he brought selected files up for perusal. The Becketts' dealings with James Thwaites were fully listed. That is to say, the files gave the dates of Thwaites' contacts, full details of the book or books he was offering them – not a complete catalogue description – that was the Becketts' job - but enough to tell the Becketts what they were buying – the dates of despatch, receipt and collection, the full catalogue description eventually arrived at, with a suggested price, and then details of the sale: collector, price paid with date, details of despatch and so on. References were used rather than names, but the Carters knew this from their previous lists. So Thwaites was S179, while the collectors to whom his acquisitions were sold were C32, C451 and so on. If the Carters had not had the list of clients with their contact details, they could not have made sense of Max's files.

Thwaites' dealings with the Beckett's were not numerous. They stretched back a number of years, but with only two or three volumes a year. The last three entries were the most revealing. They related to the nine months prior to Thwaites' demise and concerned, naturally, three books: Jean-Baptiste-Hippolyte Lamare's *An Account of the Second Defence of the Fortress of Badajoz, by the French,* in 1812, in a translation from the French – apparently only twelve pages long, but Thwaites wanted £700 for it; and a hardback first edition of Edward Jesse's *An Angler's Rambles* of 1836, for which Thwaites wanted £90. There was a short correspondence in which the parties wrangled over the price of these two volumes. The Becketts had eventually paid Thwaites £380 for the first and £62 for the second. Details of the collectors who bought these items concerned the Carters not at all. The third book was a folio edition of the King James version of the Bible from 1770, with the crowned monogram of king George III tooled on the spine. Thwaites wanted £5250 for this; the Becketts offered him £3750. There was a short correspondence, in which no agreement was reached, and the entry ended with the laconic words, 'to stay on file'. Thwaites must have been annoyed to run the risk of stealing the book and then not being able to off-load it on to his usual partners in crime. It also seemed curious to the Carters that Thwaites, despite making relatively little money out of his dealings with the Becketts, persisted in his hobby of cleptobibliomania. Then, however, Alex let out a fearful yell:

'Yes, yes, yes: we've got 'em!'

'What? how?' asked Lorna in bewilderment.

'Look, what do you see at the end of his entry?'

'I see three letters.'

'And what are those letters?'

'Come on, Alex, you can read them as well as I can: PTE.'

'And what do you suppose they stand for?'

'Not the faintest.'

'It's obvious to me.'

'Go on, then.'

'Proved Troublesome: Eliminated. Couldn't be anything else.'

22

Serenity Burnsell came away from her interview with the eccentric Miss Pyrena Hembry in no very sweet temper. The woman had dismissed her brother as a worthless excrescence on the face of the body social. Furthermore, she had accused him of ambition in the ranks of the Anti-Churchers, and Serenity was sure that that was a misreading. Miss Hembry had brushed aside, peremptorily, the idea that an Anti-Churcher could be responsible for James' death, before admitting that she could not be a hundred percent certain after all. What an idiot the woman was! For two hoots Serenity would have punched her on the nose and enjoyed it. However, she was not yet resigned to failure. She returned to the city, sat in a café with a pot of tea and a bun and thought. One obvious source of information she had neglected was the old dean, the one who had retired at about the time of the abortive assault on the cathedral by members of the Anti-Church. The present dean had mentioned his role in the affair, but Serenity had been keener to meet Dr Croft and then that Hembry woman than to follow through Reuben's original suggestion that she should contact the dean whom James knew – the old one.

After her refreshment, therefore, she walked to the cathedral and approached an attendant who happened to be walking down the aisle towards her. Did he know where she could find the old dean, the one who retired two years ago? Yes, miss, he did. Not far from here, in the close. After receiving exact directions, Serenity walked round to No. 15 and rang the bell. Her summons was answered by a tall, thin clergyman, with a gentle and wispy beard, who peered at her over his half-moon glasses. His ancient frame tottered, perhaps at the sight of an unexpected and unknown visitor, perhaps at the sight of a handsome woman in her mid-life, and he asked her courteously what he could do for her.

'Mr Challoner?' she asked, even though the person in front of her could be no other.

'Yes.'

'I wonder whether I could have a few minutes of your time. It's about the late James Thwaites.'

'Ah,' he exclaimed. 'Come in.' She declined his offer of refreshment but was grateful for it, as it showed that chivalry, or at least courtesy, remained in at least one corner of this wayward world. She explained her errand and her hopes for light on her brother's murder, bearing in mind that the man in the opposite chair could conceivably be the murderer. If the dean was in favour of the Anti-Church demonstration and James went over his head to betray the movement; if the dean was then in poor favour with his superiors and he was retired early in what was in all but name a state of disgrace; if James had deferred indefinitely the Anti-Church's chances of making any sort of mark on ecclesiastical history: the dean could well bear an irresistible grudge. On the other hand, would this elderly, seemingly frail, gentleman sitting opposite her, with his mellow and courteous ways, have been capable of overcoming her brother in an angry confrontation? Could he then sit calmly talking to her, the deceased's sister, with a frenzied murder on his conscience? She would reserve judgement until the conversation had matured.

'Look, I'm glad you called,' he told her. 'I didn't know James had a sister, although I imagine you were at his funeral. I didn't go, I'm afraid: was told to stay away; but your visit gives me a chance to discuss a very unhappy period of my life with another interested party. You don't mind my rabbiting on for a bit, do you?'

'Not at all, Mr Challoner.'

'I knew your brother well, he being a verger and all that. We saw something of each other nearly every day, I suppose. He was a stalwart of the parish: an educated, professional and sincere man who supported the cathedral and what it stood for: Anglicanism at its best, and I sometimes regretted that he'd turned his hand to teaching rather than to the church. He had a fine voice and a good speaking manner, and his sermons would, I venture to say, have been memorable. He was also a sympathetic listener and a committed Christian.'

'Did you know about his homosexuality?'

'Oh, yes, but it never bothered me. Of course, there was always a danger of scandal in the church, but James knew that. He knew that the church wasn't yet ready for full acceptance, and he understood that he had to be discreet. I must hasten to tell you, young lady, that I have absolutely no insight at all into how he managed his sexuality. Nothing untoward ever came to my notice, and I was happy for him to continue as a member of the cathedral staff. For all I know he had a different partner every day of the week or every hour of the day, but that was for his conscience, not mine, and as long as it didn't impinge – or threaten to impinge - on the work or reputation of the cathedral, well, who was I to interfere? Equally he could have been chaste from one year's end to the next. It just didn't matter to me. That's why I can't get worked up about all this argument in the church over openly gay clergy and gay bishops and the rest of it. Completely irrelevant, as far as I can see. A person's who he or she is, irrespective of their sexuality, although I know Freudians don't agree with me. However, all that's by the bye. Let me go on with my story about James. As I say, things were ticking over quite placidly, when one day he asked whether he could have a word. It was clear that he didn't mean a quick word about some minor cathedral business, but something altogether deeper. I thought it might be to return the stolen books - '

'Stolen books?'

'Yes, well, you obviously don't know about that, so I'll say no more.'

'No, please go on. I need to get as clear a picture as I can of everything James was up to.'

'But it can't have anything to do with the Anti-Church.'

'None the less ... '

'Well, some books went missing from the vestry – an ancient Bible, a leather-bound *Book of Common Prayer* from 1760-something, and a third thing – can't remember what – and James was suspected of having a hand in it. In fact it was almost certain he was responsible for the theft. The matter was hushed up because of the potential scandal if the press got hold of it, but there was some unpleasantness at the time: the interviews with staff were very awkward. If anybody'd seen anything, they weren't telling me about it. James could be a bit intimidating, you know, and some folk might have been a bit afraid of how he'd react if they shopped him. That's my guess, but as I say, I can't see it having anything to do with the Anti-Church, and I don't want to spread rumours, however well-founded; but you did ask me, you know,' he added smiling. Serenity smiled back.

'So James came to see you,' she prompted when he said nothing further.

'Yes, he did. He was very coy, almost embarrassed, although that's not a word one usually associates with him. Had I heard of a Dr Len Croft and his book *The Master*? Real dynamite. A shot in the arm. Light at last in a darkened world. Brilliant stuff, straight to the heart of the matter. And so on. I confessed I hadn't. It seems that the book was written by an academic but in such a way that it was accessible to the willing lay person and that James had been reading it and was bowled over by its clarity and energy. I asked him how he'd come to hear of it, and he told me it had been lent him by an acquaintance, a Miss Pyrena Hembry, whom I knew by name but not personally. When I told him I had neither read nor even heard of it, he gave me a quick run-down of its contents – totally enthused, he was; excited, like a schoolboy with a new bike. It soon became apparent that his embarrassment was not caused by Croft's book, which instilled in him nothing but a sense of intellectual and religious fervour that he was happy to share with all and sundry, the more the merrier. No, he wished to broach a much more delicate subject. This Miss Hembry, it transpired, had started a movement called The Anti-Church of Jesus Christ, designed to put Croft's ideas into practice. She wanted a big gesture to put the movement on the map, and she'd picked the cathedral for her victim. Because James had influence in the cathedral – not much, but some – but principally because, as I surmised, he volunteered himself for the job, it was apparently agreed that he would undertake to see me about cooperating with the demo. This had less to do with persuading me not to call the police, or anything like that, and more to do with the publicity my participation would engender. At least, that was my impression. So I went along to see this Miss Hembry, and then I bought my own copy of Croft's book: I wasn't going to take a decision without being better informed. I read it – it's not a long book. I was interested. No, more than that, I was enthused: I'd caught the bug! I therefore agreed to assist the plotters, to the extent at least of making the cathedral available to them so that they could demonstrate and publicise their views. I'm not in the business of censorship – not where sincere and well-thought-out views of Jesus are concerned, however unpopular they might be in some circles. When I requested an undertaking that there would be no violence, Miss Hembry was scandalised and appalled that the idea had even occurred to me. "Who do you think we are?" she asked in dismay. "Violence? We're followers of a deconstructed Jesus, dean, and that means peace in our hearts, on our lips and in our behaviour. Energy, resolution, firmness, yes, but not violence."'

'Didn't you risk being sacked?'

'I suppose so. The bishop and I got on well, but I was frightened he'd ban the demo if I told him about it. In fact, I don't see how he could have gone along with it, given the present state of the Church of England. Too risky for him. However, I was due to retire in six months, and I believed passionately in the church's duty to allow free speech and to let people air their views providing only that no violence was involved, in deed or language. So I told the bishop nothing, and I resigned myself to an ignominious departure from my post if, *post factum,* he required a scapegoat.'

'But Miss Hembry's intention was to occupy the cathedral, persuade her followers to withhold their offerings and, if possible, put the cathedral up for sale. You couldn't have agreed to all that, surely? – unless James wasn't honest with you and told you only half the story.'

'No, James told me all: he was perfectly open about it - at least, that was my impression - but I took it with an enormous pinch of salt. You can't sell a cathedral, can you? The idea's absurd. So I allowed a peaceful demonstration to go ahead, to air Croft's views and let people judge the results for themselves. In fact, I was rather keen that the cathedral authorities – well, that was me, really, wasn't it? – should be at the forefront of efforts to engage in debate about the person of Jesus. I couldn't see any harm. I like to think, too, that my own quest for wisdom hadn't expired with my fortieth birthday. Ever read Montaigne? He once wrote:

> If you follow someone else, you follow nothing, you will find nothing; indeed, you won't even be looking.

So I was prepared for once to be a bit of a pioneer, even though I was well gone seventy. Foolish old man, some said, but wisdom's meant to increase with age, isn't it, not diminish. Sorry, I'm wandering. I'm just trying to explain to you why I went along with the Anti-Church plot, even though that's not really what you asked about.'

'So why did James sabotage your efforts to get Jesus publicised and discussed? Was it you he was against, or that Hembry woman, do you think?'

'I don't know. I never saw him again. He went straight to the bishop – or perhaps to the archdeacon who went straight to the bishop – the demo was stopped, and then James was killed. So I never had a chance to speak to him about things.'

'Tell me frankly, Mr Challoner, in your opinion, and from what you know of the Anti-Church of Jesus Christ, could a member of it have murdered James out of revenge – pique – disappointment, something like that?'

'I can't answer that, I'm afraid. You see, the only two members of the Anti-Church I ever met were Pyrena Hembry and your brother, in reverse order. I read Croft, as I told you, and he is certainly against violence of any sort. Christians who belong to a conventional church but wish to put Croft's ideas into practice are supposed to drop their membership and retire into an attitude of expectant, innocent simplicity which makes Jesus' return as messiah more likely, if I may so phrase it. The idea of killing out of revenge for a disappointment just isn't on the agenda. No, no, put that right out of your mind.'

'Weren't you disappointed by James' betrayal of the planned demonstration?'

'Of course, for the reasons I mentioned above; but can I say something about betrayal? If you're ever wandering about the Loire valley, go to the little village of Rivière, two or three miles east of Chinon. The village runs down to the river Vienne, which flows into the Loire a few miles west of Chinon; a perfectly charming village, the outstanding features of which are the twelfth-century church, the charming *place de l'Église*, the nineteenth-century château and vineyards stretching along the river-bank. In the church, you'll see a monument to the lord of Basché, his wife and one of their children, *gisants* quite badly chipped but readily recognisable as man, wife and child. A notice explains to the visitor why a prominent local Protestant should be buried in a Catholic church. The story was this. A plague was ravaging the country, and the lords of Basché, a château a few miles to the south of Rivière, were affected. They had embraced Calvinism and were subsequently, although no one's quite sure of the derivation of the term, known as Huguenots: Protestants to you and me. Anyway, when the plague came, their local Huguenot minister did a bunk; hopped it as fast as he could; just abandoned his flock to save his own skin. That's what we're told, although, of course, he may have had perfectly good reasons of his own. The scandalised Baschés called on the *curé* of Rivière to come to their aid, which he did, "surrounding them with the liveliest charity", the notice says: *il les entoura de la plus vive charité* – what a delightful phrase that is! It even gives us the name of the *curé*: M. Vadallieu. In gratitude, the lords of Basché renounced their error and begged to be allowed to be buried in the church of their generous friend and to set up a fund in favour of the church. That all happened in 1583.'

'Yes?'

'Well, when I think of this story, I'm again reminded of how God can turn human evil to good, to his own ends. Perhaps your brother's betrayal of the Anti-Church was ultimately for the best – I don't know. I wasn't sacked – just eased out – and I'm still here, enjoying my retirement in the Close, so I at least haven't come out of things too badly.'

'Yes, Mr Challoner,' Serenity pursued, '*you*'ve not been pilloried and ridiculed, *you* may not've wished to take revenge on my brother for his betrayal, but you can't answer for everyone, can you? Croft might be an extreme pacifist, but not everyone who's picked up on his ideas necessarily shares that one.'

'You're quite right, of course you are, Serenity. Oh, dear, why is the world so violent? You know what the most lethal creature on earth is? Man, of course. I was reading some figures recently and very interesting I found them. Sharks kill 10 people a year, jellyfish 100, elephants 600 - would you believe? - snakes 100,000 – and man? Well, a rough estimate for the annual number of murders worldwide, depending on how you define murder, is – wait for it! – 520,000! And then there's war, of course. Yes, there are violent people out there, even followers of the gentle Jesus Christ, and I can't rule out that one of them, perhaps an Anti-Churcher, was skulking round the city at the time of your brother's death and saw his – or her - opportunity.'

'Can you think of an alternative? You know the situation better than I do.'

'Could it have been a burglary that went wrong?'

'But I don't think anything was stolen, was it?'

'Perhaps the burglar was surprised, or panicked, or couldn't see anything to pinch, or realised he'd got the wrong flat. There are a number of reasons why he might have entered your brother's flat with a view to stealing but then left before the job was finished. My view has been that, as the burglar stood on the landing contemplating which flat to burgle, a visitor came out of your brother's, and the burglar barged in with perhaps a polite "Thank you" to his unwitting collaborator. When he got inside and surprised the owner in his underwear, James put up resistance, and that was it. James was no spring chicken, you know – not a match for a young thief intent on mischief.'

'Did you put this theory to the police?'

'Yes, but they weren't interested. Not a shred of evidence, they commented. They preferred to pursue the sexual partner lead – even when that got them nowhere. Look, I've talked more than enough. I insist that you have a cup of tea, my dear, and then you can tell me all about yourself. I don't meet many new people now, and it's always a pleasure – especially one so personable as you, if you'll permit an old man to say so without incurring accusations of flirting.' Giving a broad and winsome smile, he pulled himself with difficulty out of his chair without more ado and made for the kitchen. Serenity had decided that this frail and delightful old gentleman could not be her brother's murderer.

23

Ravensdale and Count Drechsler continued their conversation at St Catherine's Court, until the latter pressed the private investigator to stay for lunch. In the meantime, the count took Mark round the house and the estate, chatting about the family and asking Ravensdale about *his*. The two found they had interests in common and plenty of sources of conversation. They were soon on Christian-name terms and enjoyed a stimulating luncheon with the charming and vivacious Mrs Drechsler, Éléanore or 'Ellie' to her intimates, in the couple's sumptuous dining-room, waited on by attentive staff. Ravensdale felt inclined to abandon his quest for a murderer and invite himself for a week's holiday at the Court; but he recognised that that is not usually how life works.

After lunch, the three retired to the drawing-room for coffee, and then Mrs Drechsler excused herself on the grounds of an appointment – with her stock-broker. Ravensdale pressed the count for details of the man who had rung Thwaites' door-bell as Drechsler – 'Wilhelm' – approached the block of flats to deliver his ultimatum to Thwaites the blackmailer. This was perhaps the key to the whole business. The trouble was, Wilhelm had taken no particular notice. Furthermore, two years had elapsed. He closed his eyes the better to visualise the scene.

'I went up the street quite confidently, determined to confront Thwaites and tell him to his face to do his worst, I was no longer interested. I knew exactly where he lived and which door-bell was his, as I'd been before. As I approached the door of the apartment-block, however, a man crossed the road on my left and cut in in front of me. He didn't know, of course, that I was going to ring at Thwaites' doorbell. When he pressed the button, I heard Thwaites' voice over the intercom saying, "Yes, who is it?", the man muttered something I didn't hear into the microphone, the door clicked open, and the man went in, leaving the door to shut itself behind him – which it did reluctantly. I stood there a minute, wondering what to do. I remember it was a very warm day, and I was in full sun, so I retired and began to stroll up and down, keeping my eye on the door for when this man should come out. There was absolutely no point my going up to Thwaites' flat while I knew he already had a visitor. I didn't care what he did with the information he had and threatened to use, but there was no need for me to drag a complete stranger into the business by telling Thwaites in his presence that I was done with him and his wretched threats. Anyhow, I waited a short while - '

'How long, do you think?'

'Um, a couple of minutes, something like that? and then gave up. I reasoned that if this man hadn't come back down again in a few minutes, that meant he'd gone into Thwaites' flat, and I might have to wait another twenty or thirty minutes - at least.'

'OK, Wilhelm, now describe this man to me.'

'That's just it: I can't. No matter how hard I try to remember, nothing comes to mind.'

'Not to worry. Let me take you through one or two things. Hair: what colour?'

'Don't know: he had a cap on.'

'What kind of cap: flat cap, baseball cap, Ghandi cap, casquette, beanie, beret, deer-stalker, balmoral – night-cap?' Drechsler smiled.

'No, just a cap.'

'Was he short, medium or tall?'

'Um, about my height, perhaps a bit less. Let's say about six foot.'

'What clothes was he wearing? You say it was a hot day: was he in shorts?'

'No, trousers, light trousers, sort of beige or cream, I think; light-coloured, anyway.'

'Could it have been a track-suit bottom?'

'No, I don't think so.'

'Top, now: a T-shirt? standard shirt open at the neck and sleeves rolled up? jacket?'

'Um, no, not a jacket, I don't think. No, definitely not a jacket. I know: a fitted tank top or sleeveless sweater, one of those things,' he said as he screwed his eyes up.

'Build: slight, average or heavy?'

'Well-built, quite muscular, but not bouncer-build.'

'Age, now. What age would you say?'

'Oh, I'm no good at ages.'

'Young or old?'

'Young.'

'Teenager?'

'No older than that.'

'Thirty?'

'Could be. Sorry, Mark, it's no good asking me, I've really no idea of the man's age.'

'Specs?'

'Don't know, can't remember. I don't *think* so.'

'Dark? blond? black? Mediterranean?'

'Definitely not black: I'd've remembered. Definitely not pale, either. Average.'

'Any overall impression of this man: a toughie? a smoothie – what we used to call a spiv? a kindly sort of guy or a trouble-maker? British or foreign?'

'I really don't know: all I felt at the time was impatience and frustration. To be pipped on the post like that by some pushy young guy.'

'So he was pushy.'

'Well, no, he'd just got in my way, so I was naturally not well disposed towards him. What else can I say, Mark?'

'Don't worry, Wilhelm, I shall find this man.'

'How?'

'If he walked into that block of flats, the chances are somebody saw him. If somebody saw him, we can jog memories. It could be that he'd been seen before or, if he was a local, that he was even recognised.'

'Aren't people going to think it strange, you poking about like this two years after the event?'

'So what? Most folks are only too glad to help in inquiries of this sort: gives them a sort of ersatz importance.'

24

Wilhelm and Ravensdale continued their conversation amicably, until Ravensdale told his host that he really must get going if he was to achieve anything for the rest of the day. Wilhelm drove him back into the city. He gave him a cheque for £500, to cover Matthias Biddulph's stake in the business, and a further generous £500 in cash to tide him over the next few days of the inquiry. Ravensdale promised to return for dinner in three days' time to report back. The first thing Ravensdale did was to make his way to the block of flats in question. It was a standard apartment-block, three storeys high. The entrance lobby and stairs were in the middle of the long side facing the street, with a flat on either side. Three further flats occupied the back section of the block. This pattern was repeated on the other two storeys. All fifteen flats had a bell on the street and also a letter-box, accessible to residents from within the lobby. Ravensdale began at the bottom, thinking that a resident in one of the ground-floor flats at the front would probably have a better idea of comings and goings than somebody on the top floor. He pressed the bell of No. 1 and waited. There being no answer, he tried the bell of No. 2. A querulous voice, which could have been male or female, asked who was there.

'Good morning.' The 'sir' or 'madam' remained unspoken, for fear of causing offence. 'My name's Ravensdale, and I'm investigating the death of Mr James Thwaites in this block of flats two years ago. I wonder whether you can help me by answering one or two questions.' He had considered impersonating a policeman and, alternatively, coming out with some outlandish story in order to gain entry to the various flats, or at least to have a few moments' conversation with each resident, but the first option was illegal, and the second could damage his *bona fides* in the residents' eyes if he ever did gain an interview with them. He hoped therefore that an honest, straightforward approach would work. It did on this occasion at least.

'Come in, young man. Happy to help.' The door clicked open, and Ravensdale entered the lobby. Coming out of the ground-floor flat on his right was an elderly woman in a faded housecoat.

'This way,' she beckoned. 'Nice to have someone to talk to. Can be lonely in these flats, you know. Why, I hardly see anyone from one day's end to the next, and that's not good for an elderly person. My fault, I suppose, since I don't make friends easily: just too fussy, you see. I mean, some people go on and on, and you never get a word in edgewise, and, well, why should I sit through a whole string of someone's little anecdotes, when I don't know any of the people involved? It's just boring, and people aren't interested in my little doings. I don't really blame them for that, but we could talk about the tele, or current affairs, couldn't we, but they don't seem to want to: too keen to tell me about so-and-so who did such-and-such. Oh, well, comes to all of us, I suppose. It's all me husband's fault: drank himself to an early death and left me on me own, instead of supporting me in me old age. You married, sergeant? Then you'll know what I mean. Well, mustn't keep you on the doorstep: come on in. If you don't mind me saying so, you don't look like a policeman. What did you say your name was?'

'Ravensdale, madam, and I'm not a policeman.'

'But you said you were investigating poor Thwaites' death.'

'I am, but only as a private investigator.'

'But I'm sure you told me you were a policeman. Oh, well, never mind, you're here now. What'll you have, tea or coffee? I do both, but of course tea's easier, as I'm about to make a pot for meself.'

'Tea will do fine, thank you.' Ravensdale, unsure how best to break into the logorrhoeic flow without causing offence but impatient to hear whether she had any useful information for him or not, let her continue for a bit before broaching the subject of his visit.

'James Thwaites, madam. Can you remember the day he died? He seems to have had a visitor, a young man in a sleeveless sweater, about three o'clock in the afternoon. Did you see this man at all?'

'No, why should I? I mean, I don't put me head out of me flat every time the door opens. That'd be silly, wouldn't it? I'd never get any peace. No, I ignore the door, the comings and goings, the postman, the arguing, the hours people keep, the banging of doors, the noises on the stairs – can't be bothered with it all.'

'Did James Thwaites have many visitors, do you know?' Ravensdale put in when there was the tiniest pause.

'Oh, yes, I used to see them through my window. You notice I have an arm-chair where I can see all that goes on; keeps me occupied through the day. Well, you'd do the same if you were me, young man.' She poured tea for them both with a shaky hand, her white hair escaping from the hair-pins that held most of it in place. Her house-slippers were frayed and faded, but there was an air of gentility about her that endeared her to her visitor.

'When you say "many" visitors, do you mean several a day?'

'Oh, no, not several a day.'

'One a day?'

'Well, no, not so many as that, probably. A few in the week – two or three maybe. Many, many more than I get.'

'I see. So did you notice this particular young man on the day of Thwaites' death?'

'What day of the week was it? It wasn't a Tuesday was it?'

'Yes, it was, actually.'

'Oh, dear, then, no, I wouldn't have seen anything. Tuesdays I go round to me chiropodist to have me feet seen to – gets me out of the house, you see; such a lovely girl, too – then I go on to the hairdresser's for a bit of titivating, and then I treat meself to a bun in a café in the town. It's an afternoon out, you see. Of course, getting about isn't as easy as it used to be, and I suppose one day the chiropodist and the hairdresser'll have to come to me.' She chuckled.

'Tell me, do you think the people in the opposite flat might have seen anything? I can't get an answer.'

'Oh, no, dear, most unlikely. Well, I don't like to say this - ' and here her voice dropped to a whisper – 'she works nights, if you know what I mean. Sleeps all day. I mean, she'd have to, wouldn't she, dear?'

Ravensdale had the greatest difficulty in extricating himself from the widow's clutches, but he consoled himself with the thought that he had performed one charitable action that day, even though at the expense of his nervous energy and spiritual poise. This first interview was highly unsatisfactory. It had taken Ravensdale three-quarters of an hour to extract minimal information, and he hoped that none other of the flat residents were so loquacious. Otherwise the three days before he was due to dine at St Catherine's Court would have passed without bringing him anything he did not know beforehand. On the other hand, the honest admission of his purpose had gained him entry to one flat; and according to the occupant of that flat, he would be wasting his time in contacting her opposite number, as it were. He had drawn up a table of the residents, numbered 1-15, omitting

No. 13, which he discovered was numbered 12A. Four of the residents were new, but he asked for addresses of their predecessors who might have been in residence at the time of Thwaites' death. He did not bother with Thwaites' own flat, since there was, by definition, nothing he could learn there. Two of the residents refused to speak to him, even over the intercom, possibly frightened of getting caught up in an event beyond their comprehension and control, but not before they had told him firmly that they knew nothing to tell him. He managed to contact all other seven occupants, including other members of their households, but in each case drew a blank. One was a retired postmaster who never left his flat during the day because daylight troubled his eyes; he could not have met anybody on the stairs. All the other six, who worked during the day, had been absent on the day in question and could not help him. One thing he discovered was that the police inquiry had been perfunctory, to put it no more strongly than that, since the detectives in charge of the case had not interviewed all the residents, and even those they did interview were asked only specific questions about the two visitors the police suspected of involvement in Thwaites' death: Chimes and Biddulph.

Of the four who had occupied flats on the crucial day, three had moved to other addresses in the city, and Ravensdale was able to contact them all – with no result. The fourth had moved to an address in Selby, and, with money no object thanks to the kind offices of the Duke of Jülich and Count of Somewhere Else, Ravensdale travelled nonchalantly to Selby to complete his investigation. As he stood ringing the doorbell of No. 7, Armoury Road, a head popped out of a neighbouring window.

'Wasting yer time, mate,' a male voice said. 'In 'orspital – suspected food poisoning.'

'Oh, dear, sorry to hear that. Is he likely to be back soon, do you know?'

'No idea, mate. The last I 'eard 'e was right poorly. That were yesterday, that were. Can I 'elp?'

'Er, no, no thanks,' Ravensdale said and took his leave. It probably was not important anyway. Right, back to St Catherine's Court for a dinner in delightful company, but with little to report for three days' work.

25

He took a taxi out to the Drechslers' and, having negotiated the long drive on foot, was warmly received at the house. It was drizzling, and there was the faintest hint of autumn in the air. The Drechslers had lit a fire in the drawing-room, which, while not perhaps required for warmth, was none the less cheerily welcome. A servant brought a trolley of bottles and accompaniments and disappeared unobtrusively, and the count dispensed drinks.

'Right, Mark, spill the beans. How have you got on? Ellie's as keen as I am to know what success you've had.'

'Ah, well, not much, really,' Ravensdale admitted. 'In fact, none at all, if I'm to be honest. I contacted virtually all the occupants of the flats who were in place when Thwaites met his end. You'd be amazed at how difficult people are to get hold of: either they've moved on, or they don't want to talk to you, or they're not in, or they're in a rush and can't spare you the time. However, the net result of all my interviews is zilch: a big round O; nix; diddly-squat - how else can I put it?'

'What, nothing at all?'

'Well, no, obviously I talked to people and listened: what I meant was, nothing useful. It seems that nobody saw anything.' Ravensdale was being disingenuous and purveying less than the honesty he had promised his hosts, because he here concealed a fact that was a disturbing part of his investigation. The thought had crossed his mind that the young man in his sleeveless sweatshirt pushing the bell at Thwaites' door was a creation of Count Drechsler's to distract attention from his own role as blackmail victim and murderer. Ravensdale had dismissed such thoughts as unworthy and a betrayal of the count's friendship, but, despite the fact that he was now being pay-rolled by Drechsler and despite the fact that his commission to trace the bearded man had been brought to a successful conclusion, he felt that his primary allegiance was still to Matthias Biddulph and that he should dispassionately follow ideas wherever they led him, until he could see his way more clearly. He would therefore continue to bear in mind that his host could be one colossal liar and an unparalleled knave. Fortunately these unworthy thoughts were to be kyboshed sooner than he expected.

'Perhaps that's not surprising in the middle of the afternoon,' Drechsler was saying. 'How long would it take Thwaites' visitor to get from the street-door to his flat?'

'About twenty seconds, I should think: ten seconds for each flight of stairs.'

'There you are, then. Twenty seconds up, fifteen seconds down. What are the chances of somebody else in the flats going up or down the stairs at precisely the same time, particularly given that most people probably weren't in anyway? - all out at work or perhaps having a snooze or watching television.'

'I was told that Thwaites received visitors once or twice a week, always men seemingly, usually younger than himself. He himself went out quite a bit, presumably to do duty at the cathedral, shopping, eating out, meeting friends and so on – I don't know, didn't get any information on that, but presumably the police looked into it all.'

'Don't count on it, Mark. You said you contacted virtually all the residents. What happened to the others? Might they be of help, do you think?'

'Well, I missed out on one only. Had to go to Selby to hunt him down, only to find he's in hospital – sorry, 'orspital – with food poisoning; but I don't think he'd have made any difference – not if the others are anything to go by. He'd be the only one out of, say, twenty-five inhabitants of the apartment block who saw anything – high odds.'

'You don't remember his name, by any chance?'

'His name? No, I don't, but I've got it here somewhere.' He retrieved a notebook from his inside jacket pocket and leafed through it. 'Yes, here we are: Lambert Shearsby. Mean anything to you?'

'Well, yes, it's rather curious.'

'What is: his name? Shearsby's certainly unusual. Mind you, Lambert isn't exactly common, either.'

'No, no, the fact that you've been hoping to speak to him.'

'Why?'

'Ellie, where did you put last night's paper?'

'It's here,' his wife said, pulling it from under a cushion on the sofa. She handed it to her husband, and he spent a little time searching through it.

'Yes, here we are,' Drechsler announced at length. 'A very short paragraph: funny I should remember it.'

'It was only last night's paper, Wilhelm,' his wife put in.

'Here, read it for yourself, Mark,' Drechsler went on, smiling at his wife's remark. He passed over a paper untidily folded to display the right paragraph.

Lambert Shearsby, 29, was rushed to hospital three days ago from his home in Selby, North Yorkshire, with suspected food poisoning, but tests revealed that he had ingested a fatal dose of alpha-amatoxin, which is found in certain species of mushroom. Preliminary inquiries suggest that, after a recent sports victory, Mr Shearsby received a bottle of wine and a packet of mushrooms at his door from an admirer. It was labelled as produce from a local delicatessen, but the bag had apparently been tampered with: it contained an *amanita virosa*, the Destroying Angel mushroom, young specimens of which are easily mistaken for a perfectly edible species, *agaricus campestris*. The circumstances being suspicious, police have launched a murder inquiry.

'Hm, that's interesting,' Ravensdale commented.

'Isn't it, just. You spend three days rooting around the residents of a block of flats, making it known to all and sundry that you're inquiring about a mysterious stranger as part of an investigation into the still unsolved murder of James Thwaites, and suddenly one person who might have seen something meets a suspicious death. Yes, very interesting.' Ravensdale could not see how the count could be Shearsby's murderer or, if he was, why he should draw Ravensdale's attention to Shearsby's death.

'I suppose we must go to the police with this,' was all he said.

26

Lorna Carter stared at her husband in disbelief.

'Proved Troublesome: Eliminated? You're joking, Alex!'

'Go on, then, what else could the initials beside Thwaites' name mean?'

'I don't know, do I? What about, well, what about Pretty Torrid Estimates; or Proceed To End (this contact – the man's a buffoon); or why doesn't he Produce a Transaction Every month; or Pretentious Twaddling Egghead; or Please Terminate Engagement?'

'Look, seriously, Lorna, do you think we've got enough to go to the police with, whatever these damned initials stand for?'

'No, I don't. We'd get the Becketts had up for illegal trading, but then we'd be in trouble ourselves; and no nearer getting anyone convicted for Thwaites' murder.' A silence hung between them, until Lorna spoke again. 'Do we have to resign ourselves to failure? Have we gone through all this for nothing?'

'I'm convinced in my mind that the Becketts were responsible for Thwaites' death, or at least had a hand in it. We know Thwaites had dealings with the Becketts over a number of years. We know from our own experience that it's unwise to cross the Becketts where their business is concerned, as they threatened us as well. We can guess that their business is so risky they can't take chances, and if a collaborator proves unreliable or disloyal, there might be only one solution.'

'So which of them did it?'

'It would have to be Roddy: Ava wouldn't be strong enough.'

'So how did it go?'

'Roddy gets a message to Thwaites – text, phone-call, secret rendezvous with an associate in the city, it doesn't matter to us how, although it'd probably be unsafe to leave anything written – that he's going to call to discuss matters – or he just turns up at Thwaites' flat. He rings at the street. "Yes, come on up. I'm not really presentable, but I shall be by the time you get up here." Instead, showman and narcissist that he is, he presents himself to Roddy Beckett in his underwear. Beckett doesn't give a monkey's for all that, grabs a statuette and clobbers him. Then, to finish him off, he grabs a curtain tie and throttles him. He straightens his clothes, leaves the flat and walks calmly back into the street, job done. There'd be no blood, so there'd be nothing to show he'd just committed murder.'

'Taking a bit of a risk, wasn't he?'

'Of course, but sometimes needs must.'

'And what had Thwaites done to deserve death?'

'We can only speculate. The accounts we've seen show that he and the Becketts weren't seeing eye to eye on pricing. Perhaps Thwaites began to make threats that unless his estimates were taken more seriously he'd stir up trouble.'

'But the Becketts'd be quite certain he wouldn't, because he'd get into trouble with the police himself.'

'Yes, but the penalty for Thwaites would be insignificant compared with that for the Becketts, and financially trivial.'

'The trouble is, we can't prove any of this – unless the finger-prints left on the statuette could be proved to be Roddy's. Hey, there's a thing: couldn't we go to the police with that idea?'

'Maybe, but we'd have to admit to several months working on the black market.'

'We approach the police anonymously. We drop a letter through their box suggesting they take Beckett's finger-prints.'

'After what we've read and heard, I'm not sure I'd trust that particular police-force to do the job right.'

'OK, let's just say, for the sake of argument, that the Becketts had nothing to do with Thwaites' death, that in other words we've been barking up the wrong tree. What then?'

'You obviously have something in mind, Lorna: what?'

'We haven't asked ourselves who benefits from Thwaites' death. In other words, who did he leave his money to?'

'Did he have any money to leave?'

'Don't see why not: professional man, no family, I bet he had a good bit stashed away. But how do we get a copy of his will?'

'Easy. Leave it to me.'

27

Back at home in Ripon after her visit to Dean Challoner, Serenity Bursnell poured herself a drink and sat down to think. She had not even donned her thinking-cap, however, when son Reuben put in an appearance. He threw his wet overcoat on a chair, kissed his mother and sat down on the opposite side of the gas fire, which was on low to take the chill off the room.

'Hello, mum,' he chirruped, 'you look glum.'

'I don't seem to be getting anywhere, Reuben.'

'Tell me all about it: two heads are better than one, or, as our friend The Preacher has it, "Two are better than one, because they have a good return for their work." Ah, all this Bible stuff: you shouldn't have given me such a holy name. So – oh, hold on, let me get a drink first. You ready for a top-up?' Serenity shook her head. 'Right,' he went on, 'what've you been up to?'

'I've been busy, and my head's in a whirl.'

'From the beginning!' he cautioned her.

'Well, you know the first bit: I went to see the present dean at the cathedral and learned a lot of stuff about the Anti-Church of Jesus Christ; but not enough – not enough I could understand. So I phoned Dr Croft, the author of the book which started the whole thing off, and travelled down to Nottingham to see him. Nice man. Very unassuming, helpful, friendly. Ordinary house: detached, on the outskirts of the city, rather grim style of furnishing it – but each to his own.'

'What age man?'

'Late thirties, something like that? A bit like Einstein to look at, actually. Anyway, he explained that he had nothing to do with the Anti-Church himself: that was the work of a woman who'd got hold of his ideas and wanted to make something of them. He gave me her name – Pyrena Hembry – and address, and I went along to see her. Talk about eccentric! Having negotiated a ferocious hound of the Baskervilles and a strange maid, I was granted an audience with her ladyship and subjected to a quite unwarranted assault on my personal qualities. Anyhow, she eventually told me all I wanted to know – except who might have had a hand in James' death. She was certain it couldn't have been a member of her church – sorry, Anti-Church - but when I pressed her, she admitted she couldn't be a hundred percent sure. Of course she couldn't, silly old bat. Anyway, from there I went back to see the former dean – the one who was in place when James was at the cathedral. Don't know why I didn't think of him before. Unfortunately, although he welcomed me effusively and chatted at some length – dear old chap, much too frail to be the murderer himself - he dismissed the whole Anti-Church theory as wild.'

'But he had a theory of his own?'

'No, not really. He just thought it might've been a burglary that went wrong.'

'I see. So what now?'

'Well, I'd only just got down to some serious thinking when you arrived, but - '

'Yes: but?'

'Look, what if we've been barking up the wrong tree, Reuben? What if the whacky Miss Hembry and her addle-pated Anti-Church are totally irrelevant - '

'Hold on, mum, remember uncle James was a member!'

' – and we've been ignoring what's been under our nose the whole time.'

'What?'

'Your uncle's will.'

'You don't mean - '

'Oh, but I do mean.'

28

'The police?' Drechsler sounded alarmed. 'But if you take all this to the police, you'll have to tell them about me – won't you? I don't see how you can given an account of your investigation, Mark, and leave me out of it. There must be another way.'

'Well,' Ravensdale answered slowly, 'if we can't track this presumed victim of blackmail – the one we're suggesting murdered Thwaites – who else can if not the police?'

'Look, you're really acting for Biddulph, aren't you? Your job was to clear his name. You've done that.'

'Yes, perhaps I've done that, but only by putting *you* in the frame. I can't go to the police with eye-witness evidence of a stranger ringing at Thwaites' flat without identifying the witness. They'd dismiss my evidence as fancy if I weren't prepared to name you.'

'Yes, yes, I see that, but there must be something else.' He sat for a moment looking thoughtful. 'I know!' he exclaimed suddenly. 'Did Thwaites leave a will?'

'I don't know; I suppose so: most sensible people of his age do.'

'Then we need to get hold of a copy. I don't think the police have thought of that at all, and yet greed is a very powerful motive for murder, as we all know. Perhaps Thwaites left a fortune to some guy who couldn't wait until his benefactor kicked the bucket.'

'Well, I can easily get hold of a copy. Leave it with me, Wilhelm, and we'll see whether it sheds any light on the problem.'

29

The District Probate Registry at etc.

Be it known that James Anthony Thwaites of [address] died on [date] domiciled in England and Wales and be it further known that at the date hereunder written the Last Will and Testament (a copy whereof is hereunto annexed) of the said deceased was proved and registered in the said Registry of the High Court of Justice etc.

It is hereby certified that it appears from information supplied on the application for this grant that the gross value of the said estate in the United Kingdom amounts to £935,631.00 and that the net value of such estate amounts to etc.

Dated etc.
[Signed] District Registrar

This is the Last Will and testament of me James Anthony Thwaites of etc. whereby I revoke all former Wills and testamentary dispositions made by me and declare this to be my last Will and testament

1 I appoint the Partners at the date of my death in the firm of Messrs Chauveau and Green Solicitors of etc. aforesaid to be Executors and Trustees of this my Will

2 I give the following specific bequests free of all taxes and duties absolutely:-

a) All my papers photographs other documents and articles relating to the Thwaites family including the privately-printed autobiography of our great-uncle Samuel to my sister Serenity Letitia Bursnell etc.

b) All my Hi-fi equipment and CDs and my signed copy of Gerald Moore's autobiography to Piers Blake of 21 St John's Terrace Barnards Green Truro

3 I give to Gerald Heggs of 14 Wordsworth Road Monk Bretton free of all taxes and duties whatsoever such of my books (except those hereinbefore mentioned) as the said Gerald Heggs shall select within six months of being requested by my Trustees so to do

4 I devise and bequeath in equal shares to my said sister Serenity Letitia Bursnell and to her three children Reuben, Abigail and Jocelyn all that property known as Palazzo Tormani used by me as a holiday residence situate at Ponte di Camurano in the Province of Florence along with paddocks stables and all other appurtenances thereunto belonging

5 I give devise and bequeath the remainder of my estate both real and personal whatsoever and wheresoever not otherwise effectually disposed of by this my Will or any codicil thereto (including property and assets over which I have a general power of appointment) to Martyn Spencer Wynn of Lochdhu Lodge, Altnabreac.

6 I direct that I be buried in a plain cardboard coffin without any of the rites associated with any conventional Christian church and without the ministrations of a clergyman or woman of any Christian denomination whatsoever and in the greatest simplicity in accordance with the principles of the virtuous life laid down by our Lord and Saviour Jesus Christ and to this end I charge my Executors to engage any funerary enterprise in the city which will undertake so to bury me.

7 I further declare that any Executor or Trustee of this my Will being a Solicitor shall be entitled to charge and be paid all proper professional charges for all the time expended and acts done by him or any Partner of his in connection with the proving of this my Will etc.

In witness whereof I have hereunto set my hand this twentieth day etc.

30

'Do you know,' Serenity told Reuben, 'it never occurred to me that this man Wynn had a first-class motive for murder. I was so caught up with this idea of the Anti-Church and James' involvement in the failed manifestation at the cathedral that I never gave other motives a thought.'

'Who is this Wynn guy? I've never heard of him before.'

'Well, there's a bit of a story attached to him, but I must tell you that, since I've never met him, what I'm telling you is all second-hand.'

'So what's the story? Sounds intriguing.'

'It's not much, really: I did say "a bit" of a story. Martyn Wynn was a university friend of James's: sportive, a good academic and by all accounts wealthy. Titled, too, I think, or about to be titled, but that's a detail. Martyn was reading architecture, James English, but they met at one of the sports' clubs of the university. In September 1949, the two of them decided to spend a little time in New York sight-seeing before the new academic year. Unfortunately, they got caught up in the Peekskill Riots – you know, when Paul Robeson gave concerts in the city which some white supremacists used as an excuse for some major disturbances – but you're probably too young to know these things. Martyn was hit by a badly-aimed petrol bomb. He lost his right hand; his left arm was badly disfigured; but the worst injury was the loss of his face. Surgeons saved enough to keep him alive and able to feed himself – sight in one eye, a bit of a nose and a mouth, but his life was effectively destroyed by his dreadful injuries. He bought a remote house in Scotland and, as far as I know, has lived there ever since, in almost total isolation from the world.'

'Is that the Lochdhu Lodge mentioned in uncle James' will?'

'It is. Apparently a wonderful place, if you like that sort of thing. James told me about it once, after visiting Martyn there. 1890s baronial Gothic, sixteen bedrooms, seven bathrooms, private trout-lake of twelve acres, fourteen further acres of moorland, all surrounded by forestry plantations. The private drive is fourteen miles long, and even then you've got a further twelve miles to go to get to a shop. So not a place for the faint-hearted – or the sociable. James' visits to Caithness gradually diminished in frequency – not surprising, given the length of the journey and the sombre atmosphere at the Lodge, but the main reason, I think, was that Martyn couldn't bear even his close friends to see him wasting away in the Caithness remoteness. I don't think Martyn and James had *met* for some years, although I believe they continued to correspond sporadically. Why James left all his money to Martyn, I've no idea. Out of pity, perhaps; or perhaps he still regarded him as his closest friend.'

'I've never asked you how uncle James made his money.'

'Ah, well.' She hesitated. 'I don't know, Reuben.'

'But you can guess.'

'Not really. To my knowledge he never came into any substantial legacy, and his job as a teacher wouldn't have allowed him to accumulate such wealth – a palace in Italy, indeed! So I can only guess that it wasn't legal – but, as I say, I don't know, so let's not go rushing to conclusions.'

'You're dodging the truth, mum, because you think we might have to give up the Italian property if it was the fruit of, say, well, blackmail - ' he pronounced this with a marked rise in intonation. 'Morally, I mean.'

'I'll stay in my ignorance, young man, and so will you. I don't think it was blackmail – more dealing in rare books on the black market. There was some trouble once with books from the cathedral, but I never got the full story. Anyway, it's not for us to speculate and besmirch your uncle James' memory, so say no more about it.'

'OK, so what now? If what you say is true, Martyn Wynn could hardly appear in the street outside uncle James's and ring at his door without exciting a lot of attention. Are you thinking that perhaps he tried it anyway?'

'I don't know what I'm thinking. Maybe we should leave things as they are. Maybe we've taken on too much. Or maybe we should go to the police and get them to reopen the case.'

31

Meanwhile, back at Ledsham, in the rural calm of Park Lane, Lorna and Alex Carter were perusing their latest item of post marked 'Probate Registry': the last will and testament of James Anthony Thwaites.

'Well, it's obvious,' Lorna exclaimed. 'I just don't know why we didn't think of this before: too taken up with pursuing the Becketts, I suppose.'

'No, there you're wrong, Lorna. Look, I knew Thwaites, you didn't. He worked as a hack teacher, for heaven's sake, not a merchant banker or city broker. He was retired, and being part-time verger at the cathedral wouldn't have netted him that sort of money. Of course, he could've come into some fat legacy I don't know about, but our acquaintance with the shady Becketts has shown us where his money might have come from: illegal trading in books. He may have done business the Becketts had no idea about and we haven't uncovered.'

'That's as may be, but the point is: what do we do now? Pursuing the Becketts hasn't really got us very far, but this – this is different. The main beneficiary – what's his name? - Martyn Wynn – he's right in the frame, surely, and I can't think why the police didn't spot this.'

'Perhaps they did.' Ignoring Alex, Lorna ploughed on.

'He's short of money, he travels south, clobbers Thwaites, and Bob's your uncle: he's rich all of a sudden. It's just too obvious.'

'Exactly: it's too obvious. It's not credible that the police didn't follow that line of inquiry. You don't want us to pay a visit to this chap in deepest Caithness, do you? What would that achieve?'

'We could ask him where his sudden rush of money came from.'

'Lorna, be sensible. He'd just say that they were beneficiaries in a friend's will, and you'd be no further forward. In any case, Thwaites' bequest wouldn't make Wynn rich, not by the time you've taken off inheritance tax and the Tuscan *palazzo*. Richer, perhaps.' He picked up the will again and idly cast his eye over the sheets. 'Wait a minute,' he said suddenly. 'Here's a thing.'

'What?'

'Look, the envelope's addressed to us - '

'Naturally, otherwise it wouldn't have got here.'

' – but the receipt's made out to somebody called Ravensdale.'

'Here, show me.' Lorna was as intrigued as her cousin. 'So it is. Well, whaddayaknow? What does it mean?'

'The receipt's clear that this Ravensdale had applied for the same will as we did. The clerk obviously got mixed up when she posted them off: two wills the same, two envelopes to put them in, she put the receipts into the wrong envelopes.'

'What's Ravensdale want with Thwaites' will?'

'Same as us, I suppose – looking for a motive for his murder.'

'I think we'd better get in touch with him. This could be interesting.'

32

Mark Ravensdale invited Matthias Biddulph to call in on his office next time he was in town, as he was now in a position to provide the results of his investigation. Alternatively, he was happy to pop his report in the post. Either way, he could inform him officially that there would be no fee as his invoice had been settled by a well-wisher. Matt Biddulph, seizing with both hands the offer of hearing from the private investigator's lips that he had been cleared of suspicion in the case of Thwaites' murder, made an immediate appointment to call on Mr Ravensdale at King's Staith.

'Ah, good morning, Mr Biddulph,' Ravensdale greeted his client with a broad smile. 'Do take a seat.'

'You have news, Mr Ravensdale?'

'Well, yes and no. It's like this.' He assumed a professional posture and a sleek and confident tone. 'If you remember, we undertook to identify the bearded gentleman seen by a witness lurking outside Mr Thwaites' block of flats. Well, we eventually, with no little difficulty, obtained the name and address of this witness, a fuller description of the bearded man she was said to have seen and, yes, again we located him. I'm not in a position to identify him to you – it's a matter of professional confidentiality, you understand – but I can assure you that he was perfectly innocent of any malign designs on James Thwaites. If I tell you that it's this bearded gentleman who's settled your fee for you, you won't press me for his name, I'm sure.' He smiled and paused, to give his client a chance to register relief and satisfaction. 'On the other hand, identifying and exonerating *him* hasn't done *your* case much good.'

'No. If *he*'s quite innocent, the police are still going to be suspicious of *me*.'

'Quite. But we have succeeded in unearthing several other lines of inquiry, which, with your permission, I propose to put to the police.'

'Oh?'

'In the first place, we have evidence that Thwaites was running a blackmailing business, and we think that a visitor Thwaites had that afternoon may have been calling to settle a score. We haven't been able to identify this mysterious visitor, but it's possible the police may have greater success.'

'Who's this "we" you keep talking about, Mr Ravensdale?'

'It's a professional "we", Mr Biddulph: we, the business, Jorvik Probe.'

'I see. Please go on.'

'Well, we – that is, I, if you prefer – then wondered about a will. No will was ever mentioned in the original investigation, you know.'

'No, it wasn't.'

'So I got a copy. I can tell you, as it's public knowledge since probate was granted, that a certain Mr Martyn Wynn came in for a cool half a million squid on Mr Thwaites' demise.' He placed an envelope on the table between them.

'Whew, that's quite a sum. I'd no idea James commanded that sort of money.'

'Well, er, you know, Mr Biddulph, blackmail can be quite a lucrative business – if I'm right in my surmise, of course – don't wish to be doing the deceased an injustice, but I'm pretty sure that's one way at least in which he made his money. Anyway, I've made a copy of the will for you to keep, so that you can examine it at your leisure. In the meantime, what I propose is that I go to the police, suggesting this large bequest might have acted as an incentive to murder. You'll understand that, as a mere private investigator, I can't travel to Scotland – the remote north of Scotland, to boot – to threaten this man or question him: that's definitely a police matter. However, I'm confident that I shall give the police plenty to think about. What do you say?'

'I think you've done very well, Mr Ravensdale, very well indeed. It's not been an easy situation, and if you've found other lines of inquiry – blackmail and the beneficiary of a large will – I feel greatly relieved.' He slid the will out of the envelope which Ravensdale had put on the table and, with a discreet 'May I?', glanced at the contents.

'I say,' he hazarded after a minute or so, 'have you noticed this, Mr Ravensdale?'

'What?'

'The envelope's addressed to you here, but the receipt's made out to some people called Carter: Mr & Mrs Alex Carter, from Ledsham.'

'What, are you sure? I never noticed that. How silly of me.' He took the sheets that Biddulph offered him and verified the information.

'Well, I'll be blowed.'

'What does it mean, do you think?'

'I think it means that the Carters applied for a copy of the will at exactly the same time as I did, and the clerk simply got the two envelopes mixed up. Now if the Carters are interested in Thwaites' will two years after the events, it can only mean that they too are investigating the murder – I suppose. How interesting! Well, with your permission, Mr Biddulph, I think we ought to contact these Carters just to see what their game is. They may know more than we do, you see.'

'Yes, yes, of course; but, er, shall I have to finance this further step?' He sounded anxious.

'Mr Biddulph, of course not! Your bearded patron, if I may so call him, will pay any further fees due, I'm sure, as he's as keen to clear his name as you are, and he's in a position to finance the operation. Actually, he's already been very generous, and I shan't need a further subvention, I don't think. So rest assured that the matter will be pursued without any further call on your purse. I hope, however, that you'll allow me to keep you informed?'

'Oh, yes, most certainly. I shall be very anxious to hear how you get on. I can't wait to clear my name for good and all.'

33

'Right, sergeant,' asked Detective Inspector Moat in his usual business-like fashion, 'what've we got?' DI Walter Moat, mid-forties, moustachioed, big-boned but trim, with an imposing forehead under a full head of dark brown hair, was a striking figure but a humble one.

'We've got a body, sir, and at the moment not much else.' This was Detective Sergeant Alan Stockwell, smart, presentable, not long married and keen to learn, mid-twenties, tall and well-built. It was his third case with DI Moat, and he felt he was learning the job fast, although on the two previous occasions he had not been able to match his superior's agile mind. Moat's slightly idiosyncratic *modus operandi* put emphasis on careful recording of all data for later perusal, a completely open mind combined with what de Bono is pleased to call lateral thinking, a conciliatory manner with all with whom he came in contact and a democratic relationship with his assisting sergeant. In the case triggered by the theft of the so-called Wigginton locket[5], Moat had left Stockwell far behind in identifying a particularly devious, ruthless and capable criminal. In the case of the murder of Harry Quirke, fan of the piano-music of Alkan[6], he had been able to contribute a lot of thinking – none of it right – but his use of the Popperian method of conjecture and refutation had impressed his inspector.

'I thought we had a cause of death?'

'We have, sir – partly.'

'Go on then: sock it to me.' Stockwell made a point of flourishing his note-book under Moat's nose. The two were sitting in Moat's exiguous office at police headquarters on the edge of Newby Whiske in North Yorkshire. Between them stood a pot of tea, their favourite beverage, and a plate of custard creams thoughtfully provided by Moat.

'Well, sir, Lambert Shearsby, aged 29, was admitted to hospital on 7 October complaining of severe vomiting, diarrhoea, and stomach pains.

---

[5]See Julius Falconer, *The Waif* (2012).

[6]See Julius Falconer, *The Alkan Murder* (2012).

He'd called his doctor, and the doctor, noticing a yellowing of his eyes, had had him admitted immediately to Jimmy's[7]. Further tests were conducted, and eventually the presence of amatoxins was detected. Don't ask me what they are, sir: I'm only passing on the information. The medical team carried out emergency treatment from the outset, but the patient died thirty-six hours after admission – at 09.31 on Sunday the 9th to be precise. Essentially he died of liver failure. Naturally we carried out a search of the deceased's kitchen and kitchen waste, and in the bin we found an empty packet of dried funghi labelled "Best Gourmet Funghi" at a local delicatessen. Because the shop is Polish, the funghi had been imported from eastern Europe, but we traced other customers who bought identical packets from the same batch, and none had suffered any ill-effects at all. A preliminary analysis of fragments still in the cellophane packet at Shearsby's suggested the presence of one of the amanitas, probably *amanita virosa*, but further tests will have to be carried out before certainty is ascertained.'

'You mean, "before we can be sure".'

'You see, sir,' Stockwell added confidingly, ignoring the interruption, 'the amatoxins are also found in some other species of funghi, not just the amanitas.'

'Yes, thank you, sergeant. Please carry on.'

'It seems that someone left the packet of mushrooms and a bottle of wine on his doorstep with a covering card: "Congratulations, celebrate in style!"'

'What was that a reference to?'

'Not sure. It seems he'd been the star player in his local darts team the week before. Nothing else has come up – unless it was his engagement, but that was three months before. He must have returned to his flat, cooked himself the evening meal using the new-found mushrooms and settled down to watch a bit of tele.'

'How do you know that?'

'I don't, sir. I'm guessing.'

'Anybody see the person who dropped the mushrooms off?'

'A passer-by caught a brief glimpse but wasn't really paying attention. Anyway, the first symptoms of poisoning probably manifested themselves some hours after his meal, say in the darkest hours of the night. It's apparently characteristic of amanita poisoning that there's often a period of remission after the first symptoms, and this probably explains why the

---

[7]St James's University Hospital, Leeds.

deceased didn't call his doctor until later that afternoon. By then it was too late.'

'You've been busy: well done. So who is this Lambert Shearsby?'

'He's a young bank-clerk working for Lloyds. He moved with his job to Selby about twelve months ago and rented this flat in Armoury Road. He's engaged, to a young woman called – ' there was a pause because he could not immediately find the name on the page – 'Milly Troughton. He belongs to the local Rugby Union club, his local is the Abbey Vaults in James Street, he doesn't go to church, his parents live in Sheffield. That's about it, sir.'

'Any known enemies – his proposed in-laws, for example? - sort of *The Eldest Son* in reverse? Recent difficulties at work, with colleagues or managers? Any fights at the Abbey Vaults in which he might have made himself unpopular?'

'No, sir, not that we've discovered so far, but we haven't really started an investigation: waiting for you, sir.'

'Yes, yes, but the Force is quite capable of carrying out preliminary inquiries under the watchful eye of a detective sergeant – sergeant.'

'But now, sir, we wish to be directed. We want to know how an investigation should be conducted.'

'Yes, yes, well, never mind that now. We'll get Odgers as usual to set up an incident room – you can see to that, please. I want a list of all Shearsby's contacts: family, work, friends, mailbox entries, mobile phone contacts – you know the form, sergeant. I also want a cv for him going back as far as you can. We shall need to go back to the delicatessen owner – a Pole, is he? with an impossible name, I suppose – and I shall need to see a member of the medical team that treated him at Jimmy's. We'll also interview all his neighbours.'

'Again.'

'Yes, again; and I want a print-out of his emails, texts and phone-calls over the last, say, six months – where possible, of course; plus all his letters you can lay your hands on, including bills and the like. There must be a cogent reason why a young man is suddenly murdered in cold blood, and, if there's a reason - and not some flight of fancy or a psychotic episode - reasoning can disclose it. First off, you and I'll go and see the woman who witnessed the delivery of the contaminated mushrooms. You'll drive, of course. I need to listen to some music – *bel canto*, for preference – to maintain sanity in a mad world.'

34

Moat and Stockwell ran the witness to ground in Sainsbury's supermarket in the middle of Selby, where she worked as a supervisor. Mrs Eileen Gray was a woman in her forties, neat, compact, brisk. The store manager had put an office at the detectives' disposal, with the anxious rider, 'this interview won't take long, will it?'.

'Now, Mrs Gray, this won't take long, I'm sure. My name's Moat, and this is DS Stockwell. I understand you've already been interviewed?'

'Oh, yes, as soon as I read that that poor man had died, I knew had to go straight to the police; but I told the officer all I knew – or could remember.'

'That was very public-spirited of you, Mrs Gray; we appreciate it. But if it's not too much trouble, would you just run over for *us* what you told the officer?'

'Very well. I don't know how well you know Selby, inspector, but I live in Fairfax Avenue and generally walk up Armoury Road to get to work. The day you're talking about, I was due on duty at two o'clock, so I left home at about twenty to. As I came up Armoury Road, I noticed this guy peering keenly at the house-numbers – not all houses are numbered, you see, and it's not always easy to pick on the right one straightaway. He seemed eventually to find what he was looking for, opened the gate, deposited a packet and a bottle on the step of the side door and went back out of the gate.'

'Did he look nervous?'

'No, not a bit of it: perfectly normal, as far as I could tell. Just a normal delivery.'

'And then?'

'He walked up the road a bit, going in the same direction as myself, got into a car and drove off. And that's it. So I never really saw his face, and I had no particular reason to notice him.'

'But you did notice him?'

'Yes, and I've asked myself that same question: *why* did I?'

'And what's your answer, Mrs Gray?'

'That's just it: I haven't got one. I was walking up the street, nothing particular on my mind. There were one or two other people about, but the street wasn't busy, and I suppose I just thought about this guy because he was closer than anybody else.'

'So describe him to us, as well as you remember.'

'Youngish, muscular, blondish, average height. That's about it. Not much, I know.'

'You say "youngish": how "youngish"?'

'I couldn't say more precisely: not a slip of a boy, but not middle-aged.'

'OK – so not so old as I am?'

'Oh, no, inspector, *much* younger.' Ignoring that, Moat went on.

'When you say "muscular", how could you tell that unless he wore something sleeveless and tight-fitting on top?'

'Oh, he did: a T-shirt – short sleeves.'

'Jeans? cords? tracky bums?'

'Not sure: blue jeans, I think.'

'I see. "Blondish": do you mean not really blond, just not dark?'

'Yes, I suppose so.'

'Short or long hair?' She thought for a few seconds.

'Short, I think.'

'His car, now: any idea as to make?'

'No, just a car, inspector.'

'Big or little?'

'Average.'

'Colour?'

'Um, don't know: perhaps silver – ish?' Moat gave a small sigh.

'Well, Mrs Gray, you've been most helpful and public-spirited. Do you think there's anything you can add?'

'Oh, I've tried so hard, inspector, but no, nothing else. However - '

'However?'

'Well, if I saw him, other people may have done too.'

'Yes, we'll look into that, of course, although nobody's come forward so far. In the meantime, thank you very much for your help.'

While they were in Selby, they walked through the town centre to have a look at Armoury Lane. Moat did not think there would be anything to learn from visiting Shearsby's house, but it would be a curious murder inquiry in which the investigating officer had never visited the scene of the crime. Knowing that the inside of the house had been thoroughly searched already, Moat and Stockwell contented themselves with taking stock of the outside and imagining Mrs Gray walking up the street and taking little notice of a man depositing a package and a bottle outside no. 7.

35

When the detectives were back in the car, having slaked their thirst at a convenient café in Gowthorpe, Moat instructed Stockwell to make for Jimmy's hospital in Leeds.

'We may not learn very much there,' Moat explained apologetically, 'but at the moment we've so little to go on. Anyway, it'll give Odgers time to get some material together for us.' They travelled as fast as the road and the traffic would allow them, found nowhere to park when they got there but felt justified in occupying the space reserved for a consultant. They presented themselves at reception and were asked to wait. They waited nearly half-an-hour before Mr Webb, the consultant who had been responsible for Lambert Shearsby's treatment, was available to speak with them. He looked as if he might be approaching retirement age, but there was nothing tired or perfunctory in his manner.

'There's no more I can tell you than I've told your colleagues already, inspector,' he told them firmly. 'The patient's condition was so far advanced when he came to us that there was nothing we could do.'

'No, no, sir,' Moat hurried to say, 'we're not in the least criticising the hospital's treatment of the, er, victim: we just wish to clarify the circumstances of the crime. The patient died of acute liver failure?'

'Yes, inspector – it's what the amatoxins do. So within six to twelve hours of eating his mushrooms – look, say he had his meal at seven o'clock that night. By the early hours of the morning he'd be feeling very sick. He'd vomit and have diarrhoea. He'd have a severe stomach ache and would feel very weak. Eventually all that would subside, he'd feel well enough to go back to bed, and he'd be able to sleep. He might even have something to eat. Then later that day, the symptoms would return, and he'd feel alarmed enough to call the doctor. Of course, by the time he'd got to us, the main damage to the liver and kidneys had been done. It takes time to carry out all the tests necessary for an accurate diagnosis: his condition could have other causes, you see: gastroenteritis, for example, or hepatitis, or poisoning by some other plant. There'd be blood tests to carry out, a number of other tests for liver and kidney function. The consultant also needs to look at the patient carefully, palpating, prodding and inspecting. Only when all the test-results are in - can he be sure of an accurate diagnosis. Of course, in a case like this, emergency treatment is carried out immediately on the patient's admission to the hospital – no point in hanging around doing nothing while the patient's life ebbs away slowly but surely – or perhaps not so slowly. We did what we could, inspector. Because we're not persuaded that penicillin, either on its own or in combination, is very effective, we tried silybin administered as a mono-chemotherapy, which has proved in clinical tests to be more useful than anything else - '

'I'm quite sure you did everything you could, sir. Tell me, what would be a fatal dose of amatoxin?'

'In a man of his weight, I'd say 7 or 8 mg.'

'And would a single amanita fungus contain that amount of poison?'

'I'm no expert on funghi, inspector, but yes, I'd say so.'

'And the strength of the poison wouldn't be affected by drying the mushroom out or cooking it?'

'No, I don't think so. These amatoxins are very persistent, you see, and by inhibiting RNA polymerase II - '

'Well, thank you so much, Mr Webb. You've been most helpful.'

36

On their way back to headquarters to consult the dependable and seemingly omnipotent DS Odgers, Moat mused on what they'd learnt so far.

'You see, young sergeant, if our mysterious deliveryman had left just a packet of dried funghi, his victim might have been tempted to put in a cupboard for use on some future occasion. "Gourmet funghi" would suggest use at a dinner-party, would it not? But the bottle of wine – apart from adding to the "celebration" Shearsby was meant to be having - would persuade him to start on his mushrooms straight away. At least, I think I'd be tempted. If only he'd contacted his doctor at the first onset of his symptoms … '

'But most people are reluctant to disturb a doctor at night.'

'They are, but that's what the emergency services are for. We're a civilised country, sergeant. So, to pursue my train of thought – the delivery-man, who's the murderer or someone acting for the murderer - intends his victim to die fairly soon. He doesn't want him to put the mushrooms away in a cupboard and forget about them.'

'But if he had, when death came, perhaps months later, nobody would have remembered seeing the delivery-man.'

'No, there is that. Funny way to kill someone. But tell me, do you think we could be dealing with a random accident? The packers in Poland make a mistake, and a rogue fungus finds its way into an otherwise clean batch.'

'So the present of a packet of dried funghi and a bottle of wine was a genuine tribute to a great darts player?'

'Well, couldn't it be?'

'I'd feel happier with that, sir, if the poisoned packet had been bought over the counter by a random customer and not delivered to the door of a specific individual.

'Yes, good point. Our trouble is, we're theorising in the absence of sufficient data. We'll have to wait and see what Odgers has got for us.'

Odgers had a lot for them. A search-team had combed Shearsby's rooms and extracted all his correspondence, texts and emails. It had his address-books, both physical and digital; his digital pictures; a record of all his telephone calls. It had gone through his books, papers and clothing for anything that might document the existence of an enemy. Furthermore, another team had contacted residents of Armoury Road. One or two people thought they remembered a delivery at Shearsby's house, but none of the information amounted to much. All this material would wait on DI Moat's inspection. Oh, and a chap called Ravensdale had phoned – twice – wanting to speak to him. Said it was urgent.

'What's it about, did he say?'

'Well, he asked to speak to the officer in charge of the Shearsby murder case. If it's the Mark Ravensdale from York I think it is, he's a private eye. I know him.'

'Is he reliable?'

'Oh, yes, I'd say so.'

'OK, phone him back, and I'll have a word. I'll be in my office .'

'Am I speaking to the officer in charge of the Shearsby case?'

'You are.'

'Good, my name's Ravensdale, and I think I might have some information for you.'

'Right, go ahead: I'm listening.'

'Well, Inspector – sorry, Moat, was it? Inspector Moat - it's a little difficult over the phone. Could we meet, do you think? I'd feel happier telling you face to face.'

'OK, what about tomorrow morning? You live in York, I understand: we can call in on our way to Selby, if that's all right with you.'

'That'd be fine. Thanks.'

Parking being even more difficult in York than in Leeds, Moat and Stockwell decided to leave the car at the police offices in Fulford and catch a bus into the city centre. From there they walked down to King's Staith and were warmly welcomed by the smart and personable receptionist, who ushered them immediately into Ravensdale's office.

'Gentlemen, good morning. So kind of you to visit me in my little eerie. Please take a seat, and a pot of tea will be here directly.'

'Now, sir,' Stockwell said briskly, 'what information do you have that might be relevant to the Shearsby murder case? We're anxious to make progress.'

'Yes, of course you are, sergeant. It's like this. Well, I'll tell you the story from the beginning, but I'd prefer to disguise the names – for the moment – professional confidentiality, you understand. It's all a bit difficult, you see, as the identities of those involved are not mine to disclose.'

'Yes, sir, we quite understand. Please proceed, and we can then judge for ourselves. You know DS Odgers at HQ, he tells us.'

'Yes, indeed – not well, but, yes, we are acquainted. Well, a few weeks back, I was approached by a middle-aged gentleman – shall we call him Matthew? – anxious to clear his name. He'd been involved in a murder case two years ago as a suspect. The police accepted his plea of innocence - or let me put this another way: they never gathered together enough evidence to charge him - but the local people weren't so sure, and he found life getting very difficult. He himself suspected that the real murderer was a bearded fellow seen near the victim's flat at the time of the murder, but the police either hadn't bothered to trace him or genuinely couldn't. You follow me so far?'

'Perfectly,' Moat and Stockwell replied in unison.

'So he asked me to trace the bearded man, in an effort to clear his name.'

'And did you?'

'Yes, I did. We'll call him William, shall we? He admitted being the bearded man but didn't want any publicity. You see, he's a person of some standing in society, and he'd been blackmailed by the victim, and he didn't want the whole sordid story all over the papers. Furthermore, he wasn't convinced the police would believe he had nothing to do with the murder.'

'Yes, please go on.'

'Well, William told me he'd seen a suspicious character ringing the bell to the dead man's flat and thought that if I could identify this visitor, William's own name needn't be mentioned. The police could interview this visitor, charge him with murder, and William could be kept out of it. I should perhaps explain, officers, that a set of finger-prints were found on the statuette which stunned the victim before he was strangled, and they were never identified. Anyway, I spent three days carefully questioning all the residents in the block of flats where the murder had taken place, in the hopes that someone saw something of the dead man's mysterious visitor. Nobody had, but the interesting things is this. Four of the flats out of the fifteen were occupied by people who'd moved in only after the murder, so they were no use to me, except in so far as they could tell me where their predecessors had moved. Some others had been in residence at the time of the murder but had since moved away. I managed to contact all of them – except one: Shearsby. Before I could catch up with him, he was taken ill, and, two days later, I read in the papers that he'd died – of a suspected poisoning.'

'Yes, I see,' Moat intervened. 'That's interesting – very interesting. I wonder whether there's anything in it. What do you think, sergeant?' he asked, turning to his assistant.

'Well, sir, do you remember the opening sentence of Poe's *The Mystery of Marie Roget?*

> There are few persons [it reads], even among the calmest thinkers, who have not occasionally been startled into a vague yet thrilling half-credence in the supernatural, by *coincidences* of so seemingly marvellous a character that, as *mere* coincidences, the intellect has been unable to receive them.'

'Your point is, sergeant?'

'My point is that I think we should take Mr Ravensdale's information seriously.'

'Yes, I think so, too.'

'So let's have some dates, Mr Ravensdale,' Stockwell went on. 'When did you carry out your first, um, interview at the flats?'

'Let me see. Yes, here we are,' he said after consulting his notes. 'Monday 3rd October. I kept popping back at various moments of the day, to catch everybody in, and I didn't finish the job until the Wednesday evening.'

'And Shearsby was taken ill on the 6th – the Thursday. The murderer didn't waste much time.'

'So what are we thinking, sergeant?' Moat asked.

'We're thinking, sir,' Stockwell dutifully replied, 'that, because the murderer had reason to think that Shearsby could incriminate him, he had to be eliminated. So, Mr Ravensdale,' he went on, turning back to the private investigator, 'you must have told somebody you intended to get in touch with Shearsby. It's that that put the wind up the murderer.'

'Yes, I suppose so, although I don't remember using those precise words. I suppose it was obvious to whoever I was talking to that I was going to look him up.'

'So who were you talking to?'

'Well, I can tell you that easily enough, sergeant, but the alarm could've been raised – in the murderer's mind, I mean – by my movements in general. I mean, it must've been obvious that I was making my way round all the flats and that sooner or later I should hit on Shearsby as being a resident at the time of the original murder.'

'And in fact it needn't be a resident of the flats,' Moat chipped in again. 'Anyone you questioned or got to hear of your questioning might have warned an acquaintance. What do we think Shearsby saw?'

'Presumably he saw the murderer go into or come out of the dead man's flat,' Stockwell suggested. 'Perhaps he didn't realise at the time the significance of what he'd seen, but the murderer – *our* murderer – thought Mr Ravensdale might jog his memory with his inquiries.'

'Why didn't the police pick up on Shearsby when they carried out the original investigation? Why wasn't his murderer frightened of his disclosing his information then?' Moat asked.

'Perhaps he was away from home,' Ravensdale answered. 'I have to tell you, inspector, that my inquiries revealed a less than thorough investigation by the police. I hope you don't mind my saying this.'

'Not at all, sir, these things happen. We shall no doubt find out more about that in due course if we pursue this line of inquiry. We shall need the name of the deceased, his address and the name of the original investigating officer, if you've got it.'

'There is one other thing, inspector.'

'Yes?'

'I wrote away for a copy of Thwaites' will – leaving no stone unturned, you see, in my efforts to clear my client – but the copy I got – perfectly correctly addressed - was invoiced to a couple called Carter, who live at Ledsham. They'd obviously applied for a copy of the will at the same time as me, and the clerk muddled the receipts. May be nothing in it, but I thought I'd tell you anyway – but I don't wish to get anyone in trouble unnecessarily.'

'Don't worry, Mr Ravensdale, we'll be very discreet. Have you got the Carters' address there? Good. And could we take your copy of the will, for reference? Thanks. Otherwise for the moment I don't think we need trouble you for identities. Well, Mr Ravensdale, if that's all, we'll leave you to your work, with our thanks.'

37

Moat decided that he and Stockwell should carry out further investigation in this direction immediately, before going to Selby to look round the scene of the murder. That could wait until they had clarified the circumstances of the murder of James Thwaites. They had some lunch on the way and presented themselves at the relevant police headquarters early in the afternoon. Moat detected a certain coolness in their reception, but he was not going to be deflected by *that*. Eventually they were conducted to the office of DI Kevin Barnes.

'I can't believe you're raking over all that stuff, gents,' he told them amiably enough. 'Water under the bridge.'

'But you haven't closed the case.'

'No, we haven't, and I suppose we're always open to new evidence, but the thing is, new evidence is very unlikely to be found now. Our investigation at the time was very thorough.'

'We appreciate that,' Moat said. 'We should not have expected anything else. On the other hand, if the same man is responsible for both murders – Thwaites' and now Shearsby's – we need to get as firm a grip on both murders as we can. Could you just outline the case for us, in so far as you remember it.'

'Happily give you the file, although it's a pretty hefty one.'

'Yes, thanks, that would be appreciated; but a quick break-down now? To get it from the horse's mouth?'

'It's two years back: my memory's a bit hazy, but I'll do my best. We couldn't make an arrest as we just didn't have enough evidence. One and a half chief suspects, both of them pretty dodgy characters. The legal stumbling-block was the statuette used to stun the old man before he was strangled: clear set of prints – well, a thumb-print - belonged to no one we interviewed. Dead end: how do you go looking for a complete stranger in a city as busy as this? That was the suggestion: a complete stranger. But we knew who dunnit. The other thing was motive: the only reason somebody'd want to bump off the old codger was sex. Otherwise he seemed quite harmless. No previous. Long retired. Just no motive there. All one and a half suspects had a sexual motive, but we couldn't prove it, that was the trouble. So we gave up. No point in hammering away at the same case week after week, and, to be perfectly candid, gents, the city was well rid of the old faggot, and I didn't hold it against whoever dunnit. I know I shouldn't say that, but most of the boys thought so too.'

'So how do you read the murder? Have you got exact timings?'

'It went like this. Thwaites and his usual partner – Biddulph, that's his name: it's all coming back to me now – had their usual lunch at the Black Cat in town and then went back to Thwaites' flat. They got to the flat at something like 1.25, give or take a few minutes. They then made themselves a coffee and put on some sleazy film – to get them in the mood, apparently. Their sex session then began at about 2.30 – of course, we've only got Biddulph's word for all this, but his account seemed plausible enough – and lasted for twenty minutes. Disgusting, if you ask me, but each to his own. Biddulph then got dressed and left the flat, he reckons just before 3. He met no one on the stairs, went out to do some shopping, and he was caught on camera in the main precinct ten minutes later. So far so good. The following morning, at about 10, a technician arrived, by appointment, to sort out Thwaites' internet connection, which had been playing up; couldn't get any answer. Knocked on the neighbouring flat. The woman there assured him that her neighbour was in, as she hadn't heard him go out; in any case, they could hear the TV going. Alarmed, the woman phoned us, and we sent a man along, just in case. There was the body, semi-naked, sprawled in the living-room. The pathologist placed death on the previous afternoon, between 3 and 4, although he wasn't going to rule out a slightly earlier or later death. Biddulph was questioned but denied any involvement. His argument was, why would he murder a man he had sex with every week and had done for ages? It made no sense. The other main suspect was a sad, inadequate and insignificant creature called – let me see, it's coming back – yes, wait for it - Chimes, Jonas Chimes, that's it. He'd been heard having strong words with the dead man the week previous. The story was that Thwaites had propositioned him and he'd wanted nothing to do with it, but if you ask me the bloke was guilty, guilty as hell.'

'So how do you explain that his finger-prints didn't match those on the statuette?'

'Easy. The prints were put there earlier, by some other visitor, and Chimes had the nous to use a handkerchief when he hit Thwaites with it.

Chimes came out with various stories, was in a high old state, had been heard to ramble on about doing violence to someone or other, and was generally a very unsatisfactory witness. So we banged him up to give him a chance to think things over. Had to release him because we couldn't prove anything – that stupid lawyer of his.'

'So you interviewed all the people in the flats?'

'We did, although it was so obvious Chimes was guilty, it was just a matter of observing the forms.'

'And nobody saw anybody else around?'

'No, but that's not very surprising in the middle of the afternoon, is it? People are out at work, or snoozing, or shopping.'

'But Chimes wasn't gay, was he?'

'No, but that's just the point: a clear case of straight-on-gay crime. Chimes was anti-gay, had been propositioned by one, so got his own back.'

'Didn't he have an alibi?'

'Yes, but, as I say, he came out with various stories, and in the end we didn't know what to believe.'

'Would he have been physically capable of overpowering Thwaites?'

'Didn't have to, did he? Look, this is how I see it. Biddulph leaves the flats and disappears into the town. Chimes arrives, rings the bell on the street, and Thwaites invites him up. "It's me, Chimes. Can I come in?" "Yeah, o' course, mate. It'll be a pleasure to see yer." So up he goes, to find Thwaites still not dressed after his previous bout. They chat – or not – and, while Thwaites' attention is distracted – perhaps he offered to make his visitor a cup of tea in the kitchen – Chimes bashes him over the head with something that lies readily to hand. Realising that he hasn't killed him and that he could therefore come round and have him for gbh, he makes sure by strangling him. No great strength required – just determination and patience. He then leaves, but of course, being a sad individual, his nerves are shaken and he can't bluff it out with us.'

'He never admitted the crime, we understand, even after heavy questioning.'

'No, the snivelling little shrimp; but we tried. Having failed to find enough evidence, even though he was obviously guilty, we gave up. A sighting on the stairs would've been helpful, but it wasn't to be. So that's it, gents. Now you know all.'

'Is Chimes still around?'

'Not here, he's not. Disappeared. Did a bunk. Couldn't stand the pointing fingers. Good riddance, I say. So I can't help you there.'

'Biddulph?'

'Nah, he moved away too: got too hot in the kitchen. He was never a really serious candidate for Thwaites' murder. We picked on him only because we couldn't nail Chimes or identify the alleged bearded stranger, and Biddulph admitted a sex session with Thwaites shortly before the presumed time of his murder. But the man hasn't got it in him to murder anyone.'

'Never the less, in the light of this second murder, it might repay us to have a word. You see, we know a private investigator's been stirring things up round Thwaites' old flat - '

'Oh, yeah?'

'And it seems that that put the wind up someone. Thwaites' murderer knew there was someone who could identify him – probably someone who used to live in the block of flats – and that person had to be silenced.'

'It's Chimes, then. Must be. Good. Now we've got a chance of pinching him.'

'Well,' Moat said cautiously, 'the murder we're investigating in Selby was pretty sophisticated. From what you're telling us, Chimes wouldn't be up to it.'

'Perhaps he had help.'

'Perhaps. Would this Biddulph be up to contaminating a packet of dried mushrooms with a rarer poisonous variety and delivering it to his victim's house in broad daylight?' DI Barnes shrugged his shoulders. 'Could you find his new address, do you think,' Moat went on, 'just in case he's got anything useful to say?' Barnes invited someone or other on the other end of the telephone to institute inquiries immediately, starting with the estate agent responsible for the sale of Biddulph's house two years before. Moat remained silent for a moment when Barnes had replaced the receiver. 'There's one other thing, inspector, if we may.'

'Go ahead,' Barnes invited.

'Thwaites presumably left a will, we're told. Anything of interest in it?' Moat guiltily concealed from DI Barnes that he already knew exactly what was in it. He did not wish to be thought by the representative of the city police in front of him to be criticising, much less muscling in on, an investigation which Barnes clearly considered adequate if inconclusive.

'Not to say "of interest", exactly. There were some individual bequests – his sister, for one – and the bulk of his estate was left to some guy in a remote Scottish fastness – a baronial hall a million miles from anywhere, if I remember aright.'

'Did he come into much money?'

'Yeah – a cool five hundred thou. But he couldn't have been the murderer.'

'Oh, why not?'

'We asked a member of the local constabulary to investigate for us. The constable travelled miles and miles, in increasingly lonely countryside, until he got to the drive to this house, and that itself was miles long – fourteen or fifteen miles, I think. Eventually he came to a completely isolated mansion stuck in the middle of a vast moor, with only trees and the birds – and not many of those – for company. He interviewed the owner, a man of about Thwaites' own age. Turned out he and Thwaites were university friends; but the thing is this: the owner – Winter, I think, or some such name – was badly disfigured, with only one eye and one arm, and never left the property. He couldn't conceivably have travelled hundreds of miles south to murder Thwaites – certainly not without attracting a lot of notice; in any case, it was quite apparent that he was too ill to travel far. It appears he wasn't short of a bob or two, anyway, so didn't actually need the bequest; nice to have of course, but not a necessity.'

'And presumably the prints didn't match either of the other beneficiaries.'

'Nope. They weren't all that clear, to be honest, but we couldn't match them. The murderer would have to be pretty stupid to leave no other trace behind him except a thumb print that could be used against him. So, if that's all, inspector – '

'It is. Many thanks. I'll give you a receipt for the file, of course, and I'll be in touch later if we turn up anything else.'

38

Moat realised that it made sense for them to visit Biddulph, now established as being a citizen of York, on their way back to HQ, and to visit the Carters if possible. While the police had not been able to charge Biddulph in the course of the original investigation, for lack of evidence on the one hand and because someone else was 'obviously' the guilty party on the other, the investigation of a second murder made it imperative to have a word and exclude him if possible by establishing an alibi. The Carters were in a different category: they had some interest in Thwaites' will, according to information laid by the public-spirited Mark Ravensdale, and Moat and Stockwell would need to discover what that interest was. Accordingly they drove sedately off the A1(M) at the Selby Fork, crossed the old A1 in a westerly direction and covered the final mile to Ledsham village wondering at the richness of the landscape suddenly disclosed to view as the car descended Holyrood Road (Holyrood Road?) into the village. They found the Carters' residence, parked up and knocked on the door. There was no answer. There was no car in the drive. As Stockwell knocked again, a teenage urchin, in whom readers of this chronicle will recognise the doughty teenage Max Bromley, appeared from nowhere and informed them that the Carters had gone. Gone? Where to? The lad was unable to say. Was their departure sudden? The lad asked what it was to them. Moat saw no reason not to reveal their identity and explained that they were policemen looking for information in connection with a serious crime; they thought that the Carters might have witnessed something. (This seemed a slightly more plausible and less equivocal explanation than that the Carters seemed curiously interested in the will of an old gent murdered two years previously in sleazy circumstances.) The boy promptly disappeared from view and refused to respond to repeated invitations to re-enter the dialogue.

The two policemen, intrigued, went next-door and knocked. A frowsy, overweight woman, wearing a headscarf *à la* 1950s and with a cigarette dangling from her lips, answered their summons and told them that, because she knew nothing about anything, they were wasting their time and should take themselves off whence they came, preferably with a resolution not to pollute the village again. While Stockwell surreptitiously made his way round the back of the house, Moat did his best to persuade the housewife to allow them to have a word with her boy, as it would save time and unpleasantness in the long run, but she was adamant. However, Stockwell had, without violence other than a gentle twisting of a grubby teenage ear, persuaded Max to come forward and deliver his testimony. His mother spat energetically and eloquently into the overgrown flowerbed and shut the door behind her, leaving the policemen and Max in sole possession of the front garden. Max had the presence of mind to ask to see their identification and laid it down as a condition of his cooperation that he should sit in their car. This was accomplished without further negotiation. The reason for Max's ready – well, readyish – compliance was that he feared for his friends the Carters' safety. The whole story came out. Max knew that 'Carter' and the Carters' Christian names were *noms de guerre* (not his phrase, of course – he simply said 'false names') but was unable to recall what their real names were. He told Moat and Stockwell how the Carters had moved to the village to reconnoitre the activities of a criminal couple called Beckett, who lived a few hundred yards away in Claypit Lane; how they had spied on them until they could be sure that their business was illegal trading in old and rare books, which they had suspected from the beginning but needed to know for certain; how they had infiltrated their operation and become part of it in their search for evidence that would incriminate them in the murder of some old geezer for which Mr Carter had taken the rap unfairly. (His account contained no mention of his own part in proceedings.) Max was not privy to the Carters' thinking or planning beyond this point, but he had guessed a fair bit. Mr Beckett, having been hospitalised after a car-accident, had invited the Carters to run the business in his absence, and Mrs Beckett had been happy to make a partial withdrawal to concentrate on her husband's recovery. However, Mr Beckett had returned home and discovered somehow that the Carters had gained access to the Becketts' coded files which the Carters had no need to consult. It was at that point, as young Max surmised, that the Carters had upped sticks and disappeared.

Moat felt frustrated. All this was a new complication their investigation could have done without. Should he abandon this Carter-Beckett business to colleagues more conversant with the illegal traffic in books and restrict himself to matters more germane to the Shearsby inquiry? On the other hand, might catching up with the Carters and/or the Becketts confirm an idea that was germinating in his mind? The first thing, clearly, since they were already at Ledsham, was to repair to the Beckett residence up the road and see what could be achieved there. Max insisted that no mention of his name was made in whatever encounter might ensue. He confined his role to pointing the detectives in the right direction. What explanation he gave his parents for the detectives' visit, once Moat and Stockwell had departed, is not recorded.

The two men walked up to the Becketts' house and noted its seclusion as they knocked on the front-door. There was no answer. Idly peering through the window into the study, Moat noticed signs of great confusion: scattered papers, drawers pulled out and left open, a chair overturned. Inspection through other windows revealed no further damage, and Moat considered it sufficient to telephone for a couple of men, with a warrant, to enter and search; likewise two men to enter and search the Carters' house. There was enough evidence, he thought, to justify such moves. He would institute a man-hunt, however, only if what they found warranted it. At the same time, he thought this development of sufficient interest to oblige him to communicate it to DI Barnes, on whom devolved the prime responsibility for the investigation into James Thwaites' death. His communication came bouncing back soon enough.

39

Moat and Stockwell sat in the car pondering the situation.

'I've been thinking, young sergeant,' Moat told his companion, ' – a rare but pleasurable experience.'

'Yes, sir,' Stockwell dutifully acknowledged this admission.

'Of course, I'm speculating ahead of the facts.'

'Surely not, sir: that's not like you.'

'Well, in this case, it's true. Let's just suppose that the murder the Carters are keen to probe is that of James Thwaites.'

'Seems a likely assumption in view of the fact that the Carters had applied for a copy of Thwaites' will, after two years. I mean, it's not as if the murder has suddenly hit the headlines; on the contrary.'

'Quite. Now why would they suspect the Becketts of having a hand in it? According to young Max, their spying exercise was to establish beyond doubt that the Becketts dealt in rare books, which suggests to me that Thwaites too had something to do with rare books. Perhaps the Carters suspected that Thwaites double-crossed the Becketts and was done away with – but quite what their interest might be defeats me. Do you think the Carters could have it in mind to blackmail the Becketts as soon as they've uncovered proof of their guilt?'

'But that wouldn't explain their interest in Thwaites' will, would it?'

'No, probably not; but let me go on. The name Gerald Heggs mean anything to you?'

'No, I don't think so: should it?'

'Oops, sorry, I'd forgotten that you've been driving all this time, which gave me the leisure to take a closer look at the copy of Thwaites' will which Ravensdale gave us. One of the beneficiaries – a minor one, you'd think - is this Gerald Heggs, who's invited to help himself to any books of Thwaites's within six months of the testator's death.'

'So?'

'What if Heggs knew that amongst Thwaites' books was a rare one worth thousands, or even tens of thousands?'

'But wouldn't Thwaites have sold it, as he seems to have sold plenty of others? He'd hardly keep it sitting on his shelves, would he?'

'Maybe not, but maybe he would – for some reason that's obscure to outsiders like us. Let's just say he did and continue to speculate. Heggs's funds run short, and he sees a chance to top up by bumping Thwaites off. Within six months of Thwaites' death – and that, I suppose, could almost mean the day after – he can help himself freely to any books he fancies, and bingo! he's rich again, or at least solvent. All perfectly legal – apart from the murder, I mean! You see, we can make these suggestions only in the light of the Carters' activities with the Becketts at Ledsham. Our friend DI Barnes probably didn't make any connection between Heggs and Thwaites' death because he didn't suspect that any of the dead man's books might be valuable. I've skimmed through the police file, and there's no mention in the murder inquiry of books, rare, old or brand new. I think it'd pay us to call on Heggs.'

'It's a bit of a long shot, sir, but I agree that it's a novel line nobody seems to have thought of before, even though there are a lot of ifs and buts. What a brain you are, sir!'

'However,' Moat cautioned, ignoring the soft soap, 'it's not going to be any easy thing to prove. Imagine it this way. According to the will, Thwaites' sister, Serenity, gets all the papers and photographs concerning the family history. She's duly summoned by the solicitor to collect her horde of documents; or alternatively he posts them to her, depending on how bulky they are. Likewise Piers Blake, another beneficiary, who gets one book and some hi-fi equipment. The solicitor then invites Heggs to take his pick of the rest; he's got *carte blanche*. Does the solicitor make a list of what Heggs takes? Otherwise we're never going to know. Heggs wanders in, helps himself from the shelves and wanders out with a couple of holdalls bursting with the weight – possibly under the solicitor's vigilant gaze. Alternatively, I suppose, if he murders Thwaites because he can't wait for the old codger to die, he could simply take the book off the shelf when he commits the murder and walk out with it.'

'Unless there are several valuable books he wants, and he's afraid of arousing suspicion by walking out with a bulky parcel in the middle of the afternoon on which Thwaites is later found to have been murdered. But that's not really what interests us, sir, is it? We want to know whether the finger-prints on the statuette match his: that'd surely be proof enough of his involvement in Thwaites' death, with or without any books?'

'Well, Barnes' file's got nothing in it about an interview with Heggs, so perhaps we'd better fill the gap. Come on, lad, let's be moving.'

'What, now? Too late for today, surely?'

'It's not far – an hour's run across some fascinating Yorkshire countryside.'

'Do I detect a smidgeon of irony in your tone, sir? You probably mean Doncaster or darkest Sheffield.'

'Barnsley, actually. Here, get this address in the GPS: 14 Wordsworth Road, Monk Bretton. Lovely part of the world.' (In fact, dear reader, if you are unfamiliar with it, I must tell you that Monk Bretton was a victim of the nineteenth-century's lust for coal and the architectural vandalism of the 1960s, so that of the medieval village nothing remains, and the place is just part of the sprawling Barnsley suburbs that disfigure the north of South Yorkshire. [Perhaps the local people will forgive this cheerless comment.] The Cluniac monastery, the only building of interest in the area of which mediaeval vestiges remain, was and is technically outside the village. However, this is a chronicle of our times, not a historical lament! In any case, perhaps you do not regard unusable mediaeval ruins as 'of interest'?) Moat paused.

'No, you're right,' he confessed. 'We'll shelve that idea. We'll ask our South Yorkshire colleagues to take Heggs' finger-prints, and, if they don't match those on the statuette, that's another idea that's bit the dust.'

'And they didn't do that at the time of the murder?'

'Nope, I told you, apparently not. At least, there's no mention of it in the file,' he said, patting it as it lay on his lap.

'And was Thwaites' sister interviewed as well? Perhaps it's her finger-prints on the statuette.'

'Hardly. In any case, according to Ravensdale, the person his bearded loiterer saw ringing Thwaites' door-bell just ahead of him was definitely a man. I have further news for you, young sergeant, in case your police training is so far behind you it's too hazy to recall: criminals are now faking finger-prints. I was reading about it the other day. I'm not sure of the exact technique, but it involves a plaster cast of a hand, rubber solution and a rubber glove with the fake prints on. All the criminal then does is to wipe a bit of sweat on the prepared glove, and then away you go.'

'Why not just wear a normal glove, and then you don't leave behind any evidence at all?'

'Ah, well, in that case you can't be eliminated either. If there are no finger-prints, everyone's still a suspect. If there are finger-prints and they're not yours, you're excluded. So if you wish to commit a crime for which you know you'll be suspected, add a fingerprint which isn't yours – could be your wife's or a confederate's – and you're in the clear.'

'Well, here's something I do remember from my training, sir: DNA can be extracted from finger-prints, so, by wiping sweat on the glove, you've still left evidence.'

'Yes, but it's not going to be *yours*, is it? If you choose someone who's not going to be a suspect, the police aren't going to subject them to any kind of identity test and the DNA will never be traced.'

'So we need to see this Heggs chap after all.'

'The only way he's going to be caught – because the descriptions we have are so vague – is if he hasn't got an alibi. No, let me rephrase that. Our bearded friend outside Thwaites' flat two years ago and Mrs Gray in Selby last week both saw a man who could be the same one, but even the worst defence counsel is going to tear their testimony to ribbons. The presence of rare books in his house, even if they can be proved to be Thwaites', means nothing. If he hasn't got an alibi for one of the crimes, he's still suspect; but if he has, well … where does that leave us? Empty-handed, that's where.'

'Are you satisfied that DI Barnes' did his job thoroughly: that every clue was picked up?'

'Look, sergeant, I don't know. I hate to criticise a fellow-officer, but … The thing is, it's too late to go back to Thwaites' murder now anyway. What we *can* do something about is Shearsby's. Perhaps Ravensdale's piece of news has distracted us, and Shearsby's murder has nothing at all to do with Thwaites's. Have we really scoured Shearsby's life for clues that have nothing to do with Thwaites, rare books, sex sessions after lunch, bearded loiterers and the rest of it?'

'Well, no, sir, but then DS Odgers has hardly had time to collect the material together.'

'Right, let's get back to HQ and see what he's got for us.'

40

The next day was spent ploughing through letters, emails, texts, telephone-messages, address-books and FaceBook pages in an attempt to build up a picture of Shearsby's life in the round. I daresay that, in the grand scheme of things, the pile of printed matter laid out for the detectives' inspection was not massive, but it all had to be sifted through carefully. The precise object of their search was not clear, but they presumed that a number of items would excite their further interest: threats by or against him, signs of a rift in a friendship, evidence of illegal dealings, unexplained references to a sudden influx of wealth, details of plots and intrigues ... Teams of police interviewed his family, friends, employers, neighbours and acquaintances. The net result was a blank sheet of paper: not a single suspicion. Shearsby seems to have been the quintessential nice guy, with a decent family, a circle of respectable friends and no hint of evil-doing in any of its noticeable manifestations. Moat and Stockwell were beginning to think that the lead offered by Ravensdale had after all perhaps more potential than they had so far tapped into, when they were saved further doubt by a telephone-call.

'A woman calling herself Bursnell on the line for you, sir. Will you take the call?'

'Who is she?'

'No idea, but she asked for you specifically.'

'Very well, put her on, sergeant.'

'Is that Detective Inspector Moat?'

'It is.'

'My name's Serenity Bursnell. James Thwaites was my brother.'

'Ah. (Slight pause expressive of stupefaction.) Yes, I remember your name, Mrs Bursnell,' Moat then had the presence of mind to utter smoothly down the mouthpiece. 'I'm very sorry for your loss. You came into possession of an Italian palace in your brother's will, I seem to remember.'

'"Palace" is perhaps not a very fair translation of *palazzo*, inspector. Even the Italians recognise that it sounds grander than their own equivalent.

Haven't you ever wondered why their towns go in for Palace Hotels instead of the more prosaic Alberghi Palazzo?'

'But that, presumably, is not what you phoned about, Mrs Bursnell: sorry to have distracted you.'

'Well, no, it isn't. I've been making a few inquiries of my own into my brother's death, you see, and I've come to certain conclusions.'

'You know full well, Mrs Bursnell, that DI Barnes of your brother's local Force was and still is in charge of the investigation into your brother's sad death. You should go to him with any evidence you've uncovered.'

'That's just it, inspector, he told me to come to you.'

'What?'

'He said you were exploring new leads into James' death and you'd be the best person to contact.'

'I see.' Moat contemplated this piece of intelligence with a less than flattering assessment of Barnes' motivation.

'OK, what've you got for us?'

'Look, inspector, I'm coming up to York this afternoon on business. Could we meet?'

'Yes, I think so. Hold on a minute.' Then covering the mouthpiece with his large hand, he signalled to Stockwell. 'Have we got any plans for this afternoon?' he whispered. Stockwell shook his head. 'More of the same,' he mouthed. 'This afternoon in York will do fine,' Moat spoke normally down the line. 'When and where?'

'Shall we say outside the disused loos in Piccadilly?' Moat raised an eyebrow in a gesture naturally lost on his interlocutor. 'Can't get more central than that,' the voice went on. 'Three o'clock?'

'Very well, Mrs Bursnell. Can we have a mobile phone number in case of mishaps? You'll recognise us easily, I daresay.'

41

Moat rarely turned down an opportunity to visit York, even though the city had not fared well over the previous century at the hands of its supposed guardians. He abhorred urban planners, who, in his opinion, lacked all sense of history, had no vision and were prey to the interests of big business: pusillanimous types who had fewer qualifications to tinker with the townscape than the humblest passenger on the Coppergate omnibus. However, York remained one of his favourite haunts, in which he was constantly discovering new things. He instructed Stockwell to arrive early so that they could spend time sauntering and perhaps even snatch a cup of spirit-warming tea.

As they stood outside the disused public toilets in Piccadilly, punctual for their tryst, Moat and Stockwell were approached by a handsome, full-bosomed woman sporting an elegant red hat that matched her red handbag.

'You're police,' she asseverated without hesitation. 'Spotted you at fifty paces.'

'That's very gratifying, madam,' Moat replied suavely. 'We've obviously grown into our public roles until they fit us like a skin.'

'Where can we talk?' Serenity asked.

'That's what I was going to ask you.'

'Fancy a cup of tea? Let's take a table outside the café over there. That suit?'

'Admirably, madam.'

'It's Serenity, inspector. You haven't introduced me to your companion.'

'Detective Sergeant Alan Stockwell, ma'am,' Stockwell cooperated with a bow.

'It's Serenity to you too, sergeant.'

The city was busy as it bathed in warm autumn sunshine after a week of wet weather. As the heart of York, Piccadilly is always busy. The elegant woman and the two men in sober suits took their seats, were served very quickly and settled to their conversation, sufficiently far from a band of Peruvian buskers not to be too disturbed.

'Look, I'm sorry if it turns out I'm wasting your time,' Serenity began apologetically. 'I contacted DI Barnes yesterday because I had an idea about my brother's death which I don't think the police had considered at the time. I have to tell you that DI Barnes wasn't exactly ecstatic. He admitted that the case wasn't closed, half-listened to what I had to say but clearly wasn't impressed. He then suggested I had a word with you, because you were pursuing a new lead: something about James' murder feeding into a more recent murder in Selby? Could you tell me more about what that new lead is?'

'Well,' Moat hesitated, 'perhaps it'd best if you told us first what you've come up with.' He sipped his tea.

'It's like this, inspector. My son Reuben – you look just Reuben's age, sergeant! - ' she added as she turned to Stockwell, 'wasn't satisfied with the official line that his uncle James was killed by a violent homosexual who took a dislike to him all of a sudden. Some sort of row during or after a sex bout, and things got out of hand: that's the story the police worked on and won't budge from. Anyway, Reuben persuaded me to go through James' papers for clues to an alternative – there had to be another explanation – and even if there weren't, we shouldn't have lost anything.'

'Sorry to butt in,' came the smooth, masculine and imperturbable voice of Walter Moat, 'why doesn't that explanation work? It seems plausible to me.'

'I suppose it *is* plausible, but the thing is, it didn't get the police anywhere. It didn't lead to an arrest; still hasn't, if it comes to that. They contacted all James' contacts they could find, and there were only a handful, and they all had alibis but one – a sixty-two-year-old horticultural something-or-other called Matthias Biddulph. There's no evidence at all that Biddulph was violent, or capable of overpowering James, or that there was any animosity between them. We just thought that alternative explanations are at least *possible*.'

'Yes, I see. Please go on.'

'Well, as I say, Reuben and I went through James' papers, and there we found evidence that he was mixed up in the so-called Anti-Church of Jesus Christ.'

'"Mixed up"?'

'Yes, a member, I suppose you could say, and an active one. Well, I'd never heard of this – movement - before, so I decided to make myself better informed. I went to see the present dean at the cathedral, and he explained about it. On the back of what he told me, I went to Nottingham to see the man whose ideas had started it, Dr Croft, and he gave me the name of the woman who "runs" the Anti-Church. She was dismissive of James: a creature without the courage of his convictions, a turncoat – a "pusillanimous little toad" were her exact words. However, she did fill me in on the background to the fiasco which hit the Anti-Church at this time, which she blamed on James. A demo at the cathedral was planned and organised, but someone at the last minute alerted the authorities and the cathedral was closed without a shot being fired. This Anti-Church woman blamed James and had the effrontery to declare that she thought it an abysmal act of betrayal. Well, I challenged her in my turn. I more or less accused a member of her "Anti-Church" – huh! – of murdering James out of revenge, and she was outraged. In the end, she had to admit that she couldn't exclude the possibility; and that's where we left it.'

'Let me get this straight, Serenity. The Anti-Church was set to make a splash by organising a demonstration at the cathedral. Your brother made it impossible by informing the authorities beforehand. And you think someone murdered your brother for that? A bit extreme, isn't it?'

'You obviously don't know what religious extremists are capable of, inspector. That Hembry woman – Pyrena Hembry,' she repeated, assuming a faux intonation expressive of contempt – 'is as mad as a hatter and lesbian to boot. Completely crackers. Yet she thinks she can speak for all her – members – when she denies any involvement in James' death. Dear inspector and sergeant – let's order another pot of tea, by the way – don't you read your newspapers? Riots, murder, arson, lynching, rigged trials, general mayhem, even genocide – you name it, religious extremism is at the bottom of it nine times out of ten. There's nothing these crackpots aren't capable of. A single murder is a trifle in their determination to force their views on the public. They're convinced they've heard the voice of God, and nothing, but nothing, will deflect them. They're closed to the voice of reason, which they dismiss as a human fabrication, a tool of the forces of evil. Oh, I get so impatient with it all!'

'OK, Serenity, how do you propose we discover who this Anti-Church member is who murdered your brother out of revenge for a failed coup?'

'I don't know, do you? That's your job. Miss Hembry - ' uttered with noticeable simpering, 'has a list of all her volunteers. You've only got to go through them and check their alibis.'

'How many members do you think there might be?'

'One of the notes she sent James mentioned 250 mugs willing to turn up at the cathedral to deliver one in the eye to that outworn and obscurantist establishment.'

'Hm. How long do you suppose it would take us to identify and work through 250 volunteers? Possible, I suppose, but a long haul. On the other hand, what about members of the Anti-Church who weren't available to turn up on the day? could be one of them, presumably. Rather like looking for a needle in a haystack,' he added, with one eyebrow cocked.

'So you're not going to do anything about it, either?'

'I haven't said that, Serenity. I just wish to be sure that it's a viable path to take. You see, we've every reason to believe, as DI Barnes seems, for purposes of his own, to have informed you, that your brother's death ties in with another murder in Selby last week, and, even if it doesn't, we're pursuing another line of inquiry at the moment which looks promising but doesn't include members of this Anti-Church you talk about.'

'Can you tell me about it?'

'Yes, I think I can. Stockwell, care to oblige before you lose the gift of speech?'

'Of course, sir: anything to oblige a lady.' He shot Serenity a great beam of a smile. 'You haven't mentioned this, Serenity, and you may not know it – we're not over-sure ourselves - but your brother seems to have been involved in an illegal trade in rare books.' Serenity's eyebrows rose to give weight to Stockwell's assertion. 'It's possible that the people he was working for, or with, took exception to something he did or said and decided to eliminate him. Like yourself, they live in Yorkshire, but when we called on them, they'd vanished. The circumstances of their disappearance aren't quite clear, and there may be nothing in it, but we feel we ought to investigate, and we've started on that.'

'Hold on a minute, sergeant,' Moat interrupted. 'Young Max – a neighbour,' he explained to Serenity – 'told us two things we haven't really thought about, but I've been thinking about them as you were explaining things to Serenity. The first is that – sorry, Serenity, this isn't going to make any sense to you unless I give you another piece of information. We know about these illegal book-traders only because other collaborators of theirs have recently applied for a copy of your brother's will.'

'Oh? This gets more complicated by the minute,' Serenity commented

'Where was I?' Moat went on, still feeling his way. 'Oh, yes, two things we haven't yet thought about. The first is that the collaborators I just mentioned were using false names; and the second is that, according to our informant, they were determined to prove that the book-dealers were responsible for your brother's death. His exact words were, if I remember aright, that one of them had "taken the rap unfairly" for the "murder of some old geezer".'

'Sounds like Jonas Chimes!' Serenity burst out.

'That's what I was thinking,' Moat said.

'Who's Jonas Chimes?' Stockwell asked. 'Oh, wait a minute - '

'Yes, the man accused of James Thwaites' murder, locked up for eight months and finally released without charge,' Moat explained. 'But, according to DI Barnes' file, this Chimes person was an inadequate individual, a loner and a misfit – not the married man getting involved in a black market racket we're investigating in rural Yorkshire. Serenity, what do you think?'

'Don't know,' she answered. 'I'd never even heard of Chimes before James' death; certainly never met him; but I can understand he'd wish to clear his name by finding the real murderer. I always took him to *be* the real murderer, released only because the police hadn't got any real evidence.'

'No, it seems they picked the wrong man entirely. There was no proof that Chimes had been near James' flat that day – or indeed any other day. He wasn't homosexual – or at least not known to be. The only piece of evidence ever adduced was that he'd resented James' approaches to him: slim evidence on which to clap a man in irons. It seems the police considered him an easy target because he was unstable and *might* have done it. Right,' Moat added magisterially, 'that's all in the past. Our present investigation takes on an added urgency. We need to find these people to clarify the whole business.'

'So what about my Anti-Church?' Serenity put in.

'Let's leave it on hold for the moment, shall we? We're grateful for your ideas, and we appreciate the interest you have in the matter - and for coming forward today with information, of course. If only all members of the public had your spirit of civic duty!' He sighed. 'While we're here, can I just ask you another question? Apart from your brother's main bequests, there were smaller bequests to someone called Blake and someone called Heggs. D'you know either of them?'

'No, never met them personally, but I know they were both colleagues of James' at school. Blake taught physics, I think, and Heggs maths – something like that. You don't suspect *them*, do you?'

'Don't I? No, not really, just thinking round things, you know.'

Mrs Serenity Bursnell and the two detectives eventually took their leave of each other. The latter walked back up Piccadilly towards where they had parked their car, while Serenity was swallowed up in the shoppers thronging Davygate.

42

The Beckett-Carter case which Moat and Stockwell intended to investigate as soon as information became available reached an explosive conclusion sooner than they expected. Reports came in of a high-speed chase and a crash on the M6 northbound carriageway near Carlisle. The occupants of both cars were identified as hailing from North Yorkshire, and the police there were informed accordingly so that next of kin could be identified. The story was this, according to witnesses later interviewed by the police. Two cars pulled up simultaneously at Southwaite services in Cumbria. When the two drivers got out and confronted each other, there was a violent altercation, in which voices were raised to shouting level, threats uttered and Anglo-Saxon expletives freely traded. One of the drivers jumped back into his car and headed off up the motorway. The other driver wasting no time in following suit, the two cars were soon careering towards Carlisle and thence Scotland at great speed. By dint of overtaking on the inside, blithely disregarding the speed limit and complete lack of concern for other road-users, the second car drew alongside the first and forced it off the road. Under the impact of the collision, the first car careered over the verge through a wooden fence and so into a field lying just below the level of the motorway. The wheels thrust deeply into the soil, the suspension gave and the car tipped down towards its nose with the speed of its descent. The occupants of the second car were not so fortunate: their vehicle, striking the support of a panel announcing an imminent exit, was effectively sliced in two, and both driver and front-seat passenger were killed. The police commented later that it was a mercy no other vehicle was involved in what could have been, at over 90 miles per hour, a nasty pile-up. The occupants of the first car, Mr and Mrs Alex Carter, were treated in hospital for minor injuries and then allowed home, a journey they chose to undertake by train. Moat and Stockwell interviewed them at Ledsham on the following day.

The weather was damp and blustery as the two detectives made their second journey to Ledsham. They left the old A1 at Peckfield Lodge and coasted gently down towards the village, with woods on their right and harvested fields on their left, along the so-called New Road. A glimpse of the gracious old vicarage through the trees instilled in them an impression that all was right with the world. They parked in front of the Carters' modest villa, and Moat for one wished that, rather than instigate an interview which he guessed would further ensnare him in confusion, he was, despite the drizzle, on the point of donning his walking-boots preparatory to striding up the lane, through the glorious park-land that surrounds Ledston Lodge, with its quietly cropping horses, placid herd of cows and swooping and wheeling crows, to the woods beyond, showing the first tints of autumn. He dismissed the dream reluctantly from his mind. The Carters had laid on a neat tray of coffee and biscuits and, while clearly nervous of the approaching interview, were warm in their welcome.

Alex Carter exposed the whole sorry saga of his being caught up in the murder of James Thwaites. Of the death of Lambert Shearsby he knew nothing. He explained his confusion on being suspected of killing James Thwaites, his acquaintance with whom was limited to disturbing encounters with a sexual theme and impersonal chance meetings in the cathedral precincts and corridors; his sense of personal disarray on release back into a community which looked at him askance; his restorative sessions with Mrs Tukes, the psychotherapist; the support he had received from his cousin Rita, aka Lorna, and the plan she had concocted for tracking down Thwaites' real murderer. He then described in detail his and Lorna's watch on the Becketts' house - omitting all mention of their young neighbour's valiant assistance - their approach to the Becketts and their acceptance into a subsidiary role in the Becketts' business. He told how their chance had come when Roddy Beckett was involved in a car-crash and hospitalised, and how they had succeeded in decrypting the computer password to access the couple's book-trade files. It was difficult to make no mention of Max at this point, but Alex Carter glossed over his activities in the hope that DI Moat would not ask too many questions. They had found references to Thwaites and his sudden cessation of business-dealings with the Becketts but no evidence of murder that they could place squarely in front of the police. Alex went on to relate that, after his discharge from hospital, Roddy Beckett had approached them for an account of their stewardship in his absence and that, stupidly, Alex had let fall a comment which showed his familiarity with Beckett files to which he was not supposed to have access. There had followed a show-down in which Roddy stormed out of the house in a high old – and possibly murderous - temper announcing that the Carters had not heard the end of it. Fearing the worst, the Carters piled into their car with a few belongings and headed north to give Roddy Beckett a few days in which to calm down. Alex went on to tell Moat and Stockwell further that they had noticed the Becketts following them and, rather than engage in a foolish and risky road-chase, had pulled into a service-station in the hope of being able to give the Becketts a reasoned account of their behaviour. The interview had proved explosive – and the police knew the rest. Stockwell had one question to ask: how did the Carters explain that, if their intentions were criminal, the Becketts waited until they were beyond Carlisle for their assault on the Carters' car? Alex's answer was that he could only suppose that the Becketts were waiting for a suitably lonely stretch of motorway.

Before taking their leave, Moat requested a complete break-down of all the Carters' illegal activities in the book-trade: facts, figures, names, titles. The extent of the Becketts' dealings could no doubt be recovered from their computer system at home. Moat warned the Carters that they would hear further about any legal proceedings that might ensue but assured them that their motives would be taken fully into consideration. He also expressed the wish that the Carters had gone to the police in the first place with an admission of their suspicions and intentions, even though Alex had received scant sympathy from the original police team. The illegal book-trading would be handled by officers more skilled in that area than they themselves were.

43

Moat instructed his sergeant to pull into the Best Western Milford Hotel, a mile or two from Ledsham, for a pint, a sandwich and a conference. When they were comfortably seated in a secluded corner, the inspector invited Stockwell to run over the case to see what they could make of it. Such summaries were, seemingly, a forte or at least a favoured activity of Stockwell's, whereas Moat prided himself, usually with justification, on his powers of insight once the facts were marshalled. Stockwell flourished his note book, bit the end of his biro, looked his superior full in the face, smiled conspiratorially and then bent to his task.

'Well, sir, we seem to have come late into this case, or these cases, after Tom, Dick and Harry had chewed on it and left us with the remnants. All very puzzling. Let me try to bring some order to the facts. Our first knowledge of anything amiss was the death in hospital of a twenty-nine-year-old bank clerk from Selby called Lambert Shearsby. That was on 9 October. The cause of death was mushroom poisoning, and the immediate occasion was the consumption of a small packet of dried funghi purchased at a store in the vicinity.'

'You mean they'd been bought at a local shop, and he'd eaten them.'

'Yes, sir, that's what I said,' Stockwell commented without irony. 'After the inevitable publicity, a local woman came forward to testify that she'd seen a man leaving a small parcel and a bottle the shape of a wine-bottle on Shearsby's doorstep. That was the previous Thursday, the 6th. The teams ransacked Shearsby's life – family, work, friends, neighbours, activities like pub darts and so forth – without any discernible result. Shearsby seems to have been an all-round nice guy, without an enemy in the world. We did toy with the idea of an accident, but dismissed that as unlikely in the circumstances. For example, none of the other packets of funghi in the batch was contaminated; the occasion for the gift to Shearsby was really very slight; and the timing was significant. We didn't discover this until we received information from a private dick in York, who'd been working on the hypothesis that Shearsby had witnessed something untoward two years previously and was being silenced. Shearsby's murderer was, on this theory, alerted by the investigator's stirring things up in a block of flats where a man was murdered on – let me see – ' he leafed back through his note-book - 'yes, here we are, 13 July 2009. I'm not telling this story very well, am I, sir?'

'Never mind, sergeant, I'm sure you're doing your best.' Moat smiled indulgently.

'Well, this information from the investigator, one Mark Ravensdale apparently known to us, was very helpful, as it plugged a gap in our understanding of the Selby murder; it was, however, only a hypothesis. So we went back to the original murder, if I may so term it - '

'Yes, you may.'

' – to see what we could dig up. In that original murder, the victim was a seventy-two-year-old retired chemistry teacher called James Thwaites. The case hasn't been solved to this day, despite the best efforts of the local Force. Now Ravensdale was acting for one of the people the police suspected of murdering Thwaites. This man isn't necessarily innocent: it was just that there wasn't any evidence against him, although he seems to have been the last person to see the murdered man alive – apart from the killer himself, of course. On the other hand, this suspect would hardly go to the trouble of hiring a private eye to clear his name if he were guilty: he'd just be stirring things up with the possibility of evidence being raked up after all. There was only one other suspect whose involvement was taken seriously by the police, a chap called Jonas Chimes, who disappeared shortly after being held on remand for eight fruitless months. In conjunction with his cousin, Chimes went to a lot of trouble – changing his name, pretending to be married, moving into a Yorkshire village and so on - to try to pin the murder of Thwaites on a couple called Beckett, who'd employed Thwaites in their illegal business. Although he proved beyond a peradventure that Thwaites was dealing in the black market in old and rare books, he couldn't prove that the Becketts were responsible for Thwaites' death. There was a cryptic note added to Thwaites' name in the Becketts' files, which seemed to put an end to their collaboration, but nothing that proved their involvement in his murder. Since the Becketts are now dead, we may never know the full story, and the possibility that Chimes is right must remain open.' Stockwell gave Moat a quizzical glance. 'Meanwhile,' he went on, 'as we discovered, the dead man's sister – I'm talking about the original dead man's sister – Mrs Quentin Bursnell, widow of Ripon, known to us as Serenity, had been undertaking research of her own. After rummaging through her late brother's effects – prodded by her son Reuben – she found out that her brother James had become embroiled in the so-called Anti-Church of Jesus Christ in the city. Now James was said to have torpedoed an attempt by the Anti-Church to stage a dramatic take-over of the cathedral mounted to advertise their point of view, and the suggestion – Serenity's suggestion, that is – was that James was punished by a disgruntled member – or perhaps they're more properly referred to as non-members, I wouldn't know, or perhaps anti-members - '

'Just get on with it, sergeant.'

'Yessir, of course, sir. We took Serenity's suggestion seriously, but the chances of finding convincing evidence, even where no alibi was proved, was – and is – daunting. Of course, sir, all this time, as I mentioned earlier, we've been working on a hypothesis which we've really only assumed, not tested, and that is, that the murderer of James Thwaites killed Shearsby because the latter witnessed something he shouldn't have.'

'We may not have tested it, young sergeant, but the thing is, can you think of anything better?'

'No, sir, but my point is only that we're working our way through – or not, as the case may be – a bemusing fog of obscurity and ambiguity. On top of that, we find that three people benefit from Thwaites' will: his sister – to the tune of a small Italian mansion in Tuscany – a friend – to the tune of books of his choice from Thwaites' collection – and an old university friend hiding away in a remote Scottish roost; he comes in for half-a-million smackers, give or take a quid or two, according to the only estimate we've seen.'

'I seem to remember that this Scottish guy is an unlikely suspect because of disfigurement, but remind me why we didn't investigate the other friend who carried off Thwaites' books.'

'We don't know he carried any off – the offer was made, but we've no idea whether he took it up. The point was, having old or rare books on his shelves, even ones that had once belonged to Thwaites, is not proof of murder. No, the whole Thwaites' murder business seems to hinge on a set of prints – well, a thumb print - on the statuette used to stun the old man before he was strangled, and we were told that, whoever it belonged to, it wasn't to that particular beneficiary – or to anyone else in the frame, if it comes to that. So, sir, to sum up, we have four conflicting theories to explain Thwaites' death and a sort of theory to tie Shearsby's into it: all very confusing, if I may say so, even at the risk of repeating myself.'

'Right, what are the theories?'

'Theory number one, formally peddled by the police in charge of Thwaites' case: he was killed by a sexual partner, for reasons yet to be discovered – lust, fear or revenge, perhaps. That's a quotation, by the way, sir – from Helen McCloy's 1951 whodunnit *Alias Basil Willing*. In the course of that book, the author says: "Murderers differ in detail. They kill for money or lust, fear or revenge. All sorts of things. But, essentially, they're all relieving tension. All seeking peace of mind."'

'Thank you for that, sergeant. Please proceed: theory number two?'

'Theory number two, put forward with some plausibility by one of the two chief suspects in the original case, Jonas Chimes aka Alex Carter, is that Thwaites' had got himself tied up with a ruthless gang of book-dealers who punished him for insubordination or treachery or just plain bloody-mindedness. The chief actors here are both dead, but it would be nice to be able to prove their guilt, even though they're beyond the reach of the law. Theory number three, suggested by the dead man's sister Serenity, is that her brother was killed out of revenge by a member of Pyrena Hembry's Anti-Church of Jesus Christ.'

'And what's wrong with that theory, would you say?'

'Nothing – but very tiresome to prove. We may have to have a go if we can't think of anything better. Miss Hembry herself seems to be a bit of an eccentric, and I suppose there's no knowing what one of her followers might be capable of if they're as eccentric as herself.'

'And so to theory number four.'

'And so, as you so rightly assert, sir, to theory number four. This suggests that Thwaites was killed by a man he was blackmailing as had blackmailed others. There is a plausible sighting of a man ringing Thwaites' doorbell shortly before his murder, but we have a very inadequate description of him, and no trace of him has been found. This theory depends on the evidence of another of the original suspects - Matthias Biddulph - who employed a private investigator to buttress his case. Again, quite a plausible idea, but absolutely no evidence.'

'And which of the theories do you consider to be the most probable?'

'That's the doggone cotton-pickin' trouble: they're all equally probable, in my poor estimation; but may I indulge in an aside for a minute, sir? In her *A Taste for Death*, P. D. James has a character utter these words: "Love, Lust, Loathing, Lucre, the four Ls of murder, laddie. And the greatest of these is lucre." The same sentiment, if memory serves, occurs in her *Unnatural Causes*. In *A Shilling for Candles*, on the other hand, Josephine Tey has a different formulation - but it may amount to the same thing: "Ambition," she writes, "is one of the better-known incentives to murder. It comes well up, just below passion and greed." And if we go back 150 years, De Quincey gives this some support:

> In the murderer [he muses], there must be raging some great storm of passion – jealousy, ambition, vengeance, hatred – which will create a hell within him.

Incidentally, sir, I can strongly recommend that essay, "Knocking at the Gate in Macbeth", in which the author wonders out loud why the knocking at the gate in the Scottish play always inspired in him a "peculiar awfulness and a depth of solemnity". However, I'm losing myself, aren't I? My apologies.'

'Just tell me what conclusion de Quincey comes to.'

'That the knocking breaks the spell cast by the murder and so highlights the appalling gap between human evil and normal human activity.'

'I see. Thank you. Please continue.'

'All in all, the police are probably closest to the mark with their idea that the death of James Thwaites was motivated by passion of some kind. The Carters allege punishment for stepping out of line, Serenity revenge for Thwaites' betrayal of the cathedral demo and Biddulph desire to be free of a blackmailer, but all these motives require forethought and cold determination, not the white heat of passion. On the other hand, perhaps the passion bubbles away inside them until it seeks an outlet in action that is planned, cool and cunning. Our killer – or killers – have certainly covered their tracks all right. In short, sir, I haven't a blooming clue.'

'Well, that's honest, I must say! I congratulate you on your summary, sergeant. It may well prompt one of us to produce a rabbit out of the hat before we crawl to the DCI to confess our incompetence. Leave me for a time while I cogitate; it's more than a three-pipe problem.'

44

The police-car drove sedately due south out of the town on the B870. Moat had chosen Thurso for no better reason than that it was marginally bigger than its neighbour Wick. The sky was overcast, and there was a cold westerly wind. It was mid-afternoon, and Moat hoped that he and Stockwell could make the journey to Lochdhu Lodge and back before night-time. Their driver was not loquacious, and the two Yorkshire detectives had time to imbibe the nothingness and the loneliness that is Caithness in its inner depths. At Westerdale – a scattering of a few houses, boasting an eighteenth-century mansion, a nineteenth-century chapel, a nineteenth-century stone bridge and a disused water-mill, but still bleak – they left the main road and embarked on a fierce journey into the interior, where the landscape became increasingly grim and forbidding: bare hill-sides, a few lochans, an occasional tree hiding in a hollow, but largely an unrelieved emptiness. Beyond the northern shores of Loch More, the road deteriorated even further to become no more than a track through the wilderness. After following for some miles the stream that fed Loch More from the surrounding hills, the car turned NNW for the last few miles of the long drive. Forestry plantations appeared in regimented lines, and at last, on the shores of Lochdhu, stood the mansion they had come to visit: on the left, a heptagonal four-storeyed tower; on the right a bartizan; and, in between, the sitting-room window, the dining-room windows, the front door and the drawing-room window, all facing south. The car drew up to the side of the building, the driver said he would wait, and Moat and Stockwell made for the front door. Their summons was answered by a woman of perhaps sixty-five, of average height and build, unremarkable, one would say, except for a translucency about the eyes which seemed to argue a rare wisdom, keen insight into the world's follies and deep and pitiless self-knowledge. Her face betrayed recent weeping. She expressed no surprise at their appearance on her doorstep, the approach of their marked car having perhaps been evidence in itself of their identity and errand. The visitors were happy to step inside out of the piercing wind and be ushered through the hall into the drawing-room.

'I'll get some tea,' she announced flatly, in a pleasant Scottish brogue. Moat accepted, as he thought that a relaxed atmosphere would help the imminent conversation. There was not the slightest possibility of their hostess making any sort of escape. A wood fire burned in the grate, and the large room, while not exactly cosy, was at least tolerably warm. She returned after ten minutes with a tray of tea-things, which she set on a small table by the sofa, and then said, in the same flat tone,

'Gentlemen, I'm at your disposal. It had to come to this, I suppose, but I no longer care. You'll arrest me, of course?'

'Yes,' Moat agreed gently, 'but you have time to tell us your story.'

'Have I? A whole life squeezed into the time it takes to drink a cup of tea? Hardly, inspector – it is inspector, isn't it? – but I understand you. Now that Martyn's gone, it doesn't matter where I live, and a prison cell's probably as good as anywhere else. I haven't long to go, anyway.' She folded her hands in her lap and gazed out of the window. She spoke without expression but became more animated as her narrative proceeded. 'I was brought up in Orkney, where life was straightforward – or at least I thought it was. Do you know Diderot's *La Religieuse*? An odd book in many ways. The superior goes mad trying to repress her lesbianism, and Soeur Suzanne, the tragic heroine, dies from injuries received in scaling the convent walls to join a renegade monk! I've sometimes imagined that Diderot had me in mind when he wrote that book all those years ago – or at least the first part of it, before all that drama. I had a hateful childhood. I couldn't understand why my father was always so affectionate and generous to my two older sisters and so cold towards me, and it wasn't until I left school that my mother told me he wasn't my father: I was the product of an act of indiscretion on my mother's part and a constant reproach to my father's good name in the town. School was no consolation: I was plain, untalented and virtually friendless, and, when I got to eighteen, I'd no idea what I could do with myself. My father made it quite clear that he wouldn't help me, and my mother was too frightened to act on her own behalf except for slipping me a tenner every so often. Why am I telling you all this, inspector? Because I want you to understand.

'I drifted through a number of jobs, making my own way because my father didn't want me at home any more, living in cheap digs, doing unstimulating work and eking out an existence on the fringes of society. For a time I moved south, but I didn't feel at home there and soon returned to Scotland. Can you imagine a life without landmarks, drab, relieved by nothing more exciting than the occasional film at a cinema? Probably not.

But that was me, declining steadily with the advancing years. Eventually I decided to go for a post as a lady's companion, offering "care and support", as the advertisement put it, to an elderly woman living on her own in Glasgow. It wasn't very lucrative, but somehow I enjoyed it. Here was something useful, board and lodging catered for and small wages. "Care and support" covered all sorts of unpleasant jobs, as I discovered, but my employer was a kindly woman, undemanding and sympathetic. Eventually she became so infirm she had to go into a nursing home, because I could no longer provide all she needed at home, and I found another similar job – but nothing like my first one. The woman was rough-tongued and exigent beyond belief: do this, do that, hurry up, I'm paying you enough, heaven knows, and so on. I became a sort of slave, at her beck and call night and day, until I made plans to find a place of my own and some other sort of work, but I jibbed at the problems involved. You smile, I daresay, but I was timid, not practised in the world's ways and frightened. Scanning the papers one day, I came across an advert by a care agency inviting applications, and I wrote off to them with a cv. To my surprise I got an interview and was put on their books. Of course, I didn't know it at the time, but the agency accepted more or less anyone who could walk in and sign their name, but I was glad to have an alternative in front of me. I made some excuse about leaving my present post and claimed to be available for work immediately. My first new posting, and, as it turned out, my only one, was - to happiness, writ large.

'The agency told me they had a request from a gentleman for temporary care because of a recent illness. The client apologised that the house was isolated and quiet, but he assured them that the work would be light and wouldn't be for more than a few weeks. The hospital, he said, refused to let him return home until he had arranged some sort of support to cover his convalescence. Was I interested? the agency asked. I saw no reason not to accept, even though I'd hoped for something permanent, and along I went. I can tell you my heart sank as the taxi carried me and my little suitcase further and further into the Caithness hinterland. I kept on asking the driver whether he was sure this was the right road. This can't be right, I kept on telling him. There can't be anywhere inhabitable out here, surely? Eventually we came in sight of the house, and it looked bleak and depressing in the rain: another House of Usher perched gloomily on the side of a lake ready to crumble into the black waters. I told myself that it was too late to turn back without jeopardising my new position with the agency, that it was only for a few weeks, that there was no alternative. The taxi waited only to see the front door opened and then shot off at speed. It probably didn't, but that's what it seemed like to me: not even a taxi-driver was willing to hang about in such a cheerless spot!

'When I knocked, the door did indeed open – eventually – and I nearly died on the spot. The person facing me was repellent in appearance, utterly repellent: a tall man, lean, carelessly dressed, with only one hand and with the other badly scarred. What shocked the onlooker, however, was the ghastly face, like that of some beast from hell dreamt up by Hieronymus Bosch. I stared in horror, but, as I stared, almost rooted to the spot by the gruesome sight, I imagined a great plea for understanding and sympathy welling up in his one dark eye. The man put out his one hand and said simply, "Hello, welcome to Lochdhu!" I hesitated, but if I refused to go in, what could I do: walk back twenty miles through the wilderness? Not to be thought of. I plucked up all my courage, took the extended hand, picked up my suitcase – which he took off me at once – and stepped into unimaginable joy. He showed me up to a suite of rooms reserved for my use and then excused himself on the grounds that he no longer felt able to stay up and would retire back to bed. I was to wander round at will and get my bearings, and he hoped I could see my way to producing some sort of meal at supper-time. It was bizarre. I was completely out of my depth: stuck in a rambling godforsaken mansion miles from help, with only a monster for company. The kitchen was nearly bare. The house was cold. Evening was already drawing on. I felt more frightened and alone than I'd ever done in my life before, but I kept on telling myself there was no alternative; I simply had to stick it. I could possibly arrange for a taxi to take me away again the following morning, but that would be utterly unjust to my new employer. I had to convince myself somehow to stay the course. A few weeks only: get a grip, woman!

'I rustled up some sort of meal from what was in the kitchen, and laid a place for one in the dining-room. The dining-room here is a large roughly square room at the front of the house – quite gracious in its way - and the single place-setting seemed absurd in that great space. When my employer appeared, he asked me whether I should care to eat with him: "a bit of company for a sick man", he half-joked. I accepted, although inside I felt nothing but revulsion. As we sat at table, I had in all civility to look at him when he spoke to me, and for the first time I began to see beyond the awfulness of his face the gentleness and melancholy and loneliness that lay beyond. Even at that first meal, I began to warm to him: this strange man who had apparently, and for a reason that was only too obvious, chosen to isolate himself so completely from the outside world. He asked me about myself and my family and my interests, and before I knew where I was, I was unburdening myself of all my ordinariness, disappointment and dreariness. He pecked at his food, and I could sense that he was tired. I cleared away, and he expressed the hope that I would join him for breakfast at eight in the morning. In the meantime, would it be too much to ask me to do the washing and some ironing, as he was running out of clean clothes? There were other housekeeping tasks, but there was time for those. I went to bed that night with some of my gloom lifted.

'After breakfast, my employer again retired to his room, and I was left to explore the house further in daylight and to look around outside. In the middle of the morning, a van from the little supermarket in Halkirk called with some supplies, but most of them were quite unsuitable. I arranged with the shop that I should phone in a proper order in time for the next delivery. At lunch, my employer – Martyn Wynn, or Martyn as he told me to call him – invited me to use his library whenever I wished and the piano in the music-room if I fancied. (The library was stocked way beyond anything I could need: novels, ancient history, philosophy, political theory, natural history, music, humour, literary criticism, cartography, theology, spirituality, biography, autobiography, history, poetry, drama, a bit of science ... There were also odd volumes on a further range of subjects: witchcraft, philology, calligraphy, architecture, archaeology, as well as plenty of works of reference, including dictionaries in six or seven languages. My employer's tastes were wide-ranging and impressive.) He said he had no specific duties for me: just to keep the house ticking over and see to the right medicaments at the right times until he was properly back on his feet. And so those first weeks went by. The doctor called, the van came back with proper supplies, life took on a rhythm of its own, out in that bleak remoteness. One day at supper, he asked whether he might drop the formal Miss Grant and call me Daracha. That was the start of a mutual romance that has lasted until now.' She stopped short, engulfed in great sobs that shook her entire frame. With difficulty she mastered her grief.

'When the time foreseen for the end of my tenure as temporary "care and support" came round, Martyn asked me diffidently whether I should consider staying on a bit, as he had, in his usual understated phraseology, "got used to having me about the place". I accepted gladly; and I've been here ever since, blissfully happy with a man as gentle as he was wise and as warm as he was unsightly. I'm not expecting you to believe all this, gentlemen; and if you knew what he looked like, you'd believe it even less; but I'm trying to explain to you why I killed that odious Thwaites and am glad to have done so.

'I've been here for over thirty years. One day, a year or two ago, Martyn explained that his money was running low. The upkeep of the house was an enormous drain on his resources. The planners had refused him permission to change some of the windows to double-glazed pvc – out of keeping with the baronial style, he was told loftily - while the single-glazed Victorian windows didn't keep out the draughts and let out the heat. There were always parts of the roof that needed attention; or a boiler needed servicing; or a door replacing – and so on: an endless call on his funds. And of course, since the house is so far from anywhere, tradesmen charged us extra. Martyn thought of installing a wind-turbine, but that takes a considerable financial commitment. He told me that his old friend James Thwaites had promised to leave him a substantial sum in his will, but that windfall might not materialise for years. In the meantime, they might have to contemplate selling up and moving. "But you can't leave this place," I cried, "it's been your home for decades. Where could you go where people wouldn't stare at you? You're too old to adapt. And in any case, who'd buy this grotesque old house?" I was thinking of myself too, of course, as I'd grown to love the old mansion, but I was serious that any move would be the end of the Martyn I'd come to know and love. I asked more about this James Thwaites, whose name I was hearing for the first time. It was an utterly dishonourable story – a scandalous tale of carelessness, cowardice and desertion. Martyn told me that there was an "official" version the two of them put out to save Thwaites' reputation and the real version of what happened. I was so incensed I could've murdered Thwaites on the spot with my bare hands!

'As he told me the real story for the first time, all Martyn's grief and pain, pent up for fifty years, poured out in a stream of sobs and cries that nearly tore him apart. For a moment, I feared for his sanity. How do you value a human life? At twenty, Martyn was well-to-do, handsome, talented and the heir to a barony. At twenty-one, he was a monstrosity, an outcast, unfit to be seen in public, shunned by all who saw him. And yet he hadn't changed: he was still Martyn Wynn, the same witty, charming, affectionate and generous person his family and friends had known for years. Such a rich and interesting personality! So he hid away, burying his scarred face and hands in a harsh wilderness where only the birds and the fishes could see him; and it was there, by chance, that I found him and made him my own. He was kind enough to tell me, on numerous occasions, that my love for him had given him back his self-respect. Inspector, we were happy, so happy, and yet, for lack of money, our life was being taken away. I couldn't let it happen.

'So I wrote to Thwaites, asking him whether he would please consider advancing us some of his bequest to Martyn so that our continuation at

Lochdhu wasn't jeopardised. He replied coldly, informing me that his money was all tied up and couldn't be released before his death. I wrote again, asking him to untie some of it, but got no reply. I determined to travel down to plead with him face to face: I, who hadn't set foot out of Caithness for thirty years! The journey was a nightmare: busy trains, people hurrying everywhere, signs I couldn't interpret, noise – awful, just awful. Eventually, with the help of kindly fellow-travellers and passers-by, I got to Thwaites' flat. He was obviously expecting someone else, as he stood there in his underpants, looking stupid and flabby. I was shy and intimidated, but I wasn't going to let his manner stand in the way of Martyn's peace of mind. I went in, ignored his state of undress and put my case as eloquently and vehemently as I could. "Sorry, dearie," he told me patronisingly, "you're too late." I asked him what he meant. He explained that he was on the point of changing his will: in fact, his solicitor was drawing up the revised version even then, ready for his signature in a few days. He'd had second thoughts. To honour his promise to Martyn – huh! – he was leaving him an Italian *palazzo* he owned in Tuscany. This property was apparently discreet, easy to heat in the Italian climate and much more manageable in every respect. It came with a small fund for onward maintenance. The bulk of his money he'd decided to give, not to his family or friends but to some organisation dedicated, it seemed, to toppling not just the Church of England but all the Christian churches. He thought that this was a cause he could and should support whole-heartedly. Martyn's welfare was of concern to him, but this Anti-Church thing was much, much more important in the cosmic scheme of things. I pleaded with him, almost on my knees, but he was adamant. He warbled on about the supreme value of Jesus Christ's legacy, that the world was in its death throes – or would be if enough people prayed for it to happen – that the churches were obstacles in the path of this final development of world history, and lots more besides. I mentioned Diderot a while back; a terrible story. In the middle of that book, Soeur Suzanne says:

> Je puis tout pardonner aux hommes, excepté l'injustice, l'ingratitude et l'inhumanité.

> I can pardon people everything except injustice, ingratitude and inhumanity.

I'd long made this sentiment my own, but now it took on a new edge and a new urgency. Thwaites turned to show me the door, and I seized the first heavy thing I saw and struck him hard. I just saw red. Why should this insufferable, smug and pompous old fool hold Martyn's fate in his hands, when he'd caused all Martyn's pain and sorrow himself – a life-time of distress and fearful ostracism? I refused to let him live another moment and strangled him with his own curtain-tie. I'm not strong, but he put up no resistance – of course he didn't, he was out. I twisted the cord and kept twisting and held on until I knew he was dead. I let myself out, knowing that I'd done a good work and saved Martyn's future. I came back home. And that was that.

'Except that of course it wasn't. Some months later, Martyn's legacy came through, and the future looked rosy again – or perhaps I should say less bleak. We would be together at Lochdhu as long as we wished – until the end. I had a single friend from my school days in whom I confided because I was uneasy in my mind. I wanted to know that the police had no means of identifying Thwaites' killer, and the reports were encouraging. Then all of a sudden this friend came up with different news. I'm not sure of the details, because the mechanics of the thing didn't concern me, but it appeared that the dean of the cathedral where Thwaites worked was visited by Thwaites' sister, stirring things up. Two years down the line, I ask you! Now the dean knew that someone in the flats had seen something but told the police nothing because he didn't wish to get involved. The dean didn't wish to get involved, either, but wondered whether the time hadn't come for this witness to step forward if he had any information worth imparting. Of course, I guessed who this witness was. I'll tell you what happened when I first arrived at Thwaites' flat. The street-door was open. I'd consulted the list of occupants and learnt that Thwaites was on the third floor, but when I got there, I couldn't remember which number he was: too nervous to concentrate, I suppose. I knocked at random – remember, I didn't have murder in mind at all at that point; it didn't seem to matter who saw me - and a young man answered the door. He put me right, and I then knocked on Thwaites' door; but, thinking about things in the light of this recent development about the dean, I realised that, if I didn't do something drastic, this young man, whoever he was, could tell the police that a woman with a Scottish accent had been asking for Thwaites at about the time he was murdered. My number would have been up; even the local police could have put two and two together to make four. My friend undertook to sort the problem out, and that's how I was responsible for the second murder. Inspector, I have no regrets. If I'd been found out, Martyn's life would have been ended, and I couldn't allow that to happen. Life's been horrible to him, and I was absolutely determined his last years at least should be spent in the peace he'd gradually been getting to know – inner peace, I mean, spiritual peace. No one was going to stand in the way of that. And I defy you, inspector, to tell me I was wrong.'

45

A deep silence fell on the room at the conclusion of this narrative. Moat and Stockwell were greatly moved by this woman's unflinching devotion to her stricken husband; and for a time neither spoke. Then Moat said,

'Mrs Wynn – Lady Wynn, I should say – thank you. This has all been very difficult for you, and I admire your courage. If the decision were mine alone, I'd leave you in peace, but there are two people out there under false suspicion of having a hand in Thwaites' death, and I owe them justice as well. And I shall need to know the name of your friend so that we can trace Shearsby's murderer.'

'Never, inspector! You can charge me with obstructing the police, with contempt of court and any number of years in prison, but I won't give you the name. The doctors give me between twelve and eighteen months to live, so the future's of no concern to me. Without Martyn, my future just doesn't exist. In any case, I'm the murderer; anybody else involved was just doing me a favour – nodding to my pull on the strings.'

'When did your husband die?'

'Four days ago, still imagining that we should see out our days here in this lovely house. He'd been ill for some time. My poor, poor Martyn: total, eternal peace at last.' She sobbed loudly, hunched in her chair, looking old beyond her years, lonely and fragile.

46

As Moat and Stockwell waited in the buffet at Thurso railway station for their return train to Inverness, the sergeant asked his superior how he had guessed that Daracha Wynn was responsible for Thwaites' and Shearsby's deaths in her husband's behalf.

'I didn't *guess*, laddie,' Moat retorted, 'I used my reasoning. You should try it some time. Works wonders.'

'OK, sir, to humour you, how did you reason to it?'

'Well, of course, I have you to thank for presenting the case to me so clearly. Such a brain you have, sergeant! You'll remember that you outlined the various possibilities and assessed their likelihood. I sat down in a quiet corner and considered all the evidence dispassionately, in the light of your summary. As my beloved Walter Scott has it, "We reason ill while our feelings are moved." That's *Woodstock*, by the way. I admired the ingenuity and determination which had led our three, well, I might call them predecessors in this business, to look for a solution to Thwaites' murder. Jonas Chimes and his cousin, Matthias Biddulph and his hired private investigator, and the redoubtable Serenity Burnsell on her own all did well. Of course, we can't condone the Carters' illegal activities, but they were undertaken in a good cause. The fact that none of them got anywhere suggested to me that they were barking up the wrong tree. Well, I'll qualify that in a minute. Then you've got to add in the original police investigation. I say nothing about that except that I somehow couldn't take seriously DI Barnes' assertion that his team had carried out a "thorough" inquiry. So, had our three amateurs come up with anything useful? I thought not. Black-market book-dealers Becketts was probably the best bet, but there seemed no possibility of getting proof. If the solitary thumb-print in Thwaites' flat had matched either of them, we'd've had quite a good case against them, but even then their counsel might've come up with a perfectly plausible explanation to baffle the witless jury. The Anti-Church business I couldn't see working. OK, religious fanatics are an odd bunch and can get up to some very nasty things, but how'd we ever prove it without a very tiresome procedure? And there again, a ready explanation could be provided for the finger-prints: a friendly visit to Thwaites' flat the day before, that sort of thing. As for Mr Biddulph's blackmail hypothesis, I argued to myself that surely Barnes' men or Serenity and Reuben would've have uncovered more evidence if Thwaites were engaging in blackmail on any great scale – unless he kept his evidence locked away in a deposit-box which nobody's yet found: possible, I suppose; but then we could always return to this hypothesis at a later date. A sex attack? Well, DI Barnes' theory seemed to have as much going for it as any of the others, although he queered his own pitch, if you'll pardon the phrase in the context, with misdiagnoses and tergiversations. Contemplating the frailty of these four theories, I came back to Thwaites' will, which at least Barnes had had the sense to look into.'

'May I interrupt there a minute, sir? If the police constable from Thurso had been met by Lady Wynn at the door of Lochdhu Lodge, DI Barnes' investigation might've taken a very different turn, mightn't it? It seemed to me from DI Barnes' account that there was no inkling of the existence of a second person on the premises, apart from the disfigured owner.'

'My reading of that particular scene is that the Wynns had seen the police-car coming and agreed that Lady Wynn should remain hidden. Normally, I suppose, Martyn would've been very reluctant to be the object of scrutiny. Anyway, to return to my, um, reasoning. Money's always a sound motive for murder. Three main people benefited from Thwaites' will: the testator's sister - and I didn't think she'd approach the police if she'd been guilty. Double bluff? She didn't seem the type to me – Gerald Heggs the book-lover – perhaps we should've investigated further, but, as I stated at the time, I couldn't see how it would be possible to obtain a conviction on the sole evidence of Thwaites' book or books on his shelves; in any case, Barnes assured us that the finger-prints weren't his – and finally the reclusive Wynn.

'The more I looked at Wynn, the more suspicious I became. He didn't work for a living, seemingly – unless it was permanently online - and lived in a mansion the upkeep of which must've been a huge drain on his wallet. Would a man so incapacitated as he was have holed himself up alone and have still managed to look after himself and maintain the property in such inhospitable surroundings? Could Wynn have employed a companion? Was there someone else on the premises - a caretaker perhaps? Was there a cottage in the grounds which another hermit might inhabit? Another consideration weighed with me at this point. DI Barnes told us that the local constable in Scotland found out that Wynn was ill, over and above his obvious handicap, and I thought that might have added urgency to his need for funds, as well as urgency to his need for a companion. I imagined, perhaps, a male nurse hired to look after a disabled patient. So although Wynn could not feasibly have made the journey to Thwaites' flat and back without exciting considerable attention, the unknown companion I was conjecturing might. At that point, I also conjectured contrariwise that the companion was expecting to inherit from his boss and frightened that Wynn wouldn't outlive Thwaites; in which case he could kiss goodbye to his own inheritance. I was extremely surprised in the event to find Wynn married. I admit I hadn't considered a woman in the role of murderess.

'I carried out some research. ScotRail confirmed that a passenger had caught the 07.15 from Altnabreac to Inverness on the day Thwaites died. It's a request stop, you see, and passengers are a rarity. Lady Wynn could have travelled south by other means, but I argued to myself that rail was the quickest and easiest way. This train, with three changes, would enable the passenger I surmised to alight at the rail station near Thwaites' flat later that afternoon. The timing's right. Biddulph leaves the flat at 14.50, forgetting to close the street-door properly behind him. Daracha Wynn arrives hot-foot from the station, say ten minutes later, to have it out with Thwaites. She's with him, oh, I don't know, say fifteen minutes, probably less than that. She kills him in frustration and leaves. Then the bearded man puts in an appearance, let's say – and we know this to be right - to discuss blackmail but is pipped at the door-bell by a young man in a sleeveless sweatshirt – presumably another client of Thwaites's. This second man climbs the stairs, knocks and gets no answer, hangs about a bit, knocks again and then leaves. Meanwhile, the bearded man has given up and gone off too. Shearsby sees and talks to Lady Wynn at the top of the flats; an elderly woman sees the bearded gentleman pacing up and down in the street. Neither sighting leads to police action, for different reasons: in the one case because Shearsby doesn't wish to get involved, in the other because the hunt for a bearded man seems too difficult to the police. Daracha Wynn couldn't get back home on the same day – trains don't run that often – so she'd have had to stay overnight somewhere, but I couldn't hope to guess where. ScotRail then confirmed that a passenger had asked to be dropped off at Altnabreac at 13.42 on the following day. It all fitted. I suppose she told Martyn Wynn what she'd done, and he'd be an accessory after the fact; I doubt that would have disturbed him very much, after all he'd suffered over the years.

'When it comes to providing evidence to a jury of hard-bitten British citizens, we shall be able, I've no doubt, to trace Lady Wynn's journey exactly, particularly her overnight stay somewhere *en route*, and I don't think she'll find it easy to argue her way out of her finger-print on Thwaites' statuette. By the way, do we know who the statuette was of?'

'Yes, sir: Atalanta, appropriately enough.'

'Hm. Well, I think our redoubtable Lady Wynn will plead guilty, anyway: she won't want to escape justice, even though she seems to have nothing but contempt for Thwaites. Shearsby's a different matter.'

'What do you think those mysterious letters after Thwaites' name in the Becketts' books meant: "P. L. E."? Alex Carter suggested "Proved Troublesome: Eliminated." Got quite exercised over them, seemingly.'

'Yes, well, I think they were much less melodramatic than that; probably something quite simple like Partnership To End. The Becketts were trafficking in stolen goods, but we've no reason to think they were guilty of murder. Of course, running the Carters off the road at high speed might have put a different slant on things. That was after high words.'

'Another question, sir – if I'm not getting tiresome, that is.'

'Go ahead, young sergeant.'

'How *had* Thwaites made his money, do you suppose? His own sister seems to have had no idea of the extent of his wealth.'

'Possibly his book-dealing, possibly a lucky win on the Premium Bonds, possibly a generous benefactor – a past pupil, perhaps – who knows? He certainly wasn't going to share it with Serenity in his life-time.' He paused. 'Well, that's it, then,' he went on. 'Case solved – not very happily, perhaps. You know, I can't help thinking of the ominous words that end Act I of the *Duchess of Malfi:*

> Whether the spirit of greatness or of woman
>
> Reign most in her, I know not, but it shows
>
> a fearful madness; I owe her much of pity.'

About Julius Falconer

Warwickshire-born Julius Falconer completed six enjoyable years of university studies abroad before working as a translator back in the UK. Thinking that he could earn more as a teacher, to fund his lavish life-style, he took a PGCE at Leeds University and duly turned to teaching. He slaved away at the chalk-face for twenty-six long years in both Cornwall and Scotland before retiring to grow cabbages in Yorkshire, where he still lives. His wife of thirty-three years died in 2000. He has one daughter, married. In 2009, looking to fill his new-found leisure profitably(?), he started to write detective novels and is still happily scribbling away fifteen books later. He is a member of the Crime Writers' Association.

Connect with Julius Falconer

Facebook: *https://www.facebook.com/pages/Julius-Falconer/110217579009699*

Other Books by Julius Falconer

The Spider's Banquet, ISBN 9781905809462

A young woman goes to an isolated monastery to visit her brother, who is a monk there. She is dropped off at the door, meets her brother in the parlour; they say goodbye and part; and she is never seen again. The monks, however, have a cast-iron alibi. The diffident and cultured Inspector Wickfield is called in to investigate.

A Death Twice Avenged, ISBN 9781905809615

From the top of the stairs, a little girl of five overhears an argument between her father and a visitor. Frightened she dared not descend the staircase. Her father is killed. She did not see the killer but remembers the killer's voice. Twenty years later she recognises the voice, identifies its owner and sets out to take her revenge.

The Longdon Murders, ISBN 9781905809707

On the night of a blizzard an elderly couple are urgently summoned to their daughter's cottage two and a half miles away. When they reach the cottage they find it warm but empty. Unable to face the journey back home that night, they retire to bed in their daughter's cottage. The following morning, they are found dead.

The Unexpected Death of Father Wilfred, ISBN 9781905809714

One February evening, Fr Wilfred, the parish priest of the Sacred Heart Catholic church in Droitwich, tumbles out of his confessional, stabbed to death. His sister demands the best detective in the force, and Stan Wickfield is appointed to the case. Unfortunately he cannot identify the means or motive, much less the murderer.

Mr Carrick is Laid To Rest, ISBN 9781905809752

A respected teacher at a private girls' school in rural Worcestershire, physically attracted to one of the Sixth-Form leavers, discloses his feelings for her. Convinced that he has mishandled their final meeting, he writes a letter of regret and then kills himself. The coroner's verdict is suicide but Inspector Wickfield is called in to investigate.

The Bones of Murder, ISBN 9781905809769

While renovating the derelict twelfth-century chapel attached to their new house in rural Worcestershire, Grace and Benjamin Hothersall uncover three skeletons, which have clearly been the victims of murder. The Inspector is called in to investigate.

A Time to Prey, ISBN 9781905809837

On the morning following 1 September 1966, the Bishop of Worcester, the Right Reverend Giles Wyndham-Brookes is found slumped and lifeless in his study at Hartlebury Castle, his official residence. He had seemingly tripped on an edge of carpet and hit his head on the fender; but there is a distinct whiff of murder in the air.

Troubled Waters, ISBN 9781905809899

Inspector Wickfield and Sergeant Hewitt find themselves caught up in a saga of murder, illicit money-making and racist thuggery as a young girl's body is found one morning on the banks of a canal.

Tempt Not the Stars, ISBN 9781905809950

The Hon. Mr and Mrs Bede Lambton, of Abberton Hall in Worcestershire, persuade their nephew Gregory to enter a competition run by the Syrian Ministry of Tourism. Gregory, a student in the archaeology department of Bristol University, produces a paper called 'The Syrian Sapphire'. Subsequently Gregory's housemate Sheena Morrison is murdered.

Jagger, ISBN 9781905809998

Lionel Jagger, head of English at Mincliffe College in rural Worcestershire, is found dead in bed one morning, with his throat slit. Twenty-eight years old, erudite, talented, popular: an unlikely victim of murder. Inspector Wickfield and his assistant Sergeant Spooner trawl through his life, leaving no stone unturned to catch the cunning killer.

The Wichenford Court Murder, ISBN: 9781907728037

The peaceful estate of Wichenford Court, in deepest Worcestershire, is convulsed by a bizarre murder which mirrors a murder committed on exactly the same spot in 1791. Inspector Wickfield undertakes an investigation in which the killer's tracks are covered so successfully that the case is in danger of remaining unsolved.

A Figure in the Mist, ISBN 9781907728235

When Lady Amelia Walden is murdered at Monk Fryston Hall Hotel in Yorkshire on the night of her eightieth birthday, the chief suspect is Robert Purbright, a bachelor in his fifties engaged at Farlington Hall to catalogue her extensive collection of stamps. He is found not guilty but Lady Amelia's son, Toby, vows to prove the verdict wrong.

The Waif, ISBN 9781907728341

The discovery of the body of a petty criminal one winter's night in 2011, in a quiet Yorkshire hamlet, sets in train a series of events which stretches Inspector Walter Moat's capabilities to the utmost. His wily opponent, as he eventually discovers, is an elusive master-criminal called Lomax.

The Alkan Murder, ISBN 9781782281832

The wealthy and reclusive Harry Quirke is stabbed to death in his country house outside Tadcaster. Only one of the obvious suspects seems to have much of a motive: his alibi is shaky, it is true, but there is no proof of his involvement. Finally, the murderer makes the smallest of slips, and the penny drops - but it's a close thing!

Lightning Source UK Ltd.
Milton Keynes UK
UKOW052009050513

210208UK00001B/42/P